THE COURTYARD OF DREAMS

If we want things to stay as they are, things will have to change.

GIUSEPPE DI LAMPEDUSA, *The Leopard*

ANNA MONARDO

The Courtyard

of Dreams

D O U B L E D A Y

New York   London   Toronto   Sydney   Auckland

PUBLISHED BY DOUBLEDAY
a division of Bantam Doubleday Dell Publishing Group, Inc.
1540 Broadway, New York, NY 10036

DOUBLEDAY and the portrayal of an anchor with a dolphin are
trademarks of Doubleday, a division of Bantam Doubleday Dell
Publishing Group, Inc.

A portion of this book appeared in the November 1989–January 1990 edition
of *Special Reports: Fiction.*

Library of Congress Cataloging-in-Publication Data

Monardo, Anna.
The courtyard of dreams/Anna Monardo.—1st ed.
     p.   cm.
1. Italian American women—Fiction. 2. Italian Americans—Fiction. I. Title.
PS3563.O5164C68   1993
813'.54—dc20   92-45576
CIP

ISBN 0-385-42606-2

10   9   8   7   6   5   4   3   2   1

To my family—
the Americans, the Canadians and the Italians;
and to the memory of my grandparents

Acknowledgments

THIS NOVEL took a long time to write, and I was lucky —blessed, really—to have the support of many fine people.

Gail Hochman, my agent, believed. And believed and believed. Deb Futter, my editor and friend, performed magic. There aren't enough words, in English or Italian, to thank them.

Frank MacShane was encouraging when this story was in its earliest stages. Liza Dawson gave good advice. My writing group—Rachel Basch, Tricia Bauer, Annette Henkin Landau, Geneve Hard Bacon, Liza O'Hanlon-Di Mino, Toby Schechter, Nancy Schuessler—gave invaluable critiques, as did Marianne Merola, Joe Levine and Michael Clayton.

Many friends kept me laughing and hoping; among them, Martha Hughes, the late Allan Barnett, Betsy Loughran, Debbie Manetti Jewell, Bonnie ZoBell, Mary Ellen Donovan and my colleagues at *Time*, especially Bob

Acknowledgments

Braine, Barbara Collier and Doug Bradley. Sue Blair and Eleanor Edgar helped make possible an important trip to Rome. Herbert Thomas has been a wise and compassionate Virgil. My workshop students have been excellent writing companions.

Baci to my parents, Alfred and Catherine Monardo. And *baci* to my brother, Paul, who gave me the music that set the stage, and to *all* my cousins, especially Anna Rossetti, Carmen Lago, Laura Monardo, Anna Monardo di Cosenza, Anna Squeo, Paolo Monardo di Vibo and Sheila, my sister-in-law, for late-night conversations.

I am grateful to the Djerassi Foundation and the Virginia Center for the Creative Arts, where parts of this novel were written, and rewritten.

Contents

Contents

THE COURTYARD OF DREAMS

In the Courtyard
of the Five Giulias

WE ARE ALL GIULIAS, the girls in our family, named, as a sign of respect and according to tradition, after our grandmother Nonna Giulia. We are the daughters of four brothers and a sister, and if we had been born in a different time we might have grown up all together, probably within the sun-bleached walls of an ancient villa, up in the mountains of Calabria or along the Mediterranean coast. My cousins and I would have never been alone.

Our days would have begun when we heard "Giulia, wake, it's time" whispered into our dreams by the low soft voices of the old women, our duennas, who looked over us night and day. Still in white nightshirts, long hair falling, barefoot, we would rush across the stone floor of our night-chilled bedrooms, up the high step leading to our windows. And in each small room the tall, crystal-paned windows would be pulled open and the heavy wooden shutters pushed out, open, and the rooms of the Giulias would fill with blue light and the soft warm breath of early morning. Leaning out on age-old windowsills of pink marble, we would call to one another until the court-yard echoed with the overlapping sounds of our names: Giulia di Nicola . . . Giulia d'Antonio . . . Giulia di Vito . . . di Rocco . . . Giulia di Sofì.

But the duennas, running up behind us with shawls out-stretched, would scold us away from the windows, lead us back into our rooms, to small cushioned prie-dieus so they could listen to our prayers. The hushed cadences of our hurried litanies as we petitioned for the health of our family, for the quiet repose of those we had lost, for the strengthening of our faith, for the forgiveness of our weaknesses, for humility, for grace. We would call on the Madonnas—del Carmine, di Lourdes, di Pompei. Beseech all the saints—San Francesco di Paola, patron saint of our land; Santa Giulia, our namesake; Sant'Antonio of the birds; San Nicola of the sea.

While we prayed, bowls of steaming chocolate would be waiting for us on trays, and by the time the duennas ended our prayers with thumb-traced signs of the cross above our eyebrows, the dark sweet chocolate would be cool enough to drink. As we lifted the porcelain bowls to our lips, the duennas, gently, would hold back our hair. When we lowered the emptied bowls, showing cheeks rouged from the steam, the women would accuse us: "What have you done to be blushing so shamefully?" "Nothing!" "Don't tell *me* nothing," they'd say, pinching us, making our cheeks even redder. "Have you forgotten that since you first pushed into this world I've known this face and its colors and I know this bashful red." Teasing us so, they would begin working our hair with their hands, braiding, twisting, pinning. And when all was smooth and not a stray hair flying, we would dress in whatever skirts and bodices had been prepared for that day and hang small pearl drops from our ears. With silk-fringed shawls wrapped around our shoulders, we would hurry through long corridors where night breezes still coiled in the vaulted ceilings. Statues and gargoyles would stare at us with their polished eyes. But already the voices of the Giulias could be heard—on the stairways, in the passageways—as we called out to one another, and then finally we would be in the courtyard all together, where we would greet each other with small kisses on each cheek.

Eager to begin our work for the day, we would arrange our low stools in a circle under the wide shade of a full-blooming tree. From the deep pockets of our skirts we would bring out small pincushions and each of us would thread a needle with a different color of silk thread. Then the duennas, all together, would lift a large, round, white cloth over their heads and, walking under this canopy, move toward our circle until the cloth hung over us like a full moon. Lowering the white cloth onto our laps, we would take up our work where it had been left the day before, our different-color threads and various stitches adding to the ever widening pattern that spiraled out from the cloth's center. The work would have been started years earlier, perhaps by only two of the Giulias as soon as they were old enough to hold needle and thread. And then younger Giulias would have added their hand, and the older Giulias, with more complicated stitches, would have elaborated on what the younger ones had begun.

There would be palm trees to represent the tranquillity of the harbor, like the tranquillity of our courtyard, and seashells to remind us of the exotic shores we longed to see. There would be flames as symbols of our faith, and deer as a sign of our innocence, and horses, which are always a symbol of strength, and grapes as a wish for plenitude, and crescent moons as a wish for long life. And

3

hearts—the youngest Giulia would add hearts as the emblem of our family, *la famiglia Di Cuore.*

At first we would work in silence, concentrating, and the moss-covered fountain in a far corner of the courtyard would seem to gurgle louder, as it did at night when it lulled us to sleep, and there would be songs of canaries in white lattice cages. And the cats, some fat and luxurious, and others wild, skinny intruders from over the wall, but all of them purring as they wandered over the intersecting arches our wide skirts made on the ground. Lush green moss pushing up between worn black stones. The sun lightening the sundial's face. A small cloud of insects hovering over the fountain. Over the tops of the walls, long vines spilling, while rosebushes climbed from the ground below.

The tree we sat under would be a clementine with limbs so low and so full we could reach up without standing to pull off its fruit. The slightest press of a fingernail would break the tender skins, and the sections of fruit inside would be warm and plump, curled together like the fingers of a baby's fist. And then with citron-scented hands we would continue our work, each Giulia embroidering with her unique-color thread, executing the stitches she did best, then handing her work on to the cousin at her left. And in this way our cloth would rotate around the circle, and in this way our mornings would pass.

And after a while, not wanting to be silent, we would ask each other, "Giulia, what did you dream?" We would listen carefully, aware and respectful of the perverse order of dreams, and we would hope to hear of death, because death in dreams always means new life coming. And we would be wary of dreams in which coins change hands, for in dreams coins are words, and words mean arguments. And if there was water in a dream we would hope for it to be cloudy, not clear. And if one of us in a dream saw dirt or mud we would smile, relieved, and anticipate good luck.

Any dream we did not understand we would save for later, when the cook came by. She would be a broad peasant woman with a good simple name of the earth, and though she might not know how to write that name she would know how to read our dreams. She would pass us on her way back from the *campagna,* and balanced on her head would be a basket filled with figs and grapes and peaches, and perched among the fruits a bundle of five or six warm eggs, and in her hand, fighting, an orange chicken. Her whole body would be given up to the job of keeping the basket steady on her head as she lowered herself amid a cloud of orange feathers to gather herbs growing at the base of our courtyard wall. And if the chicken fighting in her hand was a fat one, we would pester her until she told us who our guest for dinner would be that day. And if it was to be a young man coming to pay his respects to our fathers, the rest of the morning would pass in a flurry of words as we wove the few details we knew of the young man together with anything the cook could tell. Eagerly we would wait, our hands working more quickly, and when we heard our fathers in the corridor greeting their guest, in a single voice we would begin to sing. Softened by our songs, the fathers would come into our courtyard, stand over us, look over us all, nod at the shallow pool of embroidered cloth covering our feet and tell each of us, *"Brava."*

With our eyes lowered, we would smile for our fathers and for their shy guest who stood silent and respectful behind them. For that brief moment, while the young man's presence filled our courtyard, our longing would be satisfied, but as soon as he left us we would long for him even more. And so again we would feed our fantasies with words, build our fantasies, create the world of the young man, create the man, and with our words we would keep him alive.

And then one day the fathers would come to the oldest Giulia and tell her, "You have been asked for." Having already seen it in a dream, she would not be surprised. Our cloth, now completed, would be divided, and each Giulia would be given a portion of the cloth. Some of us would wear the cloth as a sash, and some as a tunic, and some as a veil, however we pleased, and in this way, one by one, we would pass through the door of our fathers' house.

ONE

The Contadina Ladies

THEY LIED TO ME when I was young. What they taught me had nothing to do with the truth of the world. They lied to me with their promises and with their silences, and sometimes they lied to me outright.

"Your family are the only ones you can trust."

"Believe us when we tell you this: The less you talk, the more you keep inside yourself, the better it is."

"Better for a woman to be patient than beautiful."

"Beauty is nothing if you have no one's respect. Your reputation is everything."

"Anything. Boys will say to each other *any*thing and everything. Anything you do or say, they report to one another, and then your reputation is lost."

"Save yourself for one man—we'll tell you that now, clear as day."

"The day will come when you'll be grateful you listened. You'll find a good, smart man who makes you feel like a million bucks. And what a wedding your daddy will give you! I see it already."

"I see you with many babies, a nice house. Then your father, how proud he'll be. Think of your father."

"Your mother, God rest her soul, would have told you these things if she could. She'd want you to know these things. That's why we tell you."

"We tell you because we love you and want you to be happy."

"Your happiness, Giulia, is the only thing we want."

The Italian part of me has been at war with the American me for as long as I can remember. When I was young, the Italian me was the voice of my father, Nicola, who was always trying to send me to Italy for a vacation. He wanted me to see how many relatives I had over there.

"Giulia, this summer in Italy, what do you say?" We'd be speeding home from the fruit market in his crimson Volkswagen Bug, the tiny back seat stuffed with bags of peaches, apricots, strawberries, and in the front seat a crate of grapes under my feet, which I tried to hold light and weightless on the lid so the grapes wouldn't get squashed. With opera loud on the radio and the car full of the first fruits of spring and the aroma of orchards, my father must have felt closer to Italy, because that's when he'd start. "This year, yes? You can meet Nonna Giulia and your aunts and uncles and cousins. What do you say?"

Looking away from the road, checking the rearview mirror for cops, he'd arch his heavy eyebrows at me, and I'd give him that exasperated dropped-lip stare girls do so well at eleven, twelve, thirteen. "I wouldn't understand anything that was going on."

"*Stupida,* you will learn. Would it kill you to learn a little Italian?"

"Slow *down,*" I yelled, bracing myself with a foot against the glove compartment. My father claimed he loved America, didn't miss Italy; one place is as good as another, he said. In the car, though, he gave himself away. He drove like someone trying to escape. "I don't care what you say. I'm not going to Italy." My mother had died when I was ten, and now, scary as it was inside that cramped car, the thought of going anywhere without my father was impossible. But I'd never admit that. From my grandfather, Ben, a poker player, I'd learned at a young age the value of keeping the truth wiped off my face.

"How many girls in your sixth grade have the chance for a summer in Italy?"

"Dad, nobody would want to go to Italy."

"Stop that screaming," he warned me.

"I'm not screaming," I screamed.

Quickly, like a hiss, he said, "Giulia!" And then one great dark bushy eyebrow slid closer to the other, and a deep wrinkle shivered across his forehead. *"Basta,"* he said. "Enough."

The American part of me came from my mother, Maggie, or Margherita, as everyone in the family called her. She was born on an ocean liner lurching through a winter storm as her mother, Concetta, seven months pregnant, was sailing to America to join her husband, Benedetto. The people from their village, San Giovanni, had begged Cetta not to leave until her baby was born, but Cetta had had a dream in which the Blessed Mother came to the piazza and told her it would be good luck to give birth in Ohio. Cetta took off, but not soon enough. The baby came on a dark night, in the middle of a tormented ocean that was neither Italy nor America.

Still, my mother always claimed, "American waters, that's where I was born." At eighteen, Maggie was the

9

first among all the *paesane* women of Homefield, Ohio, to learn to drive and to get a driver's license, which her father kept in his wallet.

My mother's voice was Ohio-twinged, not a strain of Italy in it, so I trusted her more than the other adults in the family when I was learning to read. One Sunday night, I was sitting on the couch with her, she was helping me sound out the words in the "Dondi" comic strip, and the rest of the family was watching "The Ed Sullivan Show," and it happened—the Beatles appeared in our living room for the first time. I slid off the couch and moved closer to the set.

Ben grimaced. "Who are those?"

Cetta answered him, *"Sono i Beagles."*

"Beatles," I corrected her and turned up the volume. *"She loves you, yeah, yeah, yeah, yeah."* Such long hair, such music. I mouthed each singer's name as it appeared on the screen below his face. "Ring-o? Mom, is that a real name?"

"That's what it says."

Under John Lennon's name: SORRY, GIRLS, HE'S MARRIED.

"Pssh," my father said. "Giulia, move from the television. You will injure your eyes."

"Oh, look at those crazy girls," my mother said, and I could hear that she was smiling. "Just like us with Frank Sinatra. Remember, Ma, that day me and Agnes went downtown to see him? How we screamed!" I turned away from the Beatles and watched my mother, who was laughing, holding up her hands just as I imagined she and her friend had reached for Frank Sinatra. She leaned over and dipped her fingers into my hair, held my head and grinned right into my eyes.

The first summer after she was gone, my little cousin Lina asked me, "Your mom's in heaven, isn't she?" We were all in New Jersey to spend a week at the beach: my father and I; Cetta and Ben; Aunt Sofia, my father's sister, and Uncle Mike, her husband, and their kids, Lina and Carl. It was a cold day of gray sky and no rain, a day when the wind was sharp, full of sand that scraped against our faces and settled into the contours of our ears. No other families were on the beach that day, but we were unable to think of anything else to do. In late afternoon, the sea mist turned into white fog. "Giulia," Lina insisted, "where's heaven?"

My father was the educated one in the family, a psychiatrist. He had studied and read and was always quoting Dante and other things no one else had heard before. With his voice deepening and making the Italian words tremble, he told us often, *"Chi si ferma"*—he paused, raising his cigarette high over his head to hold the silence—*"è perduto."* He who stops is lost. Mussolini had said that and my father believed it was true.

After my mother died, my father lost no time in moving me from the Cincinnati suburb where we lived, to Homefield, a town just outside Cleveland, so I could be near Aunt Sofia and Ben and Cetta, who all lived on North Park Street in Homefield. We were related by birth and by marriage and by baptism, over and over again, and then we became neighbors.

Four doors down from Aunt Sofia and her family and half a block up from Cetta and Ben there was an old stone Tudor that had originally been a home for elderly nuns and had later become the mayor's official residence. Even after the mayor's three terms of office, even after he retired to Florida and left the monstrous place in the negligent hands of the local government, the house was never known around town as anything but "the convent." While its stone exterior turned darker and grittier with steel-mill dirt, the maple trees surrounding it grew denser and dustier. The house was set back from the street and easy to ignore. Everyone on North Park Street had forgotten it was there, until three weeks after the funeral when my father arranged to rent the convent and he and I moved in.

The family was in shock. It made sense to them, of course, that he would want me to live near my grandmother and my aunt, but the convent had been unoccupied and untended for five years. The floors were warped, all the plumbing was green and moldy, the roof leaked, there were huge gaps in the carved wood banisters. My father ignored all that and began by hiring neighborhood kids to pull out the ivy weighing down the trellis over the patio. He hired painters to scrape the peeling chocolate brown paint from the shutters, drainpipes and the front door and repaint everything a wild cherry red.

"It's not right," Cetta told him, "in the middle of mourning to have the door painted red on your house."

"Where's your head?" Aunt Sofia asked him, angry, "Nicola, your wife isn't dead yet one month."

"We must move forward," he said. *"Chi si ferma è perduto."*

When Aunt Sofia said, "But Nicò . . ." he told her, firmly, "I do not like black, I like red."

My father spoke the law in our family, and when he did, his Italian voice had absolute authority. Over six feet, he was unusually tall for a man from southern Italy. And there was always the legend of his academic brilliance (testified to mostly by him)—at every stage, from grade school to medical school, he had graduated ahead of his class and with superlative grades. In America, finding that the traditional avenues for beginning a medical career were closed to foreigners, he went to the only hospital in the country that would let him work—a state institution for the criminally insane—and from there he was accepted into a psychiatry training program. He specialized in family work and started a private practice. The university medical school offered him a teaching position.

By his forties he had the authority of a professor and the mystery of someone who does work few people understand. He was still young when his thick, black, backcombed hair began to gray, which gave him a sheen of weary maturity. It was that weariness, that sad, persevering strength, that always got me. There was a solemnness to my father; he had that even when he was young. I could see it in the old photographs. Dark shadows puffed under and around his large eyes. A thin elegant man, he dressed in dark fine-wool turtleneck sweaters in the fifties and early sixties, long before anything like that was fashionable. By the late sixties he was one of many men in black turtlenecks walking across campus, and I often noticed women students glance at him. On closer look, though, they spotted the thin old-fashioned lapels of his gray suit jacket, his thick-soled polished wingtips, the black-framed eyeglasses raised up on his head, and the eyes, that weary look in his eyes, and they would see he wasn't hip. He was some Old World European. Growing up in Ohio, I was embarrassed at times by this foreignness in him. More than anything, though, my father fascinated and terrified me.

Nicola had arrived in America at twenty-nine, a young doctor who knew Italian, French, Latin and classical Greek but not one word of English. It wasn't long after the war when he came, 1952, and at first the English language felt to him so unpredictable and aggressive it reminded him of the enemy bomb attacks that had fallen over Naples when he was a medical student there. He spent his first months in Ohio desperately trying to outwit the language, to discover some system beneath the randomness. By the time I was born, four years later, my father had mastered the secret code of English—his grammar was faultless, his vocabulary extensive. Still, his voice came to me from someplace far away, foreign, from across an ocean of experience whose depth and breadth I could not fathom completely, even though the wish to know that foreign region (a place defined by time and memory more than geography) became, in many ways, the hidden but irrepressible force driving me through my life.

My mother had told me stories about the war, the drama of endless Monopoly games played behind blackout window shades, leg-creme camouflage, ration coupons. And the risks she'd had to take when she was young, hiding her lipstick in her pocket as she slipped out to meet her friends because her father wouldn't let her wear a touch of makeup. My mother's stories grounded me, painted a landscape I'd easily step into one day. But as a little girl sitting across the dinner table from my father, I felt his stories pulled me too far away—they slapped down a challenge that would eventually have to be met.

He had grown up in Cimalta, a peasant village in Calabria, thousands of miles away and a million years gone. He was proud of having been one of the few boys in Cimalta to leave home after fifth grade to continue school in Montemaggiore, a city he reached by riding one full day on a donkey.

"Dad, why would you go to school on a donkey?"

"Wouldn't you, rather than walk thirty miles? But then, oh, those roads from Cimalta to Montemaggiore, they are steep and slippery with rocks, so I would have to come down from the donkey and walk. But my uncle, Torquato, was with us, and he usually put me up on his shoulders.

"He was a very strong man, very tall, with shoulders

like this"—my father measured off the whole width of the kitchen table—"and the last incline before we reach the town is steep, very difficult to climb, and by then, oh, were we tired, and Zio Torquato would say to me, 'I am going to drop you now. I am going to drop you.' This really frightened me, because from his shoulders it was a long way to the ground."

"Did he ever drop you?"

"Giulia! Of course not. I was a kid. He was teasing me."

"Then what?" I asked, my fingers tracing the maze of the checkered tablecloth.

"Then we arrived at the outskirts of Montemaggiore. We stopped there to change from our farm shoes and trousers into clothes good enough for the city, and to dust ourselves off." Smiling, he patted his shoulders and head, leaving a halo of cigarette smoke all around him. "You would not believe the dust that came from our clothes after that trip. And this uncle of mine was especially concerned for how we looked. He was not married and was everywhere looking for a wife. He shook out his jacket. With saliva on his fingers, he combed back my hair, which was always sticking up. Then, when we thought we looked really good, we went into the city. Montemaggiore. Oh, the first time I saw it I thought it really was something. So *big*."

My father had fun with these stories, but all I could think of was that from October to Christmas, Christmas to Easter, Easter to June, he didn't see his parents.

He was just as cheerful when he talked about his life as a student during the war, when, to escape bombs, he and his friends regularly spent nights sleeping underground in Naples' sewers.

"Sewers? Oh Dad, how gross."

"Well, yes, it was unpleasant, but then a few of us wrote

15

a letter of complaint to Mussolini and he arranged to give us lounge chairs and stereo music and whatever else we needed."

"Don't make fun of me."

He laughed, but I sensed a longing in him always, a desire to go back, though he tried to hide it and said it didn't exist. Describing a place, he always used the present tense. "My school is in the main piazza of Montemaggiore, and from the piazza goes Corso Dante, a wide street lined with trees, and in the spring, oh, the perfume of flowers there . . ." "In Cimalta, from our balcony we can touch the windowsill of the neighbors next door, and sometimes, to play a joke . . ." "My room in Naples—*my* room! Ha! a room shared with five other students—it is in an old house that is not very far from the university . . ." In his mind, those houses and roads and rooms were still there, waiting.

I suspected that the world he created with words was a mirage. Yet, I willingly drank from it. I listened to his stories because I wanted to conquer my father's Italianness, which unsettled me, threatened me and also was my home. And I listened because I was afraid my father would wake up one morning and realize I was foreign to him. Or maybe he would decide, after one huge crashing wave of memory, that he had given up too much and it was time to go back to Italy. So, to hold on to him, I tried to travel with him. But the task was too much for me. I ended up tossed by the ocean between his life and mine, which was more vast than I'd ever imagined.

And defeating me too in my effort to join with my father's past was the part of me that wanted nothing to do with it.

Sometimes, though, when I stood in the cantina in the basement of the convent, I imagined the entire family—the

Italians and the Americans—living all together in an old farmhouse somewhere. I knew Nonna Giulia and the others only from pictures, but often when I was down in the dark, cool cantina, surrounded by shelves sagging under the weight of boxes of pasta and gallon tins of olive oil and mason jars filled with marinated eggplant and zucchini, while I breathed in the strong peppery scent wafting from the huge wheels of provolone and held a paper towel on my head in case the homemade sausages hanging from the ceiling dripped a bit of oil, I thought of those faraway relatives and longed for some dramatic event that would force us, the Americans, all to go to Italy or that would, like magic, bring the Italians to us. This fantasy was summoned up, I suppose, by the awesome accumulation of food in the cantina; that, and the loneliness and fear I felt whenever I found myself down there alone.

Hanging on the wall just above the light switch in the cantina was an Italian calendar from the shrine of San Francesco di Paola. As a fifteenth-century monk inspired by San Francesco di Assisi, San Francesco di Paola had wandered throughout southern Italy helping the poor. According to Aunt Sofia, he had performed miracles in Cimalta. She and my father were still devoted to the saint and sent large yearly donations to his shrine. In return, we got the calendars, which each month featured San Francesco standing in the midst of a different catastrophe.

My Homefield cousins and I loved him as much as we loved God, Jesus, the Blessed Mother and all the other saints, but we were a little more afraid of San Francesco than we were of the others, because our grandfather Nonno Carlo had had a personal encounter with him.

I was eleven and Lina was seven the first time we heard the story. We were helping Aunt Sofia roll the tiny balls of dough for the Christmas *pignolata,* an endless task. During jobs like this, the kind that bound us to the earth and

17

kept us for hours in the kitchen, Aunt Sofia liked to talk either about movie stars or about the saints. "It was in wartime when it happened," she told us that day, "and down there in Calabria nobody had nothing. Women crying night and day. I was a kid, about your age, Lina, but I remember. My father was in charge for the feast we have each August for San Francesco. But this particular year there's no money and no men. Every man younger than thirty-five, forty, he's gone."

"Where?" I asked her.

"With Mussolini to fight or to the *campagna* to hide. Oh, us kids, how we waited for that feast! Marching band and procession and ice cream and singing, sometimes a movie. My father says to my mother, 'I can't tell these kids there's no feast.' That bothered him; bothered him, too, that maybe my brothers might try coming from Rome and Messina. They were studying there, and during the war we saw them maybe just once or twice.

"My father, he was a calm man, but about this, he was *very* upset. He wouldn't eat, he couldn't sleep. Then one night—it was July, miserable hot, and less than one month before the feast was supposed to be—on this night, while me and my mother are sleeping, San Francesco comes to my father, sits on the chair just beside the bed and talks to him, so nice. 'Go ahead, Carlo,' he says, 'have the feast. The money will be there.' And this was no dream, because in the morning we looked and the trousers my father left on the chair the night before had big wrinkles, just like someone had sat there on them."

Lina asked her, "Who do you think it was, Ma?"

"What do you mean, who? It was the saint, Lina. The saint."

"Maybe it was some kind of a hallucination," I suggested, "you know, since Nonno was so worried and it was hot."

Aunt Sofia told me I was a little pagan. "Yeah? Well, explain this. Two days later, my father's down in the cantina helping my mother. They're trying to get the last olives out from the bottom of the barrel. I'm watching from the steps, and I know this is bad. This means we really have almost nothing now. I remember my mother telling me that during all the years of her marriage that barrel of olives never once got so low. Those barrels were big, tall, and even my father couldn't reach his hand to the bottom, so he says, 'Let's try it this way,' and he tips the barrel to its side, and my mother says, 'Car-lo, you're wasting good oil all over the floor,' but my father screams—and I can hear it like it was yesterday—he screams, '*San Francesco mio!*' because under that barrel he sees a small pile of money."

It wasn't a lot of money—Aunt Sofia never knew exactly how much—but when the Cimaltese heard about the miracle they gave what they could, and the band agreed to march for free. The feast was small but it did take place, and my father, his brothers and some of the other men made it home.

"So you see," Aunt Sofia said, her brown eyes watering and her arms elbow-deep in a bowl of *pignolata* dough. "You see how good San Francesco is to us?"

And there he was on the calendar each time I was sent down to the cantina for an errand: San Francesco draped in brown robe and hood, speared in his side, worn sandals on his feet, leaning on a tall bent staff, his eyes eternally lifted toward heaven as he offered his poverty and pain up to God. As soon as I entered the cantina I kissed my index finger and touched it to the saint's sandaled foot ("Not the mouth," they told us when they held out holy cards for us to kiss, "the feet *only,* with the saints"); then I turned my back to the calendar, picked my way across the crowded floor, stepping over bottles of somebody's homemade

19

wine, over cases of Rolling Rock beer and ginger ale, and tried to find whatever I'd been sent down there to get, which always took forever among those densely packed shelves.

Most of the food in our cantina dated back to the Cuban missile crisis and had first been accumulated by Aunt Sofia for her own kitchen. At that time, she'd been in America only one year. After Uncle Mike explained to her that the Russians were dangerous Communists who wanted more than anything to ruin life in America, and that perhaps any day now they would be approaching from the south, she went out and bought everything he'd suggested—dried soups, powdered milk, Spam—and then, to make sure they would never have to eat any of that food, not even in a crisis, she bought thirty pounds of pasta and cases and cases of tomato paste. Contadina brand tomato paste. On the red label of each small can was a picture of a farm wife happily heaving a basket of fresh tomatoes while behind her, rows and rows of tomato plants stretched into infinity, suggesting a never-ending supply of food. Uncle Mike was working night shift at the mill then, and Aunt Sofia, alone at night in their empty house, new to America and new to marriage, felt enormously reassured by the thought of her well-stocked cabinets. "All that food," she told me years later, "how good it made me feel. I had Mike make a picture of those shelves to send to show my mother in Italy."

The photograph of Sofia's kitchen circulated in Cimalta for days, made the rounds of all the mothers who had told Nonna Giulia she was crazy to send her only daughter off with an Americano, even if he was a handsome soldier; those mothers now turned green with envy. Everytime she walked out in the town, Nonna Giulia had to put her hand in her pocket and with two fingers make *corna* to protect herself from the jealous Evil Eye. The village girls looked at their village boyfriends and their stomachs soured. Everybody looked at the picture and said, "Only in America, only in America."

When I was four years old, my mother got sick for the first time and I was sent from Cincinnati to Homefield to stay with Aunt Sofia and Uncle Mike for a few months. My aunt spoke very little English then, and that, together with the fact that she wore a dress every day, convinced me I wasn't in America anymore. My mother wore slacks and pedal pushers, sneakers, loafers, sweatshirts, and she dressed me the same way, and this, I thought, made us completely American.

"Dresses are for Sunday," I told Aunt Sofia on my second day in her house.

"Then," she said, "let's go to church," and she let me put on my favorite dress and a pair of her high heels and an old rhinestone necklace, and kneeling beside their bed with our hands folded on their crocheted bedspread, we prayed the rosary in Italian together. Soon I understood almost everything Aunt Sofia said to me in Italian, but I was loyal to my mother and answered only in English.

Aunt Sofia had no children yet, and she was so young and carefree I had her attention all day long. She let me pull cans out of her cabinets and play with them on the kitchen floor, which was so clean you could have put down sheets and a pillow and taken a nap. All day long Aunt Sofia cleaned the little house Uncle Mike had bought for them. She made me an apron to match hers and together we dusted and swept. Afternoons, over and over again, we listened to her stack of Italian 45s on the record player; Aunt Sofia sang along and I learned the words, too, even though I didn't always know what I was saying.

Our days in that small side-by-side two-family house on North Park Street were happy. But then September came around and my father decided I should be enrolled in kindergarten. Holy Cross Elementary School was just down the street. Legally, I was too young to begin school, but my father drove to Homefield to argue with the nuns. He told them I needed to be with children who, if not my age, were at least close to it. "I speak to you not only as a concerned father," he told the nuns, "but as a doctor as well." They were awed by him, a psychiatrist and with an Italian accent to boot. They let me in.

Not long after kindergarten began, I came home with a school form marked Urgent. If there was an attack from Cuba, the form asked, did my family want me to be kept at school or sent home?

Aunt Sofia called my father and told him I had to quit kindergarten. "There's going to be a war."

"This is America, Sofia, there will not be a war. What does the note say?"

"Mike read and it says the nuns think the children should stay there at school. Mike called and they told him that's what most of the mothers and fathers want their kids to do. Nicola, what's wrong with these people?"

"Well, then Giulia should stay also."

"And if those Russians show up? You think I'm going to live downstairs in my basement knowing Giulia's down the street living in a basement with those nuns? Who knows what they'll feed her. No, Nicò, enough is enough. I want her to come home. It's close. I'll run. I'll get her."

"No," he said. "Giulia stays."

So, in her first official act as an American adult, Aunt Sofia signed the form that would keep me in the hands of the nuns, and away from her, when the Russians marched into Homefield. She was crying as she explained to me what the form meant. Each day as I left for school it was like leaving forever. I cried and my aunt cried again. She hung a holy medal of San Francesco around my neck. As we clung to each other, she reminded me to pray to him, pray that the Russians would stay away from Homefield, pray that my mother would get better soon.

The Russians did not attack, and my mother got better, and eventually I went home to Cincinnati and started first grade with my neighborhood friends. And though the Russians stayed away, after a time my mother got sick again, and the winter I was ten she passed away. The funeral was to be in Homefield, where my mother had grown up. She had a lot of friends there, and that's where her parents still lived.

The night I arrived on North Park Street with Ben and Cetta we drove straight to Aunt Sofia's for dinner. I hadn't seen her small house in years. My aunt was standing at the door, waiting with the same pained expression as when I left for kindergarten, but that night she was dressed all in black. She was pregnant with her third child. The button-holes of her black dress were stretched, showing her black slip underneath, and I knew that suddenly I was closer to Italy again. With my mother I had been firmly planted in America, but here I was with my aunt and with Cetta, who was also dressed in black, and they were asking me, with those echoes of Italy in their voices, *"Cara,* are you hungry?"* Their mourning dresses still held the faint scent of the cedar closets. Things from the past that had been stored away for years were being pulled out. I saw America receding.

For eight days neighbors and relatives brought platters of food and sat in Cetta's living room and stood solemnly in the kitchen until late at night. (It was during this time that I started calling my grandparents by their first names— Cetta and Ben—just like everyone else. There was little now that separated me from the adults.) When the visitors finally left, our family sat around the table, exhausted, not wanting to leave each other, until my father gently said, "Well, we all need some sleep now." During those first days his grief was as visible as everyone else's, but sometime during the second week he decided he had a mission —to make me feel safe and secure. Without a word to anyone, my father made plans for the convent to become our new home.

Aunt Sofia's food supplies started arriving almost immediately, a shopping bag at a time, and soon the kitchen cabinets of the convent were lined with cans of tomatoes and boxes of pasta and then the cantina in our basement began to fill up. One summer afternoon she and Cetta called me down to the cantina. "Giuu-u-lia, come, dear, come. Everything is ready. We want to show you."

A few times I had caught them crying in the kitchen as they unpacked my mother's pots and pans and dishes, but as soon as they heard my father, his slippers slapping the steps as he came downstairs, they wiped their eyes and got busy. That afternoon my father wasn't home; I was afraid they'd be in the cantina crying, but when I got there they were smiling, proud, disheveled from all their hard work.

"Now Giulia," Aunt Sofia started, "me and Cetta, you know we're around all the time, but if for some reason, some emergency, you need something and you can't find us, we want you to know where is everything. Just in case."

"That's right," Cetta said, "it's *you* who has to know, Giulia, because your father, about these things, he knows nothing. Less than nothing."

I tried to listen as, with great satisfaction, they took me through their inventory. "Now here, on this low shelf is your cheese. We wrap the cheeses in cloth, like this, to keep them moist and nice, not too dry. This here, in these jars, is your vegetables, picked fresh last summer from the garden. Then, your pastas . . . your olives . . ." It went on. I was eye to eye with the old cans of tomato paste, row after row of cheerful Contadina ladies, a small army assembled by my aunt and my grandmother to protect my father and me—protect us from the Russians, from hunger, from American food, from America itself.

TWO

Our Hellos and Goodbyes

EVERY DAY as I walked up North Park Street on the way home from school, my father waited for me on the front porch. When he spotted me, walking with my friend Molly Shannon or with Lina, he stood and waved his arms, crossing them slowly back and forth as if he were signaling a boat into a foggy dock.

"There's your welcoming committee," Molly teased me, so I didn't yell back, I just waved. Inside, though, I was as happy as he was every time we first saw each other—it was a sharp-focused happiness, about ninety percent relief that he was still there.

He walked across the lawn to meet me, tapped his knuckles on the side of my head. "Well, it sounds a bit fuller up here than it was yesterday. So you learned something in school today, eh?" I kissed him, he took my book-bag and carried it for me into the house.

He was on sabbatical the winter we moved to North Park Street, home during the day writing articles for jour-

26

nals and figuring out what to do next. By the fall term he was teaching at the medical school downtown and doing counseling at two hospitals. In the afternoons he began seeing patients in his office, which was in the rooms above the garage behind our house. On warm evenings when I was playing in the back yard with friends, he'd push open his office window after the last patient had left and call out, *"Signorina Giulia, si mangia!"* Time to eat.

Our kitchen in the convent was nothing but a link in the chain of command that extended from Aunt Sofia's kitchen, at the top of the hill, to Cetta's, at the bottom. Aunt Sofia cooked our meals at her house, then walked them down the street to the convent in the afternoon. Every night, we found dinner waiting for us. Just after dawn, before leaving for work, Cetta showed up to make my father's coffee and to see that I ate enough breakfast.

Mr. Shannon, who lived across the street, once said to me, "They don't make them anymore like your aunt and your grandmother." No one on the outside suspected their tyranny.

"Go back to Cincinnati," Aunt Sofia told my father when he mentioned he was thinking of getting a housekeeper. "We take care of our own houses." It was one of the few times I ever heard her raise her voice to him.

"Nicola," Cetta said softly, her high cheekbones flushed, "you want strangers in the kitchen? Is that what you want?" My father and I soon realized that by "strangers in the kitchen" my grandmother and aunt meant us.

Sometimes from her kitchen window Lina would see my father and me sitting at our dinner table late, talking, way past the time her family's dinner dishes were washed and put away. My father would be carving patterns into the fruit peels on his plate while I sat across the table brushing my bread crumbs together.

"Giulia, what do you guys talk about all that time?" Lina asked me.

"I don't know. All kinds of stuff."

"You're lucky," she told me. "My mom and dad never talk to us that much."

Our first summer in the convent my father planted fifteen small rosebushes along the low stone wall at the edge of the patio. By our second summer the patio was completely bordered with roses. Blood red roses. Translucent white ones. And roses of an extraordinary apricot color, something from a sunset, that my father produced when he crossbred two plants. Evenings, after dinner, he would go into the back yard and I would bring him a cup of espresso. Sipping his coffee, he'd look over the rosebushes, bending occasionally to pick away dead leaves and debris. Eventually he'd balance his cup on the stone wall, take up his clippers and begin trimming, cutting off roses, pinching off thorns. Then he'd bring roses to me—at the piano if I was practicing, or to my room if I was studying, or he'd just leave them there, scattered on my desk.

It was a summer night. Lina and Molly were staying over, and we woke my father with a scream that cut through his sleep. He ran down the hallway flicking on lights, threw open the door of my bedroom and found Molly crying, with a long sewing needle puncturing her ear lobe and blood dripping onto her pink nightgown.

"For the love of God," he whispered, and then he screamed, "Giulia!"

"Dad, she's bleeding so much."

"Giulia talked me into it," Molly sobbed.

"Molly, it was your idea," Lina said. "You said before,

you wished you were Italian so you could have pierced ears. Plus, you bought those earrings."

"Yeah," I said, "you bought those stupid earrings." Gold disks with an engraved M on each one. Molly had saved up for weeks.

"For the love of God," my father repeated, and walked Molly to the bathroom, holding a towel to her ear. "Sit, Molly," he ordered as he dropped down the lid of the toilet. He wet cotton with rubbing alcohol, sat on the rim of the bathtub and wiped her ear. The wide sleeve of his light-blue robe was dotted with blood.

Molly touched the sleeve. "Is that me?"

"Shh," he said. He examined the ear again.

I didn't dare speak, but Lina told him, "We used ice first." She held out the bowl of melting cubes to show him. He said nothing.

Finally he took both of Molly's hands into one of his. With the other hand he turned her trembling face toward him. "Congratulations, Molly. You have one pierced ear. Do you want to leave it that way, or do you want to have two? What do you say, Giulia? Should we make your friend into a *zingarella* or not?"

"What's that, a zinga whatever?" Molly wanted to know.

"It means gypsy," I told her.

"Come on, Molly," Lina said, "be a *zingarella.*"

Molly looked up at Dad and he was smiling.

"How will you do it?" Molly asked him.

"You will see. Giulia, go downstairs and get that bottle of anisette in the dining room."

When I came back upstairs, Molly was wearing one of her round gold earrings with the engraved M. My father was holding ice cubes to her other ear. He poured us each a small shot of anisette. Molly had two.

"Professor Di Cuore, did you ever do this before?"

"Did I ever do this? Did you know I pierced my sister Sofia's ears when she was only one week old? I was sixteen then, just a little older than you and Giulia are now."

"You held ice to a tiny baby's ears?" Molly asked.

"What ice? We had no ice. We were lucky in Cimalta when we had water. One needle, a little fire, that is all that is needed. But you have to move quickly—pop—make the hole and that is it."

Molly wanted to know what kind of earrings newborn babies wore.

"A small twig of oregano through the hole the first week or so. It keeps away the infection, they say."

"Oregano?" Molly's hands reached up to touch her earring. When four ice cubes had melted, my father made a big show of washing his hands. He told Molly that for the same price she could have a hole made in her nose, too. He put a lit match to a needle, just as I had done. "Sit by me, Giulia, and watch this," he said. "Tell me when you are ready, Molly."

"Not yet."

"Take your time," he said. "Close your eyes. Relax. Whenever you want me to begin, just say so."

I saw blood and knew he had already begun. "We will wait as long as you like." I saw the needle in the back of her ear, then it slid all the way through. Lina and I exchanged shocked looks.

Molly's eyes were still closed. "I just need a minute to relax."

"I am now rubbing alcohol onto the ear," Dad said as he put in the second earring.

"Well, I guess I'm ready. OK, Professor. Go."

"Go?"

"Yeah, go ahead."

Dad gave Lina the signal to hold the hand mirror before

Molly's face. I threw my arms around his neck and hugged hard.

But the reign of peace in our house was nearing its end.

When I was fourteen, America started to invade my father's house. The night it happened, I was lying on my bedroom floor, my feet up on the bed, reading *Love Story*. In two nights I was going to see the movie with Morrisey Moriarty. He was the younger brother of one of the high school guys who hung out with Molly's brother, Tommy. Weekends, their cars pulled in and out of the Shannons' driveway, and I stood at our hallway window, hoping for a glimpse of Morrisey's brown ski jacket, his blond curly head. Sometimes, shopping on Homefield Avenue with Aunt Sofia, I'd see him and we'd say hi. Lying on the floor that night, trying to read, I played over every encounter I'd had with Morrisey, up to the moment of that miracle when he'd appeared, standing in the snow of our front lawn while I was shoveling our walkway. His red-gloved hands offered me a snowball. He had come to ask me out.

Suddenly my father was standing over me, his face upside down and furious. He had never before come into my room without knocking.

I jumped up. "What happened?"

"Giulia!" he shouted. "Do you know a boy with the name of Morris, Morrison . . ."

I sat up. "Morrisey?"

"So you know this boy," my father accused me. "Can you explain to me, please, why did he just call you?"

"What did you say to him?"

"To please never call here again."

"Dad! We're going to the movies on Friday. I was going to tell you."

He turned wild-eyed.

"Molly and her boyfriend are going too."

31

"Absolutely not."

"Molly's boyfriend is a junior. His father lets him drive his car."

"Giulia!"

"The movie's early. Really, Dad, it's OK."

He stood blocking the doorway. "Do you actually think I am going to say it is fine for you to go in a car with these boys at night and drive God knows where?"

"Dad, I already told Morrisey I could go."

He turned away, left the room and came back armed with the telephone. "Do you want to call him or should I?"

He held out the receiver but I wouldn't take it. "If you'd just talk to Morrisey, Dad, you'd see what a nice guy he is."

"I have nothing to say to him, unless, of course you are going to marry this boy. Are you planning to get married?"

"I'm only in ninth grade. And I'm not calling him." I sat on top of my desk.

My father's eyebrows twisted, a black snake sliding over his eyes. If he had started screaming I might have had a chance. "You do not know what you are asking for, Giulia." His whisper was ominous. Maybe I *was* wrong. He threw the phone across the wooden floor. "No more phone calls from this boy, do you hear me? This has already gone too far."

I didn't cry, not until after I'd called Morrisey.

My father had overcome many obstacles in America, but it seemed the most threatening enemy he ever had to face was American teenage boys.

The next day Aunt Sofia called me into the kitchen, lured me with a friendly "Giuu-lia, come here, dear. I want to ask you something." I figured it had to do with dinner. I found her at the sink rinsing broccoli. "Yeah?" I said from the door.

"Come here." She cocked her head, pulled me in close to her, and then in a fast, hot whisper, she asked, "What did you think you were doing, telling that boy you wanted to go to the movies with him? He might try to ask you again. What are you going to do then?"

Now everyone in the family started eyeing me suspiciously. During the previous year I had grown three inches taller, one bra size larger and my hips had started to spread. I couldn't get used to my body. I gave up cookies, cake, candy, pie and doughnuts as a Lent offering. I wanted to give up pasta, too, but the family wouldn't let me. They just looked me over every time I stepped out the door.

"Those blue jeans, they're dragging on the ground."

"I like them that way."

"They're too tight for you, Giulia. You need new ones."

"I need to lose weight."

"If she gets new ones," Lina asked, "can I have those?"

"Lina, ssh. Giulia, no chewing gum when you walk in the street."

"And how come?"

"It's not nice."

Even my grandfather and Uncle Mike were quick to tell me, "Be careful. You watch out now, you hear?"

"You guys are making me crazy," I shouted, standing in the hallway, shaking my head. My hair was blond on top of brown, like my mother's had been, but overgrown and wild. Lion's hair, Aunt Sofia called it, "to go with your big mouth like a lion's."

"I'm just going down the street. Want to send a detective?" But the way they were eyeing me told me I wasn't so blameless. "What are you looking at me like that for? Stop it!" Shouting at them, I felt huge and monstrous.

A month passed. I hadn't seen Morrisey since I'd broken our date. Every day after school, I went to Aunt Sofia's and threw myself onto her couch.

Aunt Sofia came into the living room, kicking the vacuum cleaner ahead of her. "You better stop that moping around before your father has a fit."

"You know, you could have helped me. You could talk to him and tell him it's not the end of the world if I go to the movies."

"Me? Talk to your father? And then if something happens? You want to fight your father, *you* fight him. Get your shoes off my couch." She was on the floor, on her stomach, vacuuming up cookie crumbs from under the armchairs.

"Calm down," I said, trying to grab the vacuum from her. "You think Uncle Mike's going to fire you if this house isn't spotless for five minutes? Relax."

"Out of my way, Giulia. When you're married and a mother, then we'll talk about relax." She kicked the vacuum into the dining room and left me on the couch.

When Cetta stopped by on her way home from work, I was still lying there. "Giulia! What's wrong, *cara?*"

"I've got a headache, Cetta. Come here, press your hand on my head." Her wide hand was cool and covered my whole forehead.

"You poor thing. Too many brains, huh?" I closed my eyes. "It's the *malocchio,*" she diagnosed. "I can tell from your color. You're all beige. Want me to call Comare Roseanna?" Roseanna was so good at taking away the Evil Eye she could do it over the telephone, say the prayers and incantations without your even getting on to talk to her. "Yeah, I'm calling Roseanna. See what she can do."

"Cetta?"

"Yes, dear."

"I'm moving away as soon as I can."

"What's wrong? You don't like us anymore?"

"I can't stand my father."

"Shame!"

"You know, that guy who asked me to the movie, I really liked him. It's just not fair."

"Giulia. Giulia. When I was your age I was one year from being married. And now I got Ben squawking at me, night and day. You know I been working fifteen years at Reynolds Department Store and still I can't take a penny from the bank without asking your grandfather? Did you know that?" Ben wouldn't even let her register to vote. A staunch Republican, he was sure that in the privacy of the voting booth Cetta would betray him, vote like her lady friends and their Democratic husbands. "Is that what you want, *cara?*"

I pulled Cetta down to sit next to me on the couch. There was the warmth of her, then the faint scent of wool off her brown and black knit suit. On her jacket lapel, a small pin, the tiny gold profile of a praying Madonna. I looked at Cetta's soft, full profile. Her long, light hair was braided and twisted into an intricate bun at the nape of her neck. You could still see the sixteen-year-old bride in her, but talking about Ben, she looked hard, like a young girl who knew too much. What happened in marriage?

"I know you feel bad for this boy," she told me. "But you know what they say, *cara?* You miss one bus, you'll catch the next. Don't be in such a rush to leave your daddy."

"All he cares about is himself."

"No, your father's a saint. Since your mother he never looks at another woman. He never goes with anyone, doesn't bring anyone home." All this was true. "Only

35

thing he wants is to take care of you. That man loves you more than his own life."

I picked off bits of blue and yellow thread that her skirt had gathered in the department store sewing room where she worked. "I'm never getting married."

"Giulia! Bite your tongue."

"But it's crazy. All that yelling and screaming and you never get to do what you want."

"That's love, Giulia."

"That's stupid."

"That's how it is."

Now my father and I were circling each other, both of us suspicious. When I came home after being out with my friends, he looked me over, almost sniffed me for evidence.

It worked both ways. When he called from his office at the university to say he was coming home late, I listened behind his voice to hear what was going on. I looked through his mail, watched his patients come and go. I asked so many questions about his graduate students that he asked, "Are you making an investigation?"

One night around midnight as he and I walked down the street from Aunt Sofia's, a boy called over from the Shannons' porch. "Hey, Giulia, hi."

"Hi."

"Good evening," my father said, overly polite. The full-leafed branches hung over us and held his Italian voice, which was too formal for the soft, American summer night.

The boy on the porch wasn't Morrisey, but when my father and I got to our front door and he was taking out his key, he told me in a low voice, "That boy at the Shannons', you will not go on a date with him, whoever he is, so do not ask me."

"He didn't ask me out."

"Good. I am glad."

Even with all this, even though he was keeping me from everything I wanted, filling me with fear of everything I wanted, scaring me and scaring me until it seemed that the things I wanted were evil, my friends were bad, the world beyond our house, over our hedges was terrifying—even with all this, whenever I heard the garage door open or heard his footsteps walking across the gravel of the drive-way as he came toward the house, when I heard his key in the door, there was that tremendous feeling of relief—a lightening in my shoulders, a loosening in my throat. He was home, he was back from the world, and I was safe.

By the time we were juniors in high school, Molly had gone steady with three different guys, two of them in college; one said he'd like to marry her. One afternoon, a bunch of girls were sitting around somebody's kitchen sharing a joint, and Molly confessed to us that she was still a virgin, "but just by a hair."

"Just do it, Molly," Kitty Henley said, jabbing a spoon into a half-gallon of mint chocolate chip ice cream.

"Kitty, let it sit a minute." I sighed, exasperated.

"Giulia's right, Kitty."

I was always right with my friends. I had no boyfriend, so I was never confused. "Je-sus, Kitty." I had to grab her hand to stop her. "You're bending the spoon. *Wait* a minute."

"I *can't* wait. Same with ice cream as it is with sex. What are you waiting for, Molly?"

"Probably just next Saturday night," I teased. Molly gave me the finger.

"Hey, listen, next Saturday night," Kitty said, "I can get us all into a fraternity party. Mostly *grad*uate students,

Arab guys in their twenties. Total knockouts. Great parties."

Almost everyone said yeah, they wanted to go. "Giulia, coming?"

"No, I don't think."

" 'Cause of Dad-dy," Molly sang to me.

"What is it with you, Di Cuore? You'll get high—look at you with that joint—you'll hang out with us, you'll do anything as long as it's all us girls, but when we're doing something with guys you back out?"

I inhaled a long moment. "I'd rather get busted than have to deal with my father or my aunt."

I knew I had to get out of my father's house. I knew I had to get out of Homefield.

My father wanted me to live at home for college, enroll at his university in town. It was the early seventies, and in the past few years he'd had young men—students, former students, others he'd never seen before—come to him asking for psychiatric evaluations to keep them out of Vietnam. His most promising graduate student, a young woman, had been seriously injured in an antiwar demonstration. He said he wanted me where he could see me.

But I told him, "Dad, I want to go away to college."

"What is this *away*? Are you going to college or are you planning a vacation?"

"Dad, I'm sure you'll agree with me that part of the experience of college is to try your capabilities, challenge yourself . . ."

"What you are saying is that you want to meet boys."

"What's wrong with that?"

I had to get away. During the fall of my senior year I had spent hours in the college-placement office leafing through catalogs until I found St. Helena's, a Catholic women's college fenced in by a gate and the forests of

Pennsylvania, a place so conservative, so lovely and safe that when I said, "Dad, I think I'd really get a good education there," he said, "Well, I am pleased to see you are finally coming to your senses. Yes, to a school like this one you can go. I will be happy to send you."

St. Helena's was close enough to Homefield that I could come home every weekend. Once I was there, though, I wouldn't have to and I intended not to.

In May, when St. Helena's offered me a scholarship, my father decided I was a genius. He took me, Molly and a few of my other friends out to dinner and ordered two bottles of champagne. He bullied us into tasting every dessert on the pastry cart.

"You shouldn't be so afraid of your dad, Giulia," Cindi Miller told me in the ladies' room. "This dinner's great. See, he's not so bad."

An older woman putting on mascara at the mirror said, "What a nice man out there with all you girls. Now, who's his daughter?"

"I am."

"Lucky girl."

And, yes, that night I was.

A few days later, he surprised me with the plane ticket to Italy. By then I was just biding time until I could get away. "Sure," I said, "I'll go to Italy. For how long?"

"June. July. I will come in early August and we will have a month together. How is that?"

For a few weeks my father and I were best friends.

What he didn't know was that I was on the waiting list at Barnard College, and in early June, just when it seemed my father and I had bartered some peace with each other, I was accepted.

"Dad, *this* is the school I really want. Listen, my photography teacher said I'm good. If I'm in New York . . ."

"Absolutely no. There is nothing in New York that you need to take pictures of."

"But Barnard, Dad . . ."

"Yes, across from Columbia University, which was the site of criminal unrest just a few years ago. Why go to college? Why not go directly to jail?"

"But Dad . . ."

"Why, I would like to know, is it so unthinkable to stay home for college? When I was a student we would have been happy—thrilled—to stay with our families. I had to go to Naples, where there was bombing. And there were no dormitories and football and dating and nonsense. We had no food!"

My father was standing in the middle of the kitchen. His hazel eyes wide and burning, and I was staring back at him with the same angry eyes. Aunt Sofia said it was a shock to him that I argued looking right at him. She said they never said Boo to their own father. "That was long ago," I told him, "that was Italy."

"Giulia," he said, sighing, tired, "what is it you want?"

The simple American pleasure of hanging out under the streetlights, leaning against the fat fender of somebody's father's station wagon, talking to a boy and knowing that if he asked you to go for a ride, to a party, maybe to a movie, you'd be able to say yes.

"I don't want to go to St. Helena's."

"*E qual è quei che disvuol ciò che volle . . . ,*" he quoted from Dante, about some sufferer in Hell who keeps changing his mind.

"Dad, listen to me. St. Helena's doesn't feel right. I just have this feeling in my gut."

"Then take some Pepto-Bismol. It will pass."

The full-length mirror from Cetta's sewing room was propped up against the refrigerator. It was the last fitting for my traveling suit. Cetta was kneeling at my feet, straight pins clamped between her lips. Aunt Sofia sat at the kitchen table sewing buttons onto the jacket. Lina was eating spumone out of a soup bowl.

"That suit looks real good on you, Giulia," Lina said. For years she had watched everything I did and bought and said and wore. Like me, she was a Giulia. Her full name was Giulina, named after Nonna Giulia, but in kindergarten she had told her friends she was named after me. I had ignored her then. Now, almost fourteen, she was changing, turning gorgeous. Her straight, thick black hair was down to her waist. Her narrow, half-covered eyes made her look like she knew things. That night at Cetta's she said, "That dress makes you look skinny," and I was grateful.

At my knees and elbows I was still like Cetta—cushiony, soft. And the plump tops of my arms and my moon-round face were still like hers, but with all the arguing over the past months, I had lost weight. At every fitting, Cetta had had to take in the seams of the suit a quarter inch or more. Now the yellow linen fell gracefully, curved smoothly but not too much, even around my hips, around my breasts, those places where I was always afraid I looked trampy. At first the idea of a handmade traveling suit had smacked too much of Old World thinking for me —usually for the fittings I stood slouching and braless, in dirty bare feet. But looking in the mirror as Cetta pinned up the hem, I saw that the suit did things to me. I raised myself up on my toes to see how I'd look in high heels.

"Hem it shorter, Cetta. Shorter."

Slowly, she stood up in front of me. I was a full head taller than my grandmother, but she was daunting when she got mad. Red was rising over the perfect smooth skin of her high cheekbones, and the urge came, as it always did, to kiss her there, where, when she was happy, I could

41

feel her smiling. She wasn't smiling now, and I couldn't dare kiss her. I was depending on my anger to propel me out of there, away from my father, past Italy, beyond college, into some wider world where I could breathe. The only danger was in looking back for one parting glance that might leave me choking with love for them all and unable to walk out the door. "Short-er, *please.*"

"How short? Short enough to show your *culu?*" Cetta slapped my bottom. "That short?"

"Oh Cetta, please, hurry. I don't have all night."

"And where do you got to go?" Aunt Sofia demanded. She was spreading my jacket out in front of her; the empty sleeves hung helpless off the edge of the table.

"Never mind."

"Lina, where is Giulia going?"

"Leave Lina alone. I'm going to a party at the Shannons'."

"Oh no, oh no, not there. That's all we need. Can't you just leave for Italy in peace? Why do you got to start World War Three with your father?"

"It's my last chance to see these people I went to school with. And if you cared about me at all you'd tell my father to just shut up this time and let me go."

Cetta said, "I'll tell him to let you go to that college in New York City before I tell him to send you to Shannons', that wild house."

"Close that door before Lina comes in," Aunt Sofia hissed at me later that evening. She was leaning out the sewing room window into the air shaft, smoking a cigarette.

"That guilty look on your face. I wish I had my camera." Only Cetta and I knew that Aunt Sofia smoked. She had me drive her two towns away so she could buy cigarettes. She only smoked in Cetta's sewing room, hanging out the window into the dark, dank, blind air shaft, or down in our cantina.

"I thought you were in a hurry," she said, looking at me with big eyes.

I took a cigarette from her pack and lit it with the end of hers. I rolled a puff of smoke off the tip of my tongue.

"Behave yourself."

"Monkey see, monkey do." I grinned at her.

She cracked a smile, but it was wan and tired. She wedged her cigarette into the corner of her mouth, squinted at the smoke and picked loose strings from a tear in the hem of my shorts. "Oh, before I forget. Give me or Cetta the bra you're wearing for your trip so we can sew a little pocket inside to hide your money. Comare Roseanna did that when she went to Italy. Good idea, no?"

"Sure, if I wear a bra."

She sighed. "God help you, Giulia." She had found some thread and a needle on a shelf and was mending my shorts.

Standing so close to her, I noticed the orange cooking burns that streaked her white forearms. "I know what I'm bringing you from Italy. Want me to tell you?"

"The best present for me is that you come home safe."

"Okay, all right. I'll tell you. What I'm bringing you is a carton of French cigarettes, Gauloises—they're real strong —from the duty-free shop. After all the cigarettes I mooched off you . . ."

She held the needle in front of my face. "Don't you go crazy and tell them over there I let you smoke."

"I'm going to tell them everything." I finished my cigarette, tossed the butt out the window, then took two more cigarettes from her pack, buttoned them into my shirt pocket. "I should buy you a *couple* of cartons, shouldn't I?"

"And where are you going with those?"

"I told you where I'm going."

"Not with cigarettes. Nicola'll kill us all if he sees."

"No, he won't. He'll just kill me." Aunt Sofia was staring at me, her worn-out eyes sparked with something like curiosity, a look from the old days, when she was sunny and young and we had played together. Stay like this, I wanted to say to her, stay just like this.

But then she was shaking her head at me, bewildered, asking me, "You're not afraid of anything, are you?" as if that were a bad thing.

Fearless and godless, that's what Aunt Sofia thought I was. But Molly had watched me turn into a frightened fool. "Get your ass over here, Di Cuore," she had said on the phone that afternoon. "Party tonight, and Morrisey, that wimp, still wants to see you. You better be here."

"Molly, how? I can't get over there without my father finding out."

"You just got a high school diploma. You're a frigging Merit Scholar. I think you can figure out for yourself how to get across the street."

That evening, back from Cetta's, up in my bedroom, I turned up Carole King loud and sang with her, "You make me feel like a na-tu-ral woman." I pretended I was Molly. I'd watched her get ready to go out. Rubbing lotion on her legs and Jean Naté between her breasts. A clean work shirt, a pair of dirty jeans, a bandanna around her neck or a beaded headband across her freckled forehead. Once she was dressed, the power was in her purse. Humming, she'd move through the house, collecting cigarettes, lighter, chewing gum, eyeliner, car keys, gaining momentum as her brown suede pouch filled. She hitched it up onto her shoulder as she went out the door, and the long fringe flew behind her. Nobody could stop her then.

At eight-thirty, I walked out the back door into the dimming June evening, the air warm as a bath. The cigarettes in my purse felt hot against my hip. My father was in the yard trimming his roses. He heard the screen door bang shut and looked up. "Giulia!" he said, pleased to see me.

"Hi, Dad."

He snipped off a branch of rosebuds. "So what do you think?"

They were beautiful, apricot-colored, my favorites. "For you, *signorina.*"

I examined the flowers for bugs, then put them in my hair. "How's that?"

"Gorgeous. Both the flower and the young lady. And where are you going now? I thought we were going to review those Italian verbs a few more times this evening."

"Well, there's this party. Some friends from school, you know, people I want to say goodbye to."

"And this gathering is not at the Shannons', I hope."

"Actually, yeah."

"No. Molly is welcome here anytime, but that house is off-limits to you. You know that."

I hated to hear myself beg, but I sat down in the grass next to him. "Dad, come on. It's just across the street." Staring at his muddy gardening shoes, I thought of my modern-history class, pictures of Soviet troops marching into Budapest, into Prague. "Just this once?"

"My dear Giulia, do you know what goes on in that house? Do you? Parties so wild the police must come."

"That was Molly's sisters who had those parties. Not her."

"And what do you know of those sisters? Nothing."

He offered me another rose. I took it. I tossed it. I said, "What do *you* know? All you care about is yourself and what you want. That's all you care about. You know nothing about me or anybody else."

Slowly, he stood to his full height, staring down at me

45

the whole time, as if waiting until there was enough distance between us for what he was going to say next. "I know this. I know that three years ago one of those sisters came to me asking for a psychiatric statement that would allow her to get an abortion." He was whispering, but spitting as he spoke. "Did you know that?" He never broke patients' confidences, and I knew that, more than anything, he was furious at me now for having pushed him that far. "Did you know *that* about your friends?"

I was dizzy for an instant. "Dad, that's terrible."

"*Yes.*"

"Is she all right?"

He shouted, *"No,* it is not all right."

"Oh, Dad." I stood up, tried to touch his arm. "I'm not Molly, Dad. And I'm not her sisters."

"Go, go to the party with the boys. Take a bottle of Scotch. Stay all night. Don't come home."

"Dad, don't you think you're exaggerating just a little?"

He bent over to start digging, offered me nothing but the bald spot on the top of his head. "Would you like money to buy drugs, perhaps?"

"Dad," I pleaded, "cut it out."

"Go!"

"It's only a goddamn party."

He speared the dirt hard with the shovel. "Get out of here, Giulia, before I throw something at you."

"You know, someday I'm going to do something really terrible." I was crying now. "I mean really give you something to yell about."

"Giulia!"

"I hate you," I screamed.

And then he slapped me.

Later, still shocked he had done it, he came to my room. He'd never hit me before, although it had been in the air any number of times. A solemn silence ran through the house now that it had finally happened. "Giulia, you are an intelligent girl. You don't want to be involved with these kids."

"I'm a woman, not a girl. And yes, I do want to be involved with them. They're my friends."

He reminded me again that soon I would be in Italy, and then at college. He told me to think about my studies, my career. With all this in my future, he asked me, what was an evening out, a silly party?

I didn't plead. I was a solid piece of ice and I wasn't going to melt for him, not now, not anymore. Finally he gave up, stood and walked to the door. "Giulia," he said, "I feel sorry for you if you are this shortsighted, if you cannot see beyond today or tomorrow."

But I felt sorry for him, because there was no question in my mind now that I was going to leave him, and no doubt that anywhere else would be better.

As soon as he was gone, I got up and closed the door. Locked it. I stood at my window, looked out over the back yard, beyond his roses, into the bruised sky where the sun was setting into the smoke of the steel mill, turning everything orange, purple, garish.

"I'm out of here," I said softly into the evening air. "I'm gone."

THREE

The Bridge
of the Four Heads

THERE IS A BRIDGE that crosses a narrow finger of the Tiber. It is a small bridge, the oldest in Rome. Into each of its stone pillars are carved four heads, each head facing a different direction. This is Ponte Fabriccio, also known as *il ponte dei quattro capi,* the bridge of the four heads. *I quattro capi* is how Aunt Sofia referred to her four brothers, who were all older than she. "I was young when I lost my father, then I had four chiefs, all of them tripping over each other trying to tell me what I should do."

Nicola, my father, was the oldest of the brothers, *capo dei capi,* the chief of all the chiefs. After him came Antonio and Vittorio, identical twins. When they were born, in Cimalta (a place that has always valued simplicity), the twins were thought of as one person split in half. One boy was born laughing, the other crying; Anto was all action, Vito was all thought. As children, they were indistinguishable and inseparable. As young students, though, they

split over ideology. Anto was a pragmatist, capitalist, na-
tionalist. Vito accused him of being a Fascist.

"If the Fascists give me a job, of course I'm a Fascist."

"Sei senza anima, tu," Vito yelled at him, disgusted.
"You have no soul."

When the twins began their university studies in Messina it was wartime. Anto was studying law with hopes of
one day becoming a judge. Vito, the socialist, was studying medicine. For a while Vito worked as an obscure link
in a chain of partisans who helped Jews escape through
the south. Using the money his father gave him, Vito
bought food and delivered it to a woman who sneaked the
food into a safe house. Vito never actually saw any Jews.
When he was hungry he went to Anto, who at that time
had a part-time job as a municipal clerk, a job Vito said
was complicity with devils.

"But could you feed the others if I didn't feed you?
Really I am helping the cause more than you are."

"Ridiculous, those two," Aunt Sofia remembered.
"Looking so much alike and arguing like that. It was like
seeing someone fight with himself in the mirror. 'Stop it,'
I'd tell them. 'How can there be peace in the world if two
men with the same face can't get along?' And what did
they say to me? 'Sofì, go, make us a *caffè*. Sofì, this jacket,
can you sew it for me? Sofia, do this, do that.'"

In the photos I've seen of my uncles as young men, they
are like my father—tall, usually towering over whoever
else is in the picture. They are both thin, very thin, and
have that lean masculine build that the clothes of the forties hang on so nicely—loose trousers with pleats at the
waist. Their thin necks giraffe out of wide-open shirt col-
lars. In every picture, they hold cigarettes. My father is
with them in some photos, and there are features in the
faces that join them all as brothers—thick eyebrows,
heavy foreheads, long sharp chins. Though the twins have

a lyrical fall and rise of cheekbone and cheek, a movement like italic script, none of the three is really handsome. There is intelligence in their faces, and a seriousness as alluring as good looks: a woman would be complimented to be noticed by any one of these brothers.

For Vito, a young man with pain pinched into the corners of his deep-set eyes, medical school felt like an evasion. After passing two exams, he left for Sardinia to join a group of missionaries.

Anto stayed in Messina and got his law degree. One hot June day in 1947, just one week after graduating, Anto found himself in the Salerno train station with his dream of becoming a judge quickly slipping through his hands. The war had ended but was still too close for Anto to find the kind of legal position he had hoped for. Through a friend of his father's, he'd been offered a position as assistant to the director of a hospital in Bari. This was far from what he'd wanted for himself, but his father was gone now, and there wouldn't be many of these favors coming his way anymore. Anto had a girlfriend in Naples, a nice girl whose aging uncle needed a young manager for his restaurant and hotel. The uncle wanted Anto, the girl wanted Anto. Anto had no idea what he wanted, but he understood—in that profound way we know without knowing—that the Salerno train station was a crucial crossroad in his life.

All day he stood there, asking himself, "Bari or Naples, Naples or Bari? The hospital or the hotel?" Without Vito around to argue with, Anto discovered it was no longer so easy to define what it was he wanted to do. He went into the bar of the train station, drank countless cups of espresso, eavesdropped on other people's conversations, hoping for a clue, a hint to where he should go. All day, all evening, he tried to decide. He took a walk through the streets near the station. The last train of the day went to

Bari, and because he had no place else to spend the night, he took that train, and that is how Anto decided not to marry the girl in Naples, and that is how he eventually became a hospital director.

The next morning when he got off the train, Bari smelled good, full of the sea, but then the gruff undecipherable local dialect surrounded him, and he thought, I'll get out of here as soon as I make some money.

He went straight to the hospital. While Anto was waiting to be introduced to the director, a young university student came into the office with her arm hooked through her father's. Anto was already in love with the young student—it was her voice, he said, and her high-arched feet in a pair of strappy high heels—when he found out her father was Bari's chief surgeon. Within six months, Anto and the young student, Assunta, were engaged.

At the wedding, two years later, Vito, now returned from the missions, a medical student again, declared his love to Assunta's cousin Berta. The cousins' last name, Tramonto, meant "sunset"; the twins had found their home. In time, Anto and Assunta had two children, Carlo and Marigiulia; Vito and Berta had three, Giuliana, Carlino and Daniele. All the children looked alike.

When I went to Italy, the two families were living in the same building, in adjacent apartments. Their side balconies faced each other and were so close that Assunta and Berta could lean over the railings to polish each other's fingernails and help pin up each other's hair. Anto was now the director of the hospital in Montemaggiore, a position in which he was constantly volunteering medical care to the peasants who came from nearby villages. Vito was a surgeon in that hospital and a doctor for the villagers.

The fourth *capo*, the youngest brother, was Rocco,

who, unlike his brothers, was not exceptional in any way when he was a boy. He wasn't tall like them, or brilliant or very good in school.

A few years older than Sofia, Rocco was her favorite brother. "He never told me what to do. But I had to make up stories to tell our father when Rocco was out too late playing cards. He wasn't like the other three, their heads so big with studying day and night. How serious they were, with their this and their that. Politics and school and medicine. Only thing in Rocco's head was jokes. That's all. And the animals. That kid, for some reason, always loved the animals. Cats, dogs, birds. Who knows why? And in Cimalta it wasn't like here, where the Americans let the dogs sit right up on the couch and even on the bed —what a dirty habit. In Cimalta the dogs were to keep people from stealing the sheep at night. Cats were to keep the mice away. But Rocco, he was always bringing home animals, just for nothing, just to play. All the cats of Cimalta knew our house."

Sofia laughed and covered her face with her hand, just as my father did when something made him laugh too hard. When she came back to me, she was still smiling. "I have such a clear picture in my head of Rocco when he was a boy. You know how I see him? I see him lying on the bed at night with the cat on his stomach, and Rocco would hold up the front legs of the cat, and the cat, with the back legs, would walk up and down Rocco's stomach. Rocco loved this, he said this was like the cat was kneading bread dough. He'd talk to those animals. 'Come on, cat,' he'd say, 'let's make bread.' Oh, that Rocco.

"And when he went to Montemaggiore to study! The first three months, I don't think that boy went to school one time. People told the teachers they saw Rocco at this end of town, at that end, talking to everybody in the market, in the shops up and down Corso Dante, like he was running for mayor. Twelve years old, and he'd even leave town and go out to the farms, play with those dirty animals. When Rocco took the first exams—ooph, *che disastro!*—he didn't pass one test. 'Fine,' my father said to him. 'You like it outside, you don't like to study. Fine, we'll send you to the farm to work. See how you like that.' After a month of carrying wood on his shoulders and bringing food for the pigs and horses, and getting all bit up from the bees because he had to take care of the bee houses, after one month of all that he comes with this big serious face and says to our father, 'Papà, I think I want to study medicine.' " Sofia laughed loudly, then quickly, her face got stony. "Too bad. Who knows why things went the way they did for him. He was a good kid, he could have done better."

Rocco did study medicine at the University of Rome. By that time Nicola was in America, sending him money when he could, pleased that Rocco was finally getting serious. Nicola told him in every letter, "Whatever field you decide to specialize in, I will help you." It wasn't until after his graduation that Rocco told the family he had become a veterinarian. Almost everyone thought it was a good joke. Nicola, though, felt duped.

"Nicola, understand," Rocco wrote in a letter, "being a doctor for people is too serious for me. You have to work so hard, and God forbid, if you lose one, that's a life. The animals, I do my best, but if I lose one, well—let's keep things in perspective—it wouldn't be the end of the world. The truth is, I get along with animals and I hate to work hard. Being a vet comes easy to me. I think I did the best thing."

"I think you made a big mistake," Nicola wrote back. "I do not think this is what our father had in mind when he sacrificed so you could study." Nicola got over it a bit when Rocco became a professor and then one of the directors of the department of veterinary medicine at the University of Naples, the youngest ever named to such a position.

Rocco shocked the family a second time by showing up one Christmas—he was thirty then—with his best student, Claudia, and their newborn baby, Giulietta.

"Rocco, why didn't you tell us you were married?" they all shouted.

"Because I'm not."

This was the point where Rocco lost Aunt Sofia, who scornfully referred to Claudia as *"la scienziata,"* the scientific one. Claudia had become a professor in Rocco's department, and she and Rocco had a private veterinary practice on the farm where they lived outside of Naples. "I guess she's too busy to get married," Aunt Sofia said when the letter arrived saying that Rocco and Claudia had had a second daughter, Francesca. "Funny, though, how they got time for baptisms, those two."

When I arrived in Italy, Rocco and Claudia still weren't married, and I got my first lesson in the nuances of Italian moral codes. If a woman is intelligent, well educated, part of a wealthy family, and from the North—and Claudia was all these things—she could be forgiven almost anything, especially a youthful mistake. At nineteen, Claudia had married a family friend, an old widower who praised her brilliance before the wedding, then afterward demanded that she quit studying, stay home and help raise his grandchildren. She left her husband after four months and had been waiting for an annulment ever since. The man, wealthy and proud, kept paying off powerful priests to keep the marriage contract intact. Claudia had no recourse. At that time there was still no divorce in Italy.

"That tramp," Aunt Sofia said when she heard Rocco and Claudia were expecting a third baby. When we got the telegram saying it was a boy, she muttered, "She had to keep trying, didn't she, until she got a boy."

"Aunt Sofì, first of all, what's so great about having a boy? And second, how can you blame *her*? Whose children did she have? What about Zio Rocco?"

"He's no prize, that one. It's bad enough for a man, but for a woman—"

"Hey, whose side are you on? Claudia's a woman, just like you. What would you do in her situation?"

"Me? In her situation? Never. My brothers would twist my neck like a chicken. And they'd be right to do it."

"That's nice, Aunt Sofia."

"And for your information, she wanted a boy so she could hold on to your uncle, that's why. Don't you know anything? He might pick up and leave her in any minute. He could go and find somebody else, somebody he can marry. He's a handsome, good-looking guy, your Zio Rocco."

He had the heavy eyebrows like his brothers, but on him they looked comical, as if he was always about to tell a joke. He wasn't balding like them. "They all say I'm irresponsible," he told me when I got to Italy, "so that's why I have the beard. No shaving in the morning. That's one more responsibility I got rid of." He had large round dark eyes, not the heavy-lidded worried eyes of the twin brothers, not the dark circles my father had. He was the only brother without small thin hairs growing across the bridge of his nose.

He was handsome in an obvious way, with well-proportioned features. If he'd been the kind of man to pay attention to how he dressed, women would have noticed him on the street. And it wouldn't have mattered: he looked at no woman but Claudia.

I was surprised when I met her. She was not particularly pretty—she wasn't pretty at all. Across her right cheek was a constellation of small black birthmarks. Her skin had a high mountain coloring, and down in the south, her face was almost always moist and overheated. She was still plump from the baby and wearing maternity shifts, not the expensive designer outfits Aunt Sofia imagined. ("That's probably why Rocco's got to be a professor *and* keep an office for those animals, so he can buy *la scienziata* the jewelry and clothes like she's used to.") Sofia was wrong. The woman my uncle loved was quite plain, which, I thought, showed that Rocco was a good man, one who loved for the right reasons.

"You do not need to become best friends with this Claudia when you get to Italy," my father warned me before I left. "Be respectful, but just enough to be polite—as I do in my letters."

"Why don't your father and Sofia write to Rocco and Claudia as often as they write to the others?" Nonna Giulia asked me quietly one day.

I said nothing. She knew.

"Well, I'm going to tell him myself when he gets here. There's no one like Claudia. Not for Rocco. Who else would put up with him? He was always so difficult. The first time he brought her home with that baby I wanted to beat him with a stick. A big professor, he should have known better. But then, at dinner, I brought wild mushrooms to the table. It was the season for the mushrooms, and Rocco always loved them, but he's scared. It takes just one bad one, you know, to put you in the ground. But what do I see? I see Claudia tasting the mushrooms on Rocco's plate to make sure they were safe for him to eat. That's love."

Rocco and Claudia named their son Giancarlo, after Nonno Carlo, as the firstborn boy in each family was named: Zio Anto's Carlo, Zio Vito's Carlino and Aunt Sofia's Carl. Nonna Giulia's name was given to all the first girls: Giulia, Giuliana, Marigiulia, Giulietta and Giulina. The five Giulias. The youngest cousins—Daniele and Francesca—were named by the calendar, for the saint on whose feast day they were born. Zia Assunta's mother, la Signora Tramonto, called these children *i bambini dei santi,* the children of the saints, but Nonna Giulia called them *i diavolini,* the little devils.

Three of the four *capi,* two Tramonti, *la scienziata,* two nonnas, three Giulias, three Carlos and the children of the saints. That is the family I lived with during my summer in Italy.

FOUR

Via San Silvestro, No. 152

MY FIRST NIGHT in Italy I woke up out of a dreamless sleep and found myself in a room that was a solid block of darkness. I waited a second for my eyes to adjust, for shadows to appear, for the furniture to take shape, but the blackness was thick and everywhere. Several of my cousins and at least one of my aunts were asleep in that room, I knew that, but I didn't know who was there or even how far away their beds were from mine. All I remembered about going to bed was that when someone called out, *"Buona notte, Giulia,"* two of us had answered.

All that existed was the pitch-black foreign night and the thought that for the next three months everything I did and everywhere I went, I would have to speak Italian. None of my relatives spoke English. The last twelve days of June and all of July would have to tick by, second by second, before my father arrived to translate for me, to take me home.

If it was the middle of the night in Italy, in Ohio it was

evening. My father was probably walking among his rose plants. Lost in Italy, I thought of all the roses that would bloom and wilt before I saw him again, thought of him standing at the stove, alone, waiting for his coffee to perk, something I had done for him since I was tall enough to reach the kitchen counters.

I was exhausted. All my efforts to get away from my father had done nothing but drop me into this black hole of a night where it seemed my father was the only one who could save me. I felt defeated and started to cry. I covered my face with the pillow, and my chest hurt with the effort of trying not to make a sound as I cried. When it passed, I was overheated and sweating. I took the pillow from my face. The sheet was damp and cloying. I kicked it away so I could feel my legs free. I lifted one leg, but I couldn't see it in the dark. In Italy I was invisible.

I heard shuffling footsteps from down the hallway. A toilet flushed. Someone was awake in this godforsaken night. I held my breath so whoever it was wouldn't hear me, come in and talk to me in Italian. I heard chairs scraping the marble floor. I couldn't imagine who was awake, or why, but I suppose the noises comforted me, because eventually I went back to sleep.

I woke up again when I heard the two nonnas approaching my room, the overlapping sounds of their distinctive footsteps. Nonna Giulia walked slowly with a limp, a small catch that syncopated her steps. Alongside her, la Signora Tramonto, Zia Assunta's mother, moved with small excited footsteps, slippers flapping, sounding as frenzied as the second hand of a clock. What were those old women coming to say to me? I pulled the sheet up over me. I heard the doorknob turn. I made my breathing regular and slow. Sunlight slashed the room, my eyelids flinched. Somewhere, the night was over and it was day.

59

Nonna Giulia called me, accusingly, *"Dormigliona!,"* then again, making the middle syllables ring with scorn, *"Dormigggllliooo-na."* You shameless sleeper, she was saying, you shameless girl who slept too much.

There was forgiveness, though, in the quick childlike patter of la Signora's footsteps and the sound of her wooden rosary beads, like hazelnuts rolling in a bowl.

The two women stopped at the side of my bed, and la Signora, in a stage whisper, asked my grandmother if it didn't make her heart ache to see how *"bella, bella, bella"* I was in my sleep.

Nonna answered by putting a firm, hot hand on my hip, shaking me, accusing me, *"Americana, sei dormigliona."* I thought she was teasing me, but then she put both hands on my hip and shook harder, and I wasn't sure. I opened my eyes slowly, trying to screen out the bright light, and there in front of me were the two nonnas, both so short their faces were just above mine as I lay on the bed, both of them showing me their perfect sets of false teeth. There was Nonna Giulia's severe craggy face. If it weren't for her huge black-framed eyeglasses enlarging her already large eyes I wouldn't have been able to tell she was smiling at me. Beside her was la Signora, her pretty little-girl's face pleated with wrinkles, her round blue eyes misting, a white cloud of hair spilling out of her messy bun, and that crazy voice: "Ah, the *signorina* has woken up. How beautiful she is in her sleep, like a princess, like a princess in a storybook, just like a story."

"Good morning," I whispered, in Italian.

"Good morning? Ha! Good afternoon! For you, this morning was lost."

"What time is it, Nonna?"

"Guess," Nonna challenged me, "guess what time it is."

"Is it after nine," I asked, "or ten?"

"Ten? It's time for dinner! Your aunts already made the

pasta. One o'clock it is"—she shook her crooked index finger in front of me—"almost one o'clock."

Mamma mia!

"But, Nonna, it's so dark in here."

"Poor thing, poor thing, she thinks it's night, maybe she's afraid of the dark. No wonder she stayed in bed. She was afraid."

Nonna shuffled over to the window and banged her hand flatly on the horizontal wooden shutters pulled down over the window. *Persiane,* she called them. "These make the darkness. Don't you have these in America? I thought you had everything in America. Without these, how do you sleep?"

"With our eyes closed," I said, and finally Nonna laughed.

"Yes, here too," la Signora informed me, "here too, we sleep with our eyes closed."

With a motion like pulling a bucket of water out of a well, Nonna tugged on the cord that opened the shutters, let in strips of harsh, hot light. The long night vanished. The room took shape, with four beds and two tall wooden wardrobes, and high ceilings and wide stretches of uncluttered marble floor. Nonna pushed open the balcony door and a wave of heat and traffic noise rolled in. She picked up a glass of water from somebody's night table, walked to the balcony door, tossed the water out; when it hit the clay tiles, the water sizzled. "See that heat? That's the heat of noon. And you, Americana, thought it was night." With her foot, she moved a pink chunk of rock across the floor to hold open the door.

"There," she said, "now you can breathe in here. You weren't sleeping, you were half suffocated. Hurry up, your aunts want to make your breakfast. Dinner will be ready in twenty minutes."

They left.

Mattinata fa la giornata, my father used to tell me. The morning makes the whole day, but I was pleased with myself for having stayed in bed until dinner time. Maybe after dinner, I could take a nap, and before long, one day would have passed. I threw down the sheet. In the harsh light, my legs were sickly white. I wondered what I should wear. "When you're not sure," Aunt Sofia had told me, "you put on a dress." At the foot of my bed, resting on a bench, was my locked suitcase. The keys, I remembered, were in the zippered part of my purse, and my purse, last time I had seen it, was on a table in the hallway. My backpack was on the floor and open; there was nothing in it but what Aunt Sofia had made me pack: a robe, underwear and a toothbrush in case my plane got delayed in a strange city; a pair of socks and a sweater in case the air conditioning on the plane was too high; and a dozen Tampax, in case of emergency. I thought of calling out to one of my aunts to get my purse, but probably one of the nonnas would come back. I could have asked one of my cousins, but they made me nervous with their perfect Italian.

The entire Italian summer lay ahead of me. There was no way to avoid it. I wrapped my robe around me and went out to face them.

Just outside the bedroom door Giulietta and Daniele were playing cards on the marble floor. Sitting next to them was Zio Rocco's overweight, panting beagle, Topo. *"Buon giorno, Giulia,"* Giulietta said shyly and stood up to kiss me.

Daniele ran to the kitchen yelling, "She's awake, she finally woke up."

"And she's in her nightgown." Giulietta took my hand and led me down the hall.

I walked up the two tile steps into the kitchen and several voices called out, *"Giulia! Buon giorno!"* Everywhere, there were faces familiar enough to be family, but I still wasn't sure who was who. And there were oversized pots and kettles. My cousins Marigiulia and Giuliana came over and kissed me. The daughters of the twin brothers, both girls were thirteen, two months apart in age, a mismatched set of twins. Carlino, who was ten and embarrassed, shook my hand and congratulated me on my long sleep. The baby, Giancarlo, cried from his high chair. My three aunts were wrapped in big aprons. Zia Assunta, with hips and bosom that the apron couldn't quite cover, took my face in her hands, and with basil-scented fingers pinched my cheek. She was the beautiful aunt, with blond hair gone prematurely white and piled up on her head, like her mother's, and turquoise eyes ringed with long black eyelashes; and just like her mother, she had that hysteria in her voice. "You thought it was night, didn't you, poor thing? Poor little thing. How worn out you must be."

Zia Berta was the tough aunt. She was short and small, skinny from too many cigarettes. Her hair was dark, cut sharply at her chin, side-parted and falling over half her face, so you had to go out of your way to see if she was smiling or angry. With a cigarette in her hand, she took my arm and led me away from Zia Assunta. Seriously, Zia Berta asked me, How did I want my coffee, with milk or without? How did I like my milk, warm or very hot? Did I want biscuits?

The center of the kitchen was dominated by a square table, and covering the large table was a white cloth; Giulietta surreptitiously lifted the edge. "Giulia, look," she whispered. I barely had a chance to glimpse the freshly made pasta underneath before Zia Assunta snatched the cloth from Giulietta so fast the little girl jumped. With a fast proprietary hand, Zia scooped up a few handfuls of pasta, tossed them down farther under the cloth to clear a corner of the table for me. She pulled out a stool and instructed me to sit. In front of me, she put a large flow-ered napkin and a big cup with a broken handle. When Zia Assunta turned away, Zia Berta showed up.

"A cup without an arm she gave you," Berta said. "How are you supposed to drink from this?" She took the cup away and left me with none.

Two huge fast-boiling pots throbbed on the stove, clat-tering their lids. Zia Claudia was at the sink rinsing greens. As she rinsed the leaves, humming, she tossed bad ones onto the floor, completely unaware that Marigiulia was sweeping.

Zia Assunta was at my side again. Using the edge of her apron, she held a hot espresso coffeepot in one hand and a small pot of steaming milk in the other. "Did I put a cup here, or am I losing my mind?"

"You must be losing your mind," Zia Berta scolded her. "You gave poor Giulia a broken cup."

"I don't mind, really . . ."

"Ah, Giulia! Sorry, sorry, sorry. Carlo, bring a good cup to your cousin. Now! Hurry!"

My cousin Carlo was a year older than me and I was afraid of him. Afraid because the night before, when I'd arrived, it was clear the aunts and uncles expected us to become friends, to spend time together, and there was nothing I wanted less. All I knew about Carlo was that he studied a lot, that's what the letters from Italy had said for years. Reading them at the dinner table, my father would report, "Your cousin Carlo, excellent grades. Probably he will study medicine. *Bravissimo.*"

I was wary of Carlo before I even got there. When I finally met him, he was wearing white socks. What would I have to say for three months to a studious Italian who wore white socks? But here he was now walking toward me holding out a cup, smiling broadly at me; when he got close I realized he was laughing, laughing at me caught in the middle of the aunts' frenzy. *"Buon giorno, Giulia."* He kissed me on both cheeks.

La Signora Tramonto came toward me with a pan full of warm biscuits, but the pan was not quite balanced on her hands, and as she offered the biscuits to me, telling me humbly, "We make these ourselves," she left a trail of cracked biscuits behind her on the floor.

"Mamma," Assunta screamed. "Don't you see what you're doing?" She took the tray away. "Mamma, sit, rest."

With the tray out of her hands, with nothing else to do, la Signora walked over to Carlo, slapped him on the arm and said, "You! You have no manners."

"What did I do?"

"Can't you see how busy everyone is? If you want to be helpful, introduce your cousin. Did you forget your manners?"

"Ah, Nonna is right, Nonna is right," all the aunts said.

La Signora took my arm, tugged me up onto my feet, led me to the small kitchen balcony where a boy I hadn't noticed before was sitting on a low stool with his knees jutting out. He was surrounded by crates of tomatoes and big pots of basil and rosemary plants. As we walked toward him, he stood up. *"Ciao,"* he said.

"This is Carlo's best friend in the world," la Signora explained with a hand near her heart. "Since they were young, small boys, since kindergarten, even before, such good friends, every day together, always together, for so many years . . ."

"Nonna, please, without any arias, just introduce."

"But am I right, Carlo, is he your best friend, your oldest friend in the world, am I right?"

"Whatever you say, Nonna, but you still haven't told Giulia his name."

"His name? Why his name is Luca, of course, we all know that. This is Luca."

He had a scar running through his right eyebrow, a wild tangle of long, black, corkscrew-curly hair, green eyes, and he was reaching out to shake my hand. "Luca," la Signora said, "this is our Americana, Giulia, Carlo's cousin from . . ." Then her grip on my arm tightened and she held up the hem of my bathrobe and screamed. *"Madonna!* Barefoot! *Madonna mia,* doesn't anyone see that Giulia is barefoot!"

I looked up. All my cousins were standing around me, laughing. "Americana! No slippers? No shoes?" Everybody was staring at my bare feet. Luca was still holding my hand.

My first thought was that he was not attractive. He looked too much like a man, not enough like a boy. He needed a shave. His lips were full and pouty. He was no taller than me. He was bulky. Pretty soon, I thought, he's going to have to start watching his weight. So different from thin, freckled Morrisey. Not my type. I was sorry, though, when Luca went out onto the balcony with Carlo.

After breakfast, as soon as I could, I went to get dressed, but when I came back to the kitchen Luca was gone. My uncles were home from their offices. As he kissed me hello, Zio Anto asked, "So, Giulia, are you hungry?"

"Well . . ."

"I thought so." Then he told my aunts, "Let's hurry. Giulia wants to eat."

"Last night, Giulia, you were tired from your trip," Zio Anto said as he led me into the dining room—the room was long; the table, extending almost wall to wall, was set with white linen—"and it was late, so I hope you will excuse us for waiting until today to have a meal to welcome you." My uncle pulled out my chair, motioned to Carlo to come take the place next to me.

Sitting across from us were Giulietta and Francesca. Giulietta, that summer, was six, with long auburn hair curling all over the place and big dark eyes, a face already beautiful as a grown woman's. But Giulietta was timid, afraid of everything. She had Topo's head resting in her lap, her finger counting the rows of wrinkles and jowls on his face, concentrating to avoid looking at me.

Francesca, though, was tough and bold, redheaded, intimidating, four years old. She examined me closely, right into my eyes. A bottle of water was on the table in front of us, and Francesca grabbed it at its neck. "Look at this," she said, and lifted the tall green bottle to her mouth. The weight of it threw her head way back, and she took a long drink. Refreshed, she banged the bottle down onto the table. Her mouth and nose dripping with water, "Aahhh," she said, *"fresca."*

"Mamma," Giulietta screamed, "Francesca did it again. She drank from the bottle. Mamma, she's going to break her teeth."

"Francesca," Zia Claudia yelled from the kitchen, "isn't it enough that already you broke two teeth with those blessed water bottles? Franca, do you hear me?"

"They were only baby teeth, Mamma. I'll get new ones."

La Signora Tramonto pattered up to the table. Francesca wasn't la Signora's granddaughter, but she treated all the children as if they were hers. She had a way of filling her voice with tears when petitioning for sympathy or understanding in a difficult situation. That afternoon, holding Francesca's small freckled face in her hands, la

Signora appealed to me. "Look, Giulia, look," she whined, "look what this little one did to herself." Francesca stuck her tongue out through the gap where front teeth should have been. La Signora pleaded, "Little one, why? Why no glass? Why always the bottle?"

"Papà does it."

"Papà? *Bella mia,* no one should learn manners from your father. God bless him, he is an educated man, well brought up, but for manners at the table he is a disaster. Please, for the love of God, don't follow *him.*"

"So you're talking about me behind my back, eh?" said Zio Rocco, appearing at the table in an undershirt, khaki shorts and sandals, fanning himself with the newspaper. *"Mamma mia,* what heat! Giulia, it is okay with you, no?, if I come to dinner dressed this way?"

"No!" la Signora Tramonto howled. "First you teach your own children bad habits, and now you want to come to dinner half dressed, offending our guest."

"I don't care, it's all right, it's fine," I said, but nobody was listening to me.

Zia Assunta came to the table with wine bottles and saw Rocco petting Topo. "I don't care what you wear to the table, Rocco, but I'm not eating with that beast. Go, wash your hands."

Rocco held his hands out and Topo licked them with his long tongue. "There, my hands are washed. Okay?"

"Ignorante." La Signora scowled at him.

Now there was an assembly line of aunts and cousins coming out of the kitchen with bowls of pasta, and everyone took their places. Zio Anto himself was bringing my bowl to me. He took his seat at the head of the table, tucked his napkin into his collar, spread it over the front of his white shirt. He lifted his fork. *"Buon appetito,"* he said, and motioned for me to begin.

I looked down at the bowl in front of me, a Vesuvius of

pasta spilling over the edges. "This looks delicious," I stammered. "But I could never eat this much pasta." My Italian sounded like a child's in that big, echoing dining room.

Silence up and down the table. All eyes on me.

"Maybe you'd like a different kind of pasta? Maybe linguine, farfalle?"

"No! It's just too much, I . . ." Zio Anto interrupted me; he told me he was my first uncle, three minutes older than his twin brother, Vito, which made Anto the oldest brother after my father. If I didn't eat what he offered me, he said, he would be offended. Had I traveled all this way to offend Antonio, my first uncle?

Carlo was watching me, laughing. He had his mother's sharp blue eyes, but the brightness that was vigilant worry in hers was a demon taunt in his. I wouldn't look at him. I ate as much pasta as I could, but my bowl was still half full. "Is it time now for me to save you?" Carlo whispered.

"Yes," I said, "yes."

He switched our bowls so quickly no one saw. And that is the moment Carlo and I became friends.

After a few minutes in the kitchen the aunts reappeared carrying long platters of rolled chicken breasts stuffed with spinach, bread crumbs and Parmesan cheese. Before I knew it, Zio Vito was dropping one, two, three *involtini di pollo* onto my plate. He moved stiffly because he was wearing a neck brace. The doctors said he had arthritis, but Zia Berta had written to my father that Vito's pain got worse every time he and Anto argued about politics. ("Probably some psychotherapy would be of use to him," my father mumbled as he read each letter.) Vito was taking the summer off, doctor's orders: he had to be in traction for a few hours every day. Maybe it was because his neck hurt, but every time he spoke he sounded like my father at his worst. "Giulia," he commanded, "eat."

He scared me, but I had to tell him, "Zio, three is too many."

"Too many? All right," he said, and he took away two and replaced them with one, the largest piece on the platter.

After the chicken came the fish.

Zio Rocco leaned over with a platter of cold steamed flounder covered with a mayonnaise sauce and decorated elaborately with pimentos, olives and parsley. He whispered to me, "Who knows what this is. They play with this food and play with it until you don't know what you're eating. Giulia, what do you think, fish probably, eh?"

Giulietta and Francesca heard him across the table. "Oh, Papà," Giulietta said, "can't you see it's fish? How many times do we have to tell you?"

"Excuse me, but in the village where I was born, when we ate fish it looked like fish, not like a Christmas tree."

"Rocco, enough now," Zio Claudia called from the other end of the table. "Can't you see Giulia's waiting?"

"Ah, yes, of course. Here, let me serve you. If this is, in fact, fish, it must be good. Our fish is good here, fresh, not like there in Idaho."

Francesca sighed, "Ohio, Papà. Giulia is from Ohio."

"It's all the same, Ohio, Idaho, no fresh fish. Wait until you taste this, Giulia. I recommend it," and he served me a piece that was longer than my plate.

I tried to eat. I thought of Molly and how, during the years, she had made Aunt Sofia, Cetta, my father, and even Ben fall in love with her by happily tasting hot peppers, sautéed brains, tripe stew, anything they put in front of her. I was still working on the fish when Nonna Giulia pushed away from her plate at the table.

"Mamma, what do you need?"

"Nonna, where are you going?"

With a hand in the air she quieted them all and shuffled into the kitchen. A few minutes later, she came back carrying a small bowl. She stood behind me and leaned close. "These you've never eaten before. These, I made," she told me. "It was oil from olives like these that paid for your father to become a psychiatrist."

"I know these olives. Oregano and hot pepper," I told her.

"Taste one," she said.

In my fingers it was a wrinkled little pellet, but the flavor filled my mouth—peppery, smooth. Now I knew why Cetta was never pleased with the olives in the import store near Homefield. "Nonna, these olives are delicious."

"So, then eat." And I watched as a few dozen black olives rolled onto my plate.

As she walked away I heard her muttering, "At least we can see they taught her something over there."

During dinner, they all asked me important questions about America. "And at noon there, what do you eat? No pasta? And then what time do you eat again? But you, in the family, you eat like we do, no?"

In Homefield, when we were all together for family dinners, my father played Italian music. For cookouts in summer, he put the stereo speakers in the living-room windows. While hamburgers and hot dogs cooked on the grill, the back yard filled with old songs that had been popular in Italy right after the war. During my first meal in Italy there was no Italian music, just Italian voices, and the click of forks and knives. There was the tapping of my aunts' heels as they hustled back and forth over the marble floor between the dining room and the kitchen. There were a lot of flies, and, as Zio Rocco reminded us every few minutes, there was the heat.

Finally the food stopped coming and we all sat still for a few moments. Daniele said, "So, where is the fruit?"

But Zio Anto held his hand out toward the platters, which were still abundantly full, and said, "Your cousin Giulia may feel like having a little more."

"Ah, yes," Daniele said, and he held his hands out, palms up, above the food, offering it all to me. "Giulia! *Mangia!*" Eat!

I couldn't even answer. I just shook my head no.

"Then you lied to us before, you said you were hungry."

"Oh, poor Giulia is just like me," la Signora told him, then she summoned the tears into her voice and said, "Less than a bird, that's how I eat, too."

As the dishes were being cleared away, bowls full of small purple plums and white grapes and big ripe peaches were brought to the table. I told my aunts the dinner was delicious. They told me they liked the way I spoke Italian. I said, I make a million mistakes. They told me, "Don't worry. You'll learn quickly. You're very intelligent." They knew little about me, but their praise was an extension of their admiration for my father, and an extension of their awe of America. "The cars are very big, no?" Carlino asked.

"And you, Giulia, you're able to drive those big cars? *Brava!*"

They brought out small plates for cake. On the cake, in syrupy red icing was written *Benvenuta Giulia*. Welcome. And there was champagne, and after the toast, everyone, even the aunts, sat back in their chairs, to drink and relax.

I was soft from the wine and sleepy from all the food, and they smiled at me and murmured to each other, *"Bella, no? Intelligente,"* and I began to realize that with these strangers I could be anyone, become anyone, change my life.

"Giulia, do you have a young man?" they asked, and it seemed they were telling me this was a possibility, too.

Zio Anto had just lit a cigarette and was putting his lighter away when he glanced at me and said, "Ah, Giulia, excuse me, forgive me." He leaned forward, held out a pack of Marlboros, asked, *"Sigaretta?"* and right then I fell in love with them all.

We were still talking when the doorbell chimed, loud as a church bell. La Signora was asleep in her chair, her head bobbing over her right shoulder, and she didn't stir. Two of the kids ran to answer. When I looked up, Luca was standing in the archway of the dining room, wearing a bright white, freshly ironed shirt, apologizing, saying, "You're still eating. I should go," but he didn't move. He just stood there.

I looked across the table at my little cousins, but they were already watching me, waiting for something.

Zio Anto pulled a chair out for Luca. "What happened?" he asked, as Luca sat down, "didn't your mother feed you today?"

Luca's heels tapped the sides of the chair.

Zio Vito passed the bowl of fruit to him. "Three-thirty and already you're wandering around town?"

"And in this heat?" Zio Rocco said, wiping his forehead with a napkin.

Zio Anto offered Luca a cigarette. He took it, said thank you, spun the cigarette in the air a few times.

Carlo made his eyes bright slits and smirked, tossed the matches across the table and they landed on the chair between Luca's thighs. I looked away. Luca lit his cigarette, dropped the book of matches onto the table, and it was

7 3

that small sound that startled la Signora out of her sleep. "What happened?" she asked, alarmed.

"Don't worry, Signora, it's only me," Luca said, but then he exhaled gray smoke and looked sinister.

"Luca's here early today, Nonna," Carlo said, "because he's so eager to study. No, Luca?"

Luca was spinning a small round ashtray, seeing how fast he could make it go.

"Maybe he wants to study his English. Giulia, do you know our friend Luca speaks English?" Zio Anto said. "No, Luca?"

"He says he speaks English." Zio Vito's shaming voice rolled down over the top of his neck brace. With a big knife in his big hands, he was peeling the skin off a grape. He wanted the skin off of everything he ate, even tomatoes. He didn't believe the farmers at the market who said they never sprayed their fruits and vegetables; Zio Vito rarely believed anything. "That's what Luca tells us. But what do we know? He can make any noise and tell us he's speaking English."

I asked him, in English, "Is it true?"

He showed me with his thumb and forefinger spread slightly that yes, he spoke a little English.

I smiled. "Well?" I asked. He shrugged, dragged on the cigarette. My uncles were laughing at him, so finally Luca told me, "Later I will say to you."

"What did he say?" they all asked me. "He was wrong, no?"

"I understood him," I said, already feeling loyal. "He spoke well," I lied.

Luca raised his eyebrows at me.

"Eh, maybe then Luca won't fail his exams too miserably."

"Maybe yet there's hope for you," Zio Rocco said, slapping his hand down on Luca's wide back, and Zio Anto made that gesture with his thumb and forefinger to show that maybe there was a little hope for Luca.

In one month Carlo and Luca were going to have to take the exams to finish high school, they explained to me.

"Is it a difficult exam?" I asked.

"Exam? Exams," they corrected me, "many exams."

"In every subject they will be tested—Italian, Latin, Greek."

"Your father, Giulia," Zia Assunta said, walking over to me, taking my hand to get my full attention, "when he took these exams, he passed with a ten, the highest mark, and honors."

"The *best,* Giulia," Zio Vito told me, as if teaching me a lesson.

"Always the best," la Signora repeated. "What a genius that man. What a brain, what a brain, what a brain he had."

"Nonna, he *has.* Why the past tense? What a brain he *has,*" Carlo corrected her. "I'm sure Zio Nicola has the same brain in America that he had in Italy. No, Giulia? Or has your father lost his brains in America?"

"No, he's still smart," I said, "even in America."

And I got Luca's eyes back on me again. He was smiling through smoke.

Zia Assunta and Zia Berta slowly lifted themselves from their chairs to make more espresso. Zio Anto said, "What are you boys sitting here for? Carlo, go, take your cousin out, let her see something."

"But we haven't even opened a book yet today, Luca and I. We have to study."

"Eh, today is *festa* for everyone. Tomorrow you and Luca will study twice as long. Now, go."

"Yes, and if you fail your exams," Zio Rocco said, "Giulia will take you to America and find jobs for you."

And so Carlo, dutifully, asked me, "Giulia, would you like to go for a walk?"

And Zio Anto answered, "Of course she'd like to go."

Downstairs, I stepped out of No. 152, into Via San Silvestro with Carlo, Marigiulia, Giuliana and Luca, and I wondered if my relatives were poor. I'd never met anybody who lived in an apartment building. Across the street in a concrete-block hut, one wall collapsing, was a garage. The smell of benzene choked the air. An old man in racing-car overalls was limping around broken-down cars. Next to the garage was a chicken coop; next to the chickens, a sixteen-story apartment building fringed all around with balconies. Some balconies had rusty washing machines on them, and laundry hung like banners.

At street level, the walls were covered with torn, washed-out political manifestoes and semipornographic ads for *The Godfather*. This was the street where my relatives lived: no front yards, no driveways. Dark dusty children in sandals were running up and down Via San Silvestro, bringing up clouds of clay from the potholes. Just as we walked out the door, a soccer ball came at us from nowhere, and without breaking his stride, Luca kicked the ball back to the kids halfway down the road.

"Carrr-lo!" We looked up. I couldn't spot her, but I heard Zia Assunta's worried voice coming down from a balcony high above: "Carr-lo, listen, tell Luca, no motorino. Do you hear?"

"Don't worry, *signora*," Luca yelled up.

"Because, Luca, if I hear that someone saw you speeding through the streets of Montemaggiore on that motorino with my niece, Luca, I'll . . ."

He told my aunt to stay calm. *"Stai tranquilla, signo'."* Don't worry, no speeding, he promised.

We walked in a row, quickly. But even after we were

out of my aunt's sight, there were eyes. Short dark men in dark clothes standing around on corners, leaning out of windows, looking at us, muttering. I thought I heard one of them say "Americana." I knew that I was dressed okay —blue jean cutoffs, a tie-dyed tank top and moccasins, what I'd wear to walk down Homefield Avenue. Still, I felt myself sweating. My cutoffs suddenly felt too tight. After two blocks, I realized none of the girls or women we passed were wearing shorts, not even pants. Only dresses and skirts. I was grateful when Luca led us into a narrow empty street and said, "Stop. Wait here."

We watched him run down the alley and pull a blue motorino out from against the wall. He jumped on the small bike and pedaled fast until the motor picked up. He stopped in front of me.

In English, he said, "Come in, Giulia." He moved forward on the seat and said in Italian, "There's room for you, your bottom is little enough," and I sat down quickly, just so he wouldn't say anything more.

"Ready?" Luca asked as he pumped the gas.

"No!" Carlo yelled and took my hands from Luca's shoulders and put them on his waist. "That's how you ride."

The bike started forward. My face was too close to the thick tangle of Luca's long black hair. I had an urge to touch it. I moved my hands off his waist and back onto his shoulders. He rode slowly, especially around the curves, taking me through a maze of streets. "I go slow so in case your aunt is watching from the balcony," he called over his shoulder, part Italian, part English. "At least she can't get me for speeding." He looked back at me. "Don't look so serious. Eh, you are fine?"

I nodded and held myself as far from his back as possible.

We rode up a strip of unpaved road that led to a wide

avenue. Luca told me, *"Grande Corso Dante."* I looked around his head of curls and thought, I should write to my father and tell him I've seen this. We were stopped, waiting for a break in the traffic. "In this traffic I'll have to go fast. Hold on now, Giulia." *I can't, I won't.* But then he took off, and it was all I could do to wrap an arm around him to keep from tipping off the back.

"Brava," he said, and cut into the traffic. And there I was, riding up the Corso, riding fast on a speeding motorino. I was holding on tight to an Italian boy's waist. He felt so solid. I had to rest my feet up high on the rail so my toes wouldn't scrape the ground, and this brought my legs up, spread them out wide, and there in front of me was Luca's broad back. Once I was on the motorino I wasn't afraid—not of the speed, not of him.

We flew under the trees. The streets were empty. My hands were full of Luca's warm cotton shirt. At the entrance to the piazza we came to a red light. Luca looked both ways and behind him. "No police," he said, "no one, not even a dog," and we left that red light behind. The piazza was all ours and Luca did some wide figure eights, sending up a few pigeons. He pointed here and there: "This is the school, the *municipio.*"

"I've heard of all these places," I yelled back.

"Ah, yes? You are bored? Then I show you something new." He speeded up, headed for the fountain at the center of the piazza, ready, it seemed, to ride right up over the rim, into the water. "You want swimming, Giulia?" he called back to me.

"Luca!" It was the first time I ever said his name—what an odd name for a boy. Laughing, he veered away from the fountain, did a few circles around it, dipping low. I held tight.

To avoid a red light, we rode onto the sidewalk, and then onto a small island of concrete where tiny Fiats were parked in every direction, haphazardly, as if they'd been thrown there like a handful of jacks. Moving between cars we hit tight spots, and to avoid banging my knees I had to pull them close around Luca's hips, but that little motorino was passing through slickly, and our bodies moved with it.

After the mess of cars, Luca leaned around and said, "That *signora* sitting in the white car back there, she was looking at us, no?"

"Maybe. I don't know."

"Eh, she was. I'm cooked now," he said in Italian. "That *signora* is a friend of your aunt. She'll report us for sure. We have nothing now to lose," and he speeded up as we headed for the hill. "Now you will see things you not seen *be*-fore," he yelled in English. The bike climbed. He leaned forward into the hill and I leaned forward, too, into him, to fight the feeling of falling off the back. His shoulders were so wide. We reached the top and turned onto Via dei Castelli, which Luca said was the most *"elegantissima"* street of Montemaggiore. I saw a flash of jewelry stores and leather shops, but gates were pulled across their windows. There was no one, only us breaking the afternoon calm. Eventually, the road sloped gently downward, and Luca rode onto the sidewalk and took a cobblestone path into a park. Soon we were under a cooling canopy of pink flowering bushes. He turned off the motor and we coasted. Suddenly, there were bird sounds, and Luca whispered, "It is beautiful here, no?"

At the end of the cobblestones we got off the motorino and Luca chained it to a lamppost. He walked up next to me. "I see you have ridden a motorcycle before."

"No, I haven't. Never."

"That surprises me. You moved well. If I had to guess I would say you had ridden before."

"It was fun." With my hands off him, I felt shy again. I

saw we were exactly the same height; it was almost impossible to avoid his eyes.

"Ah, it must be me, then. I am a very good driver. I made you relax." I had no idea what to say next.

We walked under a trellis of lilacs and then, like a surprise, a meadow appeared, a bowl of green grass—sunny in patches, cool and shaded under the trees. And so quiet.

" *'Nel mezzo del cammin di nostra vita, mi ritrovai per una selva oscura, che la diritta via era smarrita.'* " Luca was quoting Dante, that enigmatic language my father used now and then to teach me a lesson.

"What did you just say?"

"It is speaking of a forest."

"Yes, I know." *Una selva oscura,* a dark wood. "But the rest?"

"Dante says, 'In middle of my life I found myself in a dark forest and my way had disappeared.' "

I was never aware of falling in love with Luca. What I did feel, from that first morning when we met, was an intense awareness of his body, even if I wasn't standing near him or looking at him. And when he looked at me, I felt a self-consciousness that was paralyzing. There was no peace. Either he was watching me or I was glancing at him, and I couldn't look at him without noticing his body.

Up until that time, the only boys who had grabbed my heart were casual freckled American types, boys like Morrisey, always in sweatshirts and high-top basketball sneakers, boys who wore clothes that padded them, rounded them out, hid their flesh and muscle. Luca's clothes showed so much of him. Dark shirts or white, they fit tightly around his chest. Sleeves folded up high and tight on his arms. Tight jeans riding low on his hips, rolled at the ankle. Some days he wore a white T-shirt that pulled out of his jeans, gave me glimpses of his back—wide, brown, all muscle.

In the park that first day, he had said to me, "But come, tell me of your father. He is very famous with them at Carlo's house. I am curious of this man. Say to me."

And so, stringing together more Italian words than I ever had before, I told Luca about Nicola. It came out all mixed up, with some proper Italian I'd learned from Nicola, mostly the dialect I used with Cetta and Aunt Sofia and Ben, as well as a few words I made up myself right then. A few times Luca laughed and I hesitated, but he said, "No, continue. I like how you speak. *È graziosa.*" And I believed him because he was looking right at me, following what I said so attentively he could fill in the words that were missing from my vocabulary. When I finished, though, Luca stared at me silently for a second or two, then tapped his front tooth, and I knew he meant the retainer on my top teeth, and very seriously he asked me, "That wire, does it hurt?"

Those first days, I looked at him and looked at him but I still didn't think he was attractive. He was like me, too Italian. Still, there was something electric about the way Luca moved, and he was always moving. Visiting at my uncle's, he'd juggle cigarettes or pieces of silverware, he'd spin ashtrays. Sitting in my aunt's kitchen, his heels tapped the floor, his fingers did trills on the edge of the chair. Out in the street, he shook the coins in his pockets, jiggled his keys. Tossing, spinning, shaking, tapping, twirling, he was always either making objects move or moving around himself. There was nervousness like fire running through Luca, as if he couldn't wait to go on to the next moment, or as if he needed to be calmed, soothed. I'm telling you, all that summer there was just no peace.

FIVE

The House at the Beach

I SPENT A WEEK at Zio Anto's apartment in Montemaggiore while my aunts prepared for us all to go to the beach. One day Zio Anto led me to the kitchen balcony and pointed out over the buildings, beyond the hills that dipped and rose around the town; he pointed to a strip of blue. "See that blue, that sea, that beach? That's where you will be next week, Giulia."

But as the days passed I wasn't so sure I wanted to leave Montemaggiore. There, in town, I saw Luca all the time. I couldn't ride with him on the motorino anymore; my aunt had found out.

"How could we ever call America and tell Giulia's father that she cracked her head on the pavement of Corso Dante?" Zia Assunta, wringing her hands, asked Luca. "What would we do, *caro* Luca, what? We'd all have to shoot ourselves."

"Please, Signora, I'd be very unhappy if you shot yourself. No more motorino."

But the promise that something would happen—soon—hung in the air. Luca was always showing up. I'd look around and, out of nowhere, there he was. Across the kitchen, across the dining room, across the crowd of my cousins. It seemed that every time I stepped out of the apartment, into the street, onto the Corso or walked through the piazza with my cousins in the evening, I saw Luca. What got me more than anything he actually said was the way Luca's voice got high and soft, slightly disbelieving, every time we ran into each other. "Giulia," he'd say, sort of breathless, *"venivo a trovarti."* This meant, "I was coming to find you." Not "coming to see you," or "coming to get you," but "coming to *find* you." It sounded courtly, maybe a bit desperate, and it always thrilled me.

The week went too fast. It was Saturday. The family was leaving for the beach, but Carlo and Luca had to stay in town to study.

"You'll see them soon," Zia Berta told me. "Next weekend they'll come to the beach."

By now, though, I was used to seeing Luca in the morning, in the afternoon, evening, Luca all over the place. I'd waited so long—years—how was I going to wait six days more?

The beach house they took me to was sprawling, and because its shutters were freshly painted bright blue, it looked like a regal villa when I got my first glimpse of it. As soon as our caravan of three cars (with Zio Rocco's pulling an old wooden fishing boat) stopped in the dust of the dirt road in front of the house, I saw that the white stucco was chipping away in chunks, and that cracks snaked through the walls. The balconies that jutted out all over were uneven, sagging, skewed.

Zio Anto turned the ignition off, jumped out of the car and opened his arms to the house. "Didn't I tell you? Nice and big."

"And old." Zia Assunta slammed her car door and stood with her arms crossed, heaving up her bosom. "Anto, you said he repaired it this year. You promised me. Why do you let that old man take you for a ride every year with this house? The place gets older and you pay more rent. Giulia, we must apologize to you. I begged him this time. 'Please,' I said, 'for Giulia's sake, let's at least get a house from after the war.'"

Zio Rocco got out of his car. "You want a better house? Impossible! Look, you have the beach here, two steps away."

La Signora lifted her arms so Daniele and Carlino could ease her out of the car. "Giulia, Giulia, Giulia, forgive us. But it is your uncles who insist on this barn every year. I told them, 'This is no place to bring the Americana. She is used to everything new in Ohio.' No, Giulia, aren't you?"

"Not really." Back in Homefield, after eight years in the convent, my father hadn't got around to fixing the pipes. The banister was rebuilt but unpainted. Our mailbox still sat on the porch because no one had hung it up. These Di Cuore brothers were all alike.

"Giulia's not saying anything."

"She's in shock. She's thinking, 'I traveled all this way and look where they brought me.'"

Inside the gate was a stone-paved courtyard, an enclosed world of flowers growing everywhere, wild orchids, fat-faced sunflowers, tiny roses climbing up the cracked white walls, blankets of green herbs around the edges.

Zio Anto was using his handkerchief to wipe the rust off the lock at the gate. Perspiration caught in the tiny cup above his chin—another place where he was like my father. "This house has everything," he insisted. "Two kitchens, two bathrooms. The beauty of this house, Giulia, is that really it is two complete apartments. Bedrooms, bathroom and a kitchen on each floor."

"That's the beauty of it." Zia Berta dropped her cigarette into the dust and swiveled the toe of her sandal over it. "The ugly part is that the bathrooms often have no water, the oven in one kitchen exploded last year, the other oven is big enough to cook a quarter chicken, maybe. And there is no dishwasher, and we are sixteen people and one dog living here and eating three times a day."

"With the boat, Giulia, at night, out on this water," Zio Rocco said, waving his hand toward the beach. "Beautiful!"

Zia Assunta said, "Please, do us a favor, bring your boat into the living room so we have somewhere to sit. Giulia, there is very little furniture."

"Ah, you are spoiled, all of you!" Zio Vito signaled for Carlino to help him take the luggage out of the cars. "We are at the beach. If you want furniture go to the Vatican— they have more gold chairs there than they know what to do with."

Francesca ran to Zio Anto. "Zio, Zio, please, hurry, I have to pee."

"Well, *bella,* I'm having a little trouble here with this lock."

"Hurry, Zio," Francesca pleaded.

"Franca," Zia Assunta said, "we don't even know if the bathroom will be functioning when we get in there."

"It will work. It will work," Zio Anto said calmly.

Francesca gave an exasperated "Oooh," then slipped between two bent bars of the gate. She ran to an overgrown corner of the garden, lifted her skirt, pulled down her underpants, squatted among the plants and flowers, smiled at us and peed.

"Well, Francesca has baptized it for us," Carlino said. "Now the house is really ours."

"God help us."

My aunts were right. It was a mess. But my uncles were right, too, in loving it. The house breathed with some irrepressible life of its own. Mediterranean white, it was an awkward creation, with balconies of different sizes and shapes, and all their stucco undersides rained chalk into the courtyard. But each balcony offered a slightly different view, and whenever I was upstairs I was tempted by each one, the way I was drawn to every lookout point during our drives into the mountains: I wanted to stand on this one, this one and this one. I wanted to see everything; Italy made me greedy. Bougainvillea grew in pots on the balconies, and during the day, sea breezes sent pink and white petals dancing across the cracked tiles of the bedroom floors.

And all the while, the old house made its own music.

Hanging from the pull-chain on the upstairs toilet, for some reason, was a bell that stubbornly could not be removed. Its light ringing sang through all our days and nights, a high-pitched staccato harmonizing with the slow, deep sighs of the sea. In the downstairs kitchen was a squat refrigerator, no taller than Carlino. The tiny fridge was so overburdened with food it developed a constant wheeze, a singing hum. Every so often, when it was packed too tightly, the sound would sharpen into a bird's loud caw and we'd all go quiet and listen carefully. "Is that the baby crying or the refrigerator?"

"The refrigerator."

"Are you sure?"

"Yes, yes, the baby cries a little louder."

The whimpering refrigerator had as much a voice in the family as anyone else that summer, and when it called out to us, one of the aunts, cursing, would have to run and pull out bowls of food.

Each bathroom had a shower, but the hot-water tanks were just a bit larger than glove compartments, offering enough hot water for nothing more than a sponge bath. Zio Vito went early every morning to a nearby spring to fill jugs with water to supplement our supply.

"Rocco, the house is more trouble than this beast of yours," Nonna Giulia said, booting Topo out of the kitchen.

"Mamma, attenzione! Topo will hear you and be offended. He is not a beast." He took the dog's face in his hands and nuzzled him. "Topo loves it here, the water, the beach."

What my uncles loved best was early morning, when they went out in the boat, fishing, and they could look back at the big house with everyone else still asleep inside it. What they didn't know was that often, still a little jet-lagged, I was awake, too, looking through the shutters. I'd see them out there in the blue light of the Italian dawn, my three uncles floating in the old green boat. It was shallow, sitting low in the water, skimming over the surface like a mermaid's tail. There was room in the boat for only three adults. How would my father fit in with these brothers when he arrived?

SIX

Waiting

EVERY MORNING our green-and-white-striped umbrella was planted in the sand, tilting toward the sun, and from its spokes hung our watches and sunglasses and Zio Vito's white neck brace. Everywhere I looked I saw my family.

Nobody went into the water until everyone was there. It was part of the ceremonial way the Italians inhabited the beach. First, the men entered, to test the water. Then Francesca, afraid of nothing, climbed onto their shoulders and dove. Giulietta, panicked that she'd be pulled in next, clung to her mother and called to the saints, "Madonna mia, San Francesco! Look at Franca! Make her stop."

Zia Assunta and Zia Berta linked arms, toed the shoreline, and with cupped hands poured water over their shoulders, their faces, down the fronts of their bathing suits.

"Look! The Queen Mothers!" Zio Anto said, and he and Zio Vito swam back to shore to escort their wives.

"Grazie, tesoro," Zia Assunta said to her husband—
"Thank you, my treasure." I thought of Homefield, Aunt
Sofia and Uncle Mike, when he tried to help her down
their icy driveway and she talked to him through gritted
teeth, *"Not* so fast. Are you trying to make me fall?" All
during my summer in Italy there were moments when, out
of nowhere, tears rose in me, and it happened that day
when I saw how free my Italian aunts were to be kind to
their husbands, how sweet my Italian uncles were with
their wives.

Up on the beach, none of my uncles could let the
younger kids pass by without scooping them up off the
sand, burying a kiss deep into their necks where it tickled
and made them scream, couldn't let us older girls pass
without tugging at our hair and kissing our foreheads,
couldn't let Carlino pass without wrestling with him. The
baby we handed around constantly, hugging him until he
howled.

Beyond the family, my world that summer consisted of
the beach, a wide crescent of sand closed in on both sides
with rocks, and the five or six other families who had
houses near ours. I loved the music of their names: the
Grandeleone, Buonuomini, Sanmicaeli, Signorinelli. My
cousins Marigiulia and Giuliana—thirteen years old and
dispassionate observers—were my guides in this new
place. I relied on them for the true history of everyone on
the beach.

"That one there," Marigiulia said, widening her eyes
and nodding toward the old couple planted in the sand in
front of the house next door to ours, "that old *signore* is
Maestro Buonuomini. He played the piano in some of the
biggest concert halls. In Milano, even Paris."

"And his wife?"

"His wife is dead a long time. This woman here, he
never married her. She was their maid since she was a

young girl. The maestro kept her in the house all these years."

"Not with his *wife* there?"

"Well, she *was* the maid." Marigiulia and Giuliana had the straps of their bathing suits tied with shoelaces and they wore their father's old, stained fishing hats. When I was their age, I thought about clothes all the time; I made the air around me vibrate with hysteria, like the blur you see around an airplane's propellers as it starts to take off; but my two young cousins were as calm and all-knowing as old women. "Look how well she takes care of him." The maestro's woman (no one ever did know her name), using a child's yellow beach bucket, was pouring hot sand all over the old man's body, burying him up to his chin. "He has rheumatism. The hot sand helps his joints."

When his body was completely covered, the woman laid a white handkerchief over the maestro's head and face. "So his brains won't roast," Giuliana said. Then the woman used the little bucket to bury herself.

Some days the maestro's woman sang for him, other days he hummed arias, loud, and people up and down the beach would join in with him. It was improvisational theater every day. In Italian, bathing suits are called *costumi di bagno,* or simply *costumi.* Costumes. Perfect.

That first day, I watched a wide-hipped woman sashay down to the beach wearing a black two-piece, red heels and a white turban.

"Professoressa Signorinelli," Giuliana informed me.

"Our history teacher," Marigiulia said.

She arrived carrying nothing, while behind her trailed her three small sons, fighting about who had to carry the beach chairs, swatting each other with towels, trying to pull each other's bathing trunks off.

My aunts and uncles waved and called out, *"Buon giorno, professoressa."*

She waved back with a flat hand and announced, *"Non lo faccio più."* This meant, I can't go on like this. Gesturing, raising her arms to the heavens, she cataloged for us the hardships of being at the beach with three small animals while her husband worked in town, and she didn't care at all that she was showing us—showing everyone—the wild dark patches of hair under her arms.

A lot of the women wore small revealing bathing suits, and so did the men, and the people who weren't thin seemed as at ease with themselves as the people who were. Not far from us was a family under a blue Cinzano umbrella circled by a curtain that made a sort of tent. Sitting in the center, while several bikinied young women and two babies wandered in and out, was Rinaldo Grandeleone. "A lawyer from Montemaggiore," Giuliana said. He wore narrow red bathing trunks and had a solid wide paunch, which he affectionately rubbed.

"He never came to this beach before," Marigiulia whispered and nodded significantly in the direction of the professoressa.

"You mean they're having an affair?"

My cousins raised their shoulders and gave me that Italian shrug that means, No one knows for sure, but there is reason to think . . . I was beginning to see that to be Italian in Italy was very different from anything I'd been taught at home. At the swimming pool at the Italian Club in Homefield, the teenagers made camps that were impenetrable to children or adults. The adults took over the porch with their poker games and hushed up as soon as one of the kids appeared. In Italy, though, there were no secrets.

"Rinaldo! Welcome to our beach!" Zio Anto called as he walked toward the Cinzano umbrella. "But we require that you take off your toupee before you go in the water."

Rinaldo ran his hand through his thick mass of hair and

laughed loudly. He told my uncle, *"Invidia, invidia!"*— "You're jealous, you're jealous." The men shook hands, then Zio Anto called over to me, "Giulia, come, come."

My cousins told me, "Go, go."

"This young man here is an old schoolmate of your father's, Giulia," Zio Anto said.

Rinaldo shook my hand. "So look, our Nicola has an American daughter. We thought for sure he would come back, but America swallowed him, eh? How old are you, Giulia? Seventeen? Close to the age of my youngest daughter. These are all my daughters. There, there's Loredana, with her *fidanzato*, Bernardo."

She was a very young girl in a leopard-skin bathing suit curled on a towel with a dark-bearded man. Rinaldo laughed, "Always hiding, those two." How different my father might have been if he had stayed in Italy. "Loredana, untangle yourself. Come meet an Americana. If you're nice, she'll help you pass your English exam." He whispered to us, "That girl, for studying, she's hopeless. It's a situation beyond even Saint Jude."

Loredana ran over and shook my hand. "Americana? You will teach me everything, yes?"

"But teach her good," Rinaldo warned me. "Like the British speak, don't teach her a lot of those American things."

Loredana never did speak English that summer, but those Italians on the beach were like snake charmers with their own language, pulling me out of myself, drawing me toward them. The language was part of the air at the beach, a constant breeze of vowel sounds and lulling *l-l-l*s. As I lay on the sand, Italian voices hovered over me, surrounded me, sharpening my ear, shaping my tongue, changing me as much and as quickly as the sun was changing the color of my skin. Frustrated when I couldn't understand what was being said, I raised myself up on my elbows and watched their hands and faces. A rush of words while their lit cigarettes moved through the air like stunt planes. Then a sentence interrupted, left suspended during a slow inhalation, and no one knew what would happen next. Speaking with each other, they dueled and sparred, sometimes using sounds more effectively than words: a hum deep in the throat expressed shock, a click of the tongue was a definitive no. The mothers cooed at their babies, caressed them with soft words: *bambina, bellina, gioia, carino.*

At one o'clock we all gathered towels and chairs and rafts and children and headed home for the midday meal. Everyone moved together. There were no pockets in the day when you'd find yourself alone.

"Buon appetito, buon appetito," the other families called out to us.

And we waved and called back, *"Arrivederci, ciao."*

Our family, dressed in bathing suits, gathered for dinner at a long table that stretched across the courtyard. And despite the heat, despite the small ill-equipped kitchen, the shimmying half-refrigerator, the miniature oven and the two tight burners, the aunts always came forth with a feast. There was pasta every day—pasta with tomato and basil sauce, or pasta with shrimp sauce, pasta with beans, pasta with eggplant, or risotto with seafood or mushrooms; then meat—sautéed or baked or stuffed or grilled; or maybe fish bought fresh that morning from the fishermen nearby; then there was salad, fresh greens; after everything, there was fruit and cheese, then coffee. And always there was food left for a snack later on.

In the afternoon everyone found a cool corner to take a nap. Everyone but Zio Vito, who had to sit with his neck in a traction harness suspended from a bedroom door.

"Poverino," la Signora whimpered, "strapped up, like he's hanging himself. Berta, go, make sure it's not too tight."

And occasionally, Giulietta, wide-eyed, would slip into the hallway to ask him, "Zio Vito?"

"Yes, *cara?*"

"Can you breathe? Are you still alive?"

In the evenings there were drives to the beach towns, my uncles speeding, racing the sunset, getting us to piazzas and terraces cut into the mountains so we could see the sky turn purple over the sea. Afterward, there were cafes where we sat around a few small tables and a waiter would come to us, and whether he was blond or dark, dressed in white shirt and black bow tie or in a T-shirt and jeans, he was always handsome and serious, holding a tray behind his back, leaning close to ask me, *"Signorina,* what would you like?"

"Tell her what there is," my uncles said.

"There is everything, anything she desires," and looking into my eyes as he looked into the eyes of all the women and girls who appeared before him on all those warm summer nights, he recited for me, *"Cioccolata, vaniglia, nocciuola, pistacchio, gianduia, torrone, limone, melone, ananas, fragola, cassata, spumone.* And then, *signorina,* special, tonight, for you, we have *frutta di passione."*

After the ice cream, there was the arguing as the kids figured out who would ride in which car. My uncles sped us along the unlit, narrow, curving roads. Mountains loomed above us, the sea swirled right below, but my cousins and I huddled in the back seats of those impossibly small cars, arm to arm, leg to leg, the little ones stretched across the older ones' laps. The night turned cool, but the heat of the day's sun rose up under our skin and we warmed each other and felt safe.

There was all this, and along with it, all week long, an

undertow to every minute of every day, there was the constant waiting for Luca.

One night as the family wandered around Tropea my aunts stopped in front of a store where a hundred different bikinis were displayed in the window, a kaleidoscope of colors, dots, stripes, paisleys, blocks, swirls. I had my camera with me and started to photograph the window. After I'd taken a few shots, my aunts encouraged me to go in.

"But I've got a bathing suit."

"Oh, that thing," Zia Berta scolded me. "You're the only young girl on the beach, Giulia, who wears a one-piece."

"I don't know. I'd feel so exposed."

Claudia calmly told me, "You must learn Italian logic. You must realize that people will notice you more in your practical one-piece American bathing suit. If you show more of your body, you'll fit in more and be less conspicuous."

"Listen to Claudia," the other two said. "She's a professor, she knows."

The bikinis were too small to hang up on hangers; they were lying out on shelves and tables. I chose a few and went into the dressing room, a tiny circle of denim curtains. Mercifully, the mirror was inside the dressing room.

"Well," my aunts called in. "What do you think?"

"I'm not sure yet." Except for my white stomach, I did look like others on the beach. I'd never been to a place before where so many girls had bodies shaped similarly to mine—girls with hips, full bottoms, flesh on their arms. I'd grown up always comparing myself with Molly, who was as tall as me and fifteen pounds thinner. Cetta said Molly was a stick. "Poor thing, with those skinny knees. She looks like she's connected with rubber bands."

I was sure Molly could be a *Vogue* model if she wanted. Her long hair was blond and perfect. Her eyebrows were white, almost invisible. Inside, Molly was tough. But outside she had the clean angelic beauty that haunted America, floated inaccessibly just out of reach. In Italy, there was a different aesthetic. Women were dark and textured, and seemed to have risen right up out of the earth. Italian women didn't shave or tweeze or starve themselves; they looked less plucked. In the afternoon, even skinny Loredana would come down to the beach with her stomach distended from too much pasta.

"Here, try this." Berta shoved a tiny bikini inside the curtain of the dressing room. "I had one just this color when I was a girl."

It was turquoise and red paisley on a white background. I'd always worn dark bathing suits before, usually navy blue, which Cetta said was as slimming as black. But the paisley of this bikini promised something happy. This, I decided, was what I would be wearing when Luca showed up.

Our house at the beach had no telephone. When I discovered that, I panicked. What if Luca wanted to call? "What do we do if there's an emergency?" I asked Marigiulia and Giuliana.

"You know the small piazza we pass before the farm on the way here? Did you see the bar there? We can use the phone in the bar."

"But what if one of Zio Vito's patients needs him?"

"They call the bar, then someone comes to tell us," she said, as if this made perfect sense.

I wrote to Molly: "I feel lost in space. He can't call me here without involving the whole village. There's no way to know if he wants to call me or thinks about calling or if he's forgotten who I am."

. . . .

On Tuesday, Loredana came down to the beach and sat under the umbrella with me. She was out of her leopard-skin and in a faded pink two-piece with a ruffle around the waist. She looked like a child, but with a woman's rocky voice she told me, "I'm angry as a beast."

"Why?" I asked.

"Bernardo and I quarreled last night on the phone. He wants to know do I talk to other men on the beach while he's gone." She emptied two handfuls of sand onto her knees. "Ah, Giulia, what am I going to do? Do you think I should leave him?"

"But you're getting married, aren't you? When I met you, your father said Bernardo was your *fidanzato.*"

She waved her hands in front of me, wiping that idea out. "Yes, of course, my *fidanzato,* but he's not an *official fidanzato.* Nothing is official between Bernardo and me. See"—she held out her hands—"no ring, no promises. Giulia, Madonna mia! I'm only sixteen years old."

"But, Loredana, does your father think you're going to marry Bernardo?"

She held out her hands, palms up, and gave me a high shrug that said, I'm blameless. "Well, probably. Probably he does, but that is in the head of my father." She brushed her long limp bangs out of her eyes and took my hand, as Italians often do when they're trying to educate you about something. "Look, *cara,* it's like this. A boy and a girl meet. They maybe take a *passeggiata* in the evenings. If they see they get along, they decide to stay together. Their friends know, but their parents know nothing."

"Don't the parents see the boy when he comes to pick the girl up?"

"Noooo, noooo. To the house—never." This thought even made her laugh. "We meet outside, in the piazza, in some cafe. After a few months, if we feel we still go well together, then maybe we introduce the boy to our parents, and then, to make them happy, you can say, yes, yes, he is my *fidanzato*. That way, you can walk around town and not worry about being seen." Italian mysteries no one had ever revealed to me. "Tell me, Giulia, in America with your *fidanzati* you do things differently?"

"Yes," I said, "differently."

"Ah, maybe it's better there."

One thousand years passed before Thursday evening when a phone message came from the bar. Carlo and Luca had called. They were going to arrive on Friday evening. Luca's father was driving them down after work.

Friday morning, I woke up early and washed my favorite halter dress. I shampooed my hair and shaved my legs.

At dinner Zia Assunta set aside a big portion of pasta sauce with shrimp, Carlo's favorite, so she'd be ready to feed him at whatever time he walked in.

Everyone was waiting, all day long. But the afternoon passed, the sun set, the moon rose, and Carlo and Luca hadn't arrived. Zia Assunta told Zio Anto to drive her to the bar so she could use the phone. La Signora said a rosary. All I could do was wait in the courtyard and play cards.

My cousins had taught me four different solitaires with the deck of *carte napoletane*. They were smaller than American cards, and the four suits were designed with Medieval-looking emblems. The eights were young knights who had the vulnerable look of shy suitors. The knight of clubs, though, stood looking arrogantly over his shoulder, showing his back; the knight's well-shaped bottom made me think *Luca!* every time this card landed in my hand. Waiting for news about Carlo and Luca, I laid out a solitaire and told myself, If I win this game, they'll get here tonight.

. . . .

You could always tell who wasn't awake yet by which bathing suits still hung on the clothesline. The next morning, my new bikini and two of the baby's diapers were the only things left when I stepped out onto the balcony. Carlo and Luca hadn't arrived the night before. I looked down at the beach; they still weren't there. Forget it, they're not coming. They made other plans. Something better came up for them.

I was standing behind the balcony's wooden doors, tugging my bathing suit on under my nightgown when I heard my aunt's voice from down below in the kitchen, and she was saying, "Luca, can I offer you a coffee?"

I ran into the bathroom. I put on my bikini top, tied it in back with two knots. I looked in the mirror, hated my hair, braided it and put on eye shadow. I brushed my teeth and took off my dental retainer (and never put it on again). I tried on three different pairs of earrings. Put a T-shirt on over my bikini, heard Molly's voice telling me, Take that stupid shirt off. I washed the makeup off my face. Undid the braid. Decided on a pair of gold hoops. Forgot to make my bed. When I finally got down to the kitchen, Luca was gone.

"Dormigliona," Nonna Giulia accused me. She and Zia Assunta were busy making ravioli with spinach—the kind Carlo liked.

Zia Berta straightened my straps and kissed my forehead. "Luca is here with Carlo, you know. Zio Anto was driving to pick them up and he found them on the road from Montemaggiore. They were hitchhiking."

Zia Assunta blessed herself, left a trail of white flour from her forehead to her chest to both shoulders. "Hitchhiking! Those idiots."

"And twice Luca asked for you," Zia Berta told me.

I headed for the door. Zia Assunta followed me. "Giulia, your breakfast. I can't have you fainting on the beach. What will we tell your father then?"

"No thanks, Zia."

"Americana!"

"I don't want anything."

I wanted everything that summer. *"Tu vuoi mangiare tutto il mondo,"* my uncles often told me. You want to swallow up the whole world. All week long, waiting for Luca, I'd lain awake in bed at night thinking about the beach towns and what I'd seen there. Lovers, everywhere, holding on to each other. Up on the *terrazze,* lying behind rocks on the beach, filling the niches of doorways, deep in shadows, up on balconies, sitting at tiny tables in cafes. Girls with bare shoulders, being held by boys whose shirts were open. Girls leaning their backs against stone walls, boys' hands on girls' waists, thumbs under breasts, mini-skirted legs pinned between denim knees. Every shaded, veiled or hidden corner where I didn't see a couple, I imagined Luca and me together. Imagined Luca looking at me as if there was nothing else in the world.

When I got to the beach that Saturday morning and saw that the boys were diving off the *scoglio,* a protrusion of rock jutting out of the water, I did something I never would have imagined doing in Homefield: I went to meet them.

When they saw me, paddling out on the raft, something happened that could never have happened at home: Carlo and Luca headed toward me and no one was stopping them. They were swimming in that Italian way, with their heads above the water, but covering distance fast. And suddenly, it was just like home: I stopped paddling; I let the waves take me a little farther away. Every time Luca turned his dark head from side to side, his eyes were on me. Just at that moment, he looked so Italian and so male, so completely other, that I thought, Who is this Luca, this stranger with the odd name? Who is he?

Sitting on the raft, I couldn't hide. I was all body, stretching the seams of that bikini. I crossed one leg over the other. Carlo and Luca were inches away. Then they were throwing themselves across the ends of the raft, getting water all over me. Carlo caught his breath first. "Americana!"

"There you are," Luca said. I'd never seen him without a shirt on. The small patch of dark wet hair on his chest, wet hair under his arms, purple goose-pimpled flesh around his small brown nipples. Drops of seawater were caught in the curl of his upper lip and looked like sweat.

Luca was pretending he was the Beach Boys singing "Ca-li-fornia girrrrls," making too much noise.

Carlo asked me something. I thought he said, "Did you miss us?," but I wasn't sure.

"What?"

They slapped their hands flat on the water and splashed me. "You didn't miss us? So then tell us, what was so interesting here all week that you didn't even miss us? Tell us everything."

"What do you want to know?"

"Tell us first," Luca said—his hand was gripping my ankle, tighter, I'm sure, than he realized—"do all American girls have such white stomachs?"

"Do all Italian boys ask such stupid questions?"

They dumped me off the raft.

We sat up on the beach later, and nearby, the maestro's woman was covering the maestro with sand, slowly pouring it up the length of his leg, letting it fall over his chest. The old man opened his arms against the sand and tilted back his head. Abandon. Why were they letting us see this? I tried not to look, but my eyes kept going to them.

The woman was covering her lover as completely as I imagined he had undressed her years earlier. She had probably been lovely and quick then. Now the flesh on her sides lapped over her waist, the way Cetta's bread dough dripped over the edge of the pan when it was rising. The woman was making a pillow of sand for him, serving him, and she was living in a place where no one knew her name.

Luca and Carlo were next to me, lying on towels, their low-cut bathing trunks threatening to show me their flat stomachs below their navels where their dark hair got thicker. Luca turned over and there was that dangerous point where his back cleaved into his buttocks. I sat with my knees bent and pulled close.

"How was your studying this week?" I asked, looking back at the house and the hills rising up behind, stark and mostly brown, except for small islands of green where cactus grew.

"It was terrible." Carlo stretched and yawned and rolled over into the sand. "How would you like to study in this heat?"

"It was lonely," Luca said earnestly, his mouth muffled by the towel.

That was the voice I wanted to hear, the low, private voice that spoke to me in the park the first day I'd met him. "Lonely?"

"Yes, lonely." Luca hadn't shaved, his cheeks were dark, and his eyes still sleepy. I moved closer to listen. "We have seven rooms, three bedrooms, six beds, but it is all wasted." He grinned and looked wicked. "We have no women."

Carlo was laughing. They were both waiting for me to laugh with them. How many *fidanzate,* I wondered, had Luca wandered around Montemaggiore with?

"So, Americana . . ."

"My name's Giulia."

I felt Luca and Carlo look at each other. Then we said nothing for a long time, until Luca started singing, softly, "Just like a Woman," but with a terrible accent. "She bricks just like a little girl," he kept singing, and I wanted to say, "Sing it right or don't bother."

Carlo, bored, turned away, changed his view, lay down on his stomach and looked back at the houses. Then his breath caught. He hissed, "Oh, oh, oh, Luca, for the love of God, look who's here."

Luca looked, gave a low shocked whistle. "Did you know she'd be here?"

"Who would have imagined? They weren't here last summer."

"Giulia, ciao, come va?"

"Ciao, Loredana." She and Bernardo were walking to the Cinzano umbrella. They disappeared into the tent. Carlo kept staring after they were gone. "What is she doing with that gorilla?"

"What do you think she's doing?" Luca grunted. "That's your Leoparda."

"Her name's Loredana," I said.

"To Carlo, she's Leoparda," Luca told me. "Carlo, you see how many leopard clothes that one has! Giulia, that girl makes your cousin's head spin."

"Too bad for Carlo. Loredana and Bernardo are engaged."

"Bernardo, *il signor dentista.* He went to high school with my brother, and just like my brother, he's an idiot."

"Oh," Carlo moaned, "why is she with him?"

Luca pointed with his chin toward the tent, where only the tight bundle of their four legs stuck out. Luca told Carlo, "I'm sorry to tell you, my friend, but it looks like *il signor dentista* is conducting an examination. Carlo, listen," Luca taunted him. "I can hear them. He's saying,

'*Bella,* you have a toothache? I'm so sorry. Well, come, let's take off this little leopard bathing suit top and see if we can find the problem.' "

Luca's voice. It pulled me in, it made me want to run away.

Carlo mimicked Loredana: " '*Si, si dottore.* Right away,' " and I was sure they were mocking me along with her. " 'I'll take it off right away, *dottore,*' " Carlo laughed.

"As if Leoparda needs an excuse to take off her clothes," Luca said, as if he knew.

"How unimaginative you two are," I said. "Loredana's pretty but she's an idiot as soon as she opens her mouth." I'd never used Italian before to say anything so mean.

"Well," Luca said, laughing, "intelligence is not one of her assets."

Carlo laughed. I put on my sunglasses and turned away from them.

"Being here has made the Americana a bit antisocial," Luca said, "hasn't it?"

That evening, friends of Luca's and Carlo's came by on motorcycles. They all took off together, headed for some nightclub. No matter where they were, they always seemed to know where to go. From up in my room I heard the aunts ask Carlo, "Aren't you taking Giulia with you?"

"I'm sure she's not interested," he said.

I heard those slippery Italian male voices, then the engines revving. Then the silence when they were gone.

The night air is dangerous, my family in Italy told me. Even on the hottest nights, they said we had to sleep with the windows shut tight and the shutters pulled in. To keep air running through the house, all the bedroom doors were held open with chunks of marble. The uncles' and the nonnas' snoring reverberated through the night.

That Saturday night I lay in my narrow cot, listening, waiting to hear Carlo come home, trying to dissect every point where things with Luca had gone wrong: Was it on the raft, in the water, on the beach?

Colicky Giancarlo had been crying for hours. The aunts were meeting in the hallway every half-hour to discuss what to give him, what to do for him: a warm bath, a cool bath, camomile, milk, a drop of whiskey. I heard Zia Berta going up to the roof terrace. During the day it was too hot on the roof, but at night, when they were desperate, the aunts took turns up there with the baby. I felt desperate, too, so I went up and joined her. She was singing, marching, bouncing Giancarlo, but he was crying inconsolably, as if he, too, had just suffered a huge disappointment.

"Zia, you look so tired."

"Me? You should see Claudia. She hasn't closed an eye in two nights. What are you doing up so late? It's almost four o'clock."

"I couldn't sleep. Here, let me help you." I took the baby from her. He kept crying, but his strong fist gripped my fingers, held tight. I brought his hand to my mouth, kissed his arm where the fat bubbled over his wrist. I held his damp head against my face, and softly into his ear I sang Beatles songs. "Listen, do you want to know a secret?" That did it for him. Giancarlo nodded onto my shoulder, heavy and peaceful.

Berta was astonished. "You did it," she whispered, and clapped her hands soundlessly.

We stood there a long time. I swayed and rocked the baby; Zia lit a cigarette. She must have felt me wishing, because she offered it to me.

I nodded yes. She held the cigarette to my lips and let me inhale deeply twice. Both of us held our heads back and exhaled up at the stars. The dark sky was endless, with a skinny moon.

"When Carlino was little," Zia Berta told me, "he asked us once, 'Can Zio Nicola in Ohio see that moon?' We told him yes. For a long time, whenever there was a moon he used to say, 'Look, it's Zio Nicola's moon.' " We laughed, then she said, out of nowhere, "It's been hard these days for you, hasn't it, waiting?"

"But I'm not waiting for anything."

"No?"

"No," I lied.

"And in Ohio, isn't someone waiting for you? Some nice young man?"

"I prefer not to get seriously involved with anyone at this point."

"Oh," my aunt said, using her burnt-down cigarette to light a fresh one. "I see." She smiled at the tip of the cigarette, which was poised, as always, near her chin. There was something unmistakably glamorous about my aunt. That night, she had on a dark blue belted robe over her slip (all my Italian aunts slept in their satin slips and their jewelry) and was still wearing her gold watch and her earrings—hanging pearls circled with a ring of small diamonds. Her figure was slim, curving, perfect for evening gowns, and something about her made me feel sure there had been a time in her life when she'd stood on the terraces of *palazzi* all over Europe. What had she given up to marry Zio Vito? Or had he saved her from some life she needed to escape?

"Beautiful earrings, Zia," I whispered.

"Hmm." She leaned on the railing and told me vaguely, "A gift from long ago." Who had given them to her?

After a while she turned to me and brushed the hair away from my eyes. "Seven years I was engaged, did you know that?"

I was less curious about her epic-length engagement than I was about why she was telling me this. "Why so long?" I finally asked her.

"Oh, we had to wait for many things. First, of course, Zio Vito had to finish medical school—he lost two years when he went with the missions. Then, his specialization —another two years. Then he was working with a doctor in Torino."

"Why couldn't you just move with him to Torino?"

"And leave my mother? Oh, look—" She pointed up at a light in the sky, maybe a shooting star, but it was just a far-off plane. "Besides, Vito and I had no money, no house. Then we had two more years until he got an assignment in the south. All together, seven years." She sighed, then smiled from behind her curtain of hair. *"Stari a tavola e non mangiare, stari a lettu e non dormire, aspettari a cu' non mbena, su tri cuosi da morire.* Did you ever hear this?"

"Yes." Cetta said it all the time: To sit at the table and not eat, to lie in bed and not sleep, to wait for someone who never comes are three things to die from.

"It's crazy to wait, if you find something you want," she said, and I looked at her. "Yes! Really. Especially today, you young people, you can have anything you want. There's money, no war. And that's how it should be. Why wait? Live today. Grab your chance."

Did all the world feel this much freedom, or was it only in Italy?

I could see Berta, younger, with her short dark hair and her cigarettes, not hiding like Aunt Sofia and me, but going out into the night like Carlo and Luca, free.

Carlo never came home until the next morning. He said he had spent the night at Luca's. Who knows where they went or what time they got home or if they went home at all. Carlo brought his *caffè* out to the courtyard and sat down next to me. He asked, whispering, "Why are you angry with us? What did we do?" Alone, without Luca, Carlo seemed less dangerous.

"The way you two were talking about girls yesterday, it's terrible." Still, I cringed when I heard myself saying anything important in Italian. I sounded so childish. "How do I know, maybe you talk about me that way, too."

"Giulia, how could I talk about you in that way? You're a different type of girl. Besides, you're my cousin."

"But I'm not Luca's cousin."

"Yes," Carlo said, smiling, "aren't you glad?"

Sunday morning passed, hour by hour. Luca didn't show up. It was almost time to leave the beach for dinner when I saw Luca walking with a man and a woman, coming over the ledge of rock and onto our beach. "Ou-ou," the woman yodeled to me, waving red-fingernail-polished hands. Her gold jewelry glimmered in the sun. Her long hennaed hair was parted straight down the middle and pulled back severely into a ponytail that swung out from behind her back then disappeared again as she walked. Tall and dark-skinned, walking across the beach in her black bikini, the woman looked like *Playboy*'s idea of an Aztec priestess. The man was shirtless and wearing small black trunks and a gold wristwatch. He was carrying a pack of cigarettes and the tape deck from a car. How did Luca know these people?

"I am Renata," the woman said, walking straight up to me, stretching out her hand. "I am the *fidanzata* of Luca's brother."

"And I am the brother." He held his hand out, too, but more stiffly. "Mauro."

Luca was shorter than either of them. His dark tennis

shirt was stretched out at the neck, and he looked as miserable as a small boy who'd been woken up from a nap. By now, Luca had gained such power over my thoughts, my nights, my sleep, it was satisfying to see him dwarfed by his brother and Renata. Before he even said hello, Luca explained why they were there, "Mauro wanted to visit Bernardo."

"You are the daughter of the psychiatrist in America, no?" Mauro asked me. "And you, do you study medicine?"

"No. She studies photography," Renata told him. "Don't you remember Luca told us?" I couldn't see her eyes, but her mouth looked friendly, and I wanted to tell her, Help me. Luca talked to you. What did he say? What is he thinking? What should I do?

"Whatever you do, if you're learning Italian," Mauro told me, "don't listen to Renata. You don't want to learn her ugly Romanaccio."

Renata ignored him. *"Che fortuna!"* she exclaimed. "What luck! My family's house isn't three minutes away from you." I couldn't hear anything ugly in the way she spoke. My ear wasn't good enough yet to pick up a different dialect. I was just grateful that she was speaking clearly. She snapped her fingers in front of my face. "Like this, in a second, we walked here. You'll come to visit us often, no? We're in the small house with the brick oven out in front, my mother, my aunt and I—so I can be near Mauro."

Mauro was unmoved by this declaration. "Anyway," he said, "how are you finding things, Giulia, down here in the south of Italy?" I'd never before faced a man handsome the way Mauro was handsome—dark, all cheekbones and jaw, blue-black hair with strands of gray, shoulders even rounder and wider than Luca's, thick arms, chest soft with dark hair, hazel-tan skin. Like

Renata, Mauro was a specimen, but he spoke a stiff, educated, formal Italian. "What have you found of interest to do down here?" There was a challenge in Mauro's voice: I had to figure out the right thing to say, then I had to say it in perfect Italian.

"Well," I began, "I like the beach, and . . ." Then I heard my words trampled by Mauro's as he shouted up toward Bernardo and Loredana. It was embarrassing to hear my voice, my weak Italian, lingering in the air.

They all hugged and kissed on both cheeks. We sat in the sand under the Cinzano umbrella; they lit cigarettes for each other and started talking loud and fast.

I listened, tried to keep up, and I kept an eye on Luca. He had gathered together the stones from around the umbrella pole. He was balancing small flat stones on top of a larger one. Using a sharply pointed rock, he was cracking the flat stones neatly in half. One after another; he was concentrating, working systematically. If he got the stones in just the right spot, they fell in two at the first strike. He wasn't saying a word.

To stay in the shade we all had to sit close, and the tips of Luca's curly hair reached the ends of my frizzy hair. This small connection was bigger than my anger at him. His perfect hand played in the sand, fingers darker than the sand. Bits of sand under his pink fingernails.

"Luca," I said in a low voice, "you never told me, how did your studying go this week?"

"Ah! You two are speaking English. *Che bello!*" Renata exclaimed. "Luca, this is for you a good opportunity to practice your English."

"*His* English? Who is he now, Prince Charles?" Mauro said.

I laughed.

Luca broke a stone with one quick angry jab, and I realized I'd made another mistake. Luca stood up, asked

me in a voice so low and angry I barely heard him,
"Where's Carlo?"

"What?"

"Is he at the house?"

"Yes," I said, "yes." Then he left us.

Renata shook her head at Mauro. "You had to start,
didn't you?"

"Don't *you* start," he warned her sharply. "If he's so
immature he gets offended at the slightest remark, let him
go."

"But Mauro, he loves English. So what? Leave him in
peace." Renata turned to me, "In Mauro's book it is a
tragedy and a personal shame that Luca wants to study
languages and not medicine."

Mauro closed his eyes and sighed. "But what is the
point of getting a degree in these languages? There is no
point."

"It is important to be able to talk to people."

"Tell him, Giulia," Renata said.

"Psssh," Mauro said, and sounded just like my father.
"What do I have to say to people on the other side of the
earth? Eh? I'm fine, right here." He leaned back on his
elbow, balanced the tape deck on his hip. "I have never
been to a foreign country, I've never been north of
Rome," he said proudly. "I consider myself lucky." He
reached over and pinched my cheek. *"Bella,* relax, there is
no place better than where you are right now." There was
a thrill in his touching me, but Mauro's good looks were
starting to turn—like overripe fruit. "Renata will talk
about Rome the way Dante described the Paradiso, but
that city is, excuse the expression, a toilet."

"Oh, Mauro, shut up." She lifted her sunglasses. I was
shocked. Her eyes were naked—no makeup—and looked
so tired.

"Just be glad that for the summer I got you out of that

cave, that bar you work in. There's no place like Calabria."

"First, I don't work in that bar. I own it. And second, all I ever said is that I like my home, which happens to be Rome. Giulia, what about you? You must miss America. I'm sure of it."

Renata was the first person during my weeks in Italy to ask me that. Just that morning, there had been half an hour when I'd considered getting my plane ticket changed, so I could fly back early, but that was because I was upset about Luca. "No, I don't miss Ohio. I like it here."

Mauro's face cracked. He was not as handsome smiling as he was frowning. *"Brava! Bravissima!"*

Loredana's foot crawled out of the sand and landed on top of mine. "What I want to know, Giulia, is when are you going to teach me English? How will I pass this exam in September if you don't help me?"

"Forget it, *bella,*" Mauro told Loredana, and kissed her nose. "Exams aren't for you. For exams, you're hopeless."

She kicked sand at him. "Hopeless? Now we'll see who's hopeless." Loredana sprayed Mauro until he had to cover his face, then she grabbed the tape player and ran toward the water. "Loredà!" Mauro and Bernardo went after her.

"That Loredana," Renata said as she and I sat watching them. Now that we were alone, she looked harder, sharper, older, darker. I realized that her cheerfulness around Mauro cost her. "She's too young and she's taking Bernardo for a ride. She'll drop him soon." Then Renata looked at me and smiled weakly. "Ha," she said, "that Loredana could teach us all a lesson, no?"

I knew I had to do something, say something, but first I had to find a way to talk to Luca alone.

Just before dinner I was upstairs in the spare kitchen

getting bottles of water from the fridge. The rooms were empty, baking from the sun. Luca found me. Downstairs, everyone was preparing for the afternoon meal. He came and leaned in the door frame of the small kitchen. He was wearing a pair of Carlo's jeans and no shirt.

"My brother is a fool, you know. Why would you sit down there and listen to him? Him and that gorilla, Bernardo?"

"I like Renata."

"She's a fool, too, if she marries my brother."

Where Mauro's skin was covered with dark hair, Luca's skin was smooth and taut. He looked more fragile than Mauro, less dangerous.

"I used your razor," he said, "and it's not sharp enough."

"How do you know it was mine?"

"It was pink, and only American girls use razors."

"My aunts want to know if you're staying for dinner."

"Carlo and I are leaving right after dinner. How do you stand it here all week? It's dead as a tomb at this beach."

"Where are you going?"

"With friends."

Friends? Women? *We have seven rooms, three bedrooms, six beds, but no women.* "You could have asked me before you used my razor."

"Well, it's too late now." He walked away.

"*Lu*-ca."

He wouldn't come back, but he stopped in the other room. "What?"

"Luca, why didn't you ask me? About the razor."

He stood in the doorway and stared at me. "Giulia, you turned crazy like my brother. These two days, what have you been trying to do? I don't understand."

"Just ask me next time." I handed him a water bottle. "Please take a couple of these downstairs when you go."

He took the bottle, but then he stepped toward me and put his hand on the side of my neck.

Finally, I thought.

His fingers trailed down my throat. Then his face moved closer, hung right over mine and with just three fingers on my neck he pulled me toward him, and then, finally, his lips so light, and my mouth widened to let him know it was okay, so his face came closer and there was the scratch of his beard. And I put my hands on his arms, then his shoulders, his neck, and I was thinking, This is Luca, I'm kissing Luca.

Luca. But even as I was thinking that, something had changed. With his other hand, he pressed the icy bottle against my thigh. He was heavier now as he leaned over me, his hand moving free as I imagined him riding through the night. His fingers went straight over the rise of my chest and inside one of the paisley-print triangles of my bathing-suit top. I tried to pull back, but his tongue in my mouth was like a rope pulling on me, not letting go. There was hot breath everywhere. The damp water bottle was bumping against the backs of my thighs, but I didn't feel the coldness anymore. I just worried about glass breaking, making noise, about being heard, seen, found.

His knee found my crotch and I tightened my legs to keep him still, but he pushed harder and his hand dipped inside the other triangle of my top, and his mouth slid to my neck. He kissed me, soft again, and I thought, okay, and I ran my hands down his sides, over skin soft as a child's, but I felt wetness there—sweat. His tongue was in my ear, pressing. I held his face, but his fingers were squeezing my nipple. "Luca!"

His fingers let go, then hands again on my waist, hips, stomach, so fast. "White belly," he muttered, then he was inside the elastic of my bikini and before I could do anything he touched crisp hair. "Luca, stop!"

I pulled away, saw the tip of his tongue twitching between his lips, and to cover it up I kissed him again.

"Hey, hey, hey." He pushed me slightly, pushed me away. "You said stop, so stop. Stop."

"Luca." He wouldn't come back, but his eyes were on me, like he was about to say something. He took a drink from the bottle.

"What, Luca?"

He shook his head. "Forget it." He left the water bottle on the counter and walked away.

"Where did you go for that water," Zio Anto asked me when I got to the table, "to Ohio?"

Everyone was eating. My bowl of pasta was waiting for me.

"Leave her alone," Zia Berta told him. "She wanted to change her clothes." I'd torn off that bikini and thrown it under the bed. Berta smiled at me. "Doesn't she look nice in her sundress?"

"Excuse us, Giulia," Zia Assunta said. "The boys have to leave soon so we started without you."

Zia Claudia walked past me with a bowl of freshly roasted hot red peppers that left behind a biting aroma that made me nauseous. Claudia was bringing the peppers to the men's end of the table, offering the bowl to Zio Anto, but he said, "Please, to the scholars first, the young men," and the bowl of peppers went to Luca. "They need to keep up their strength."

Luca was helping himself to a heaping forkful of hot peppers to put on his pasta, and Zio Vito told him, "Take more, Luca, take more."

SEVEN

Big Changes in the Future

AT NIGHT in the courtyard la Signora recited for us the stories of the saints. In her mind, they were divided into two categories: the saints who were great for their miracles, and those who were great for their penitential suffering. La Signora's favorites were those of the monumental penances. San Francesco di Assisi, she informed us, mixed ashes with his food to spoil the taste of anything good. Sant'Andrea, if he committed the smallest transgression—a sip of water between meals—would run to his confessor and cry. "Enough tears to make a puddle at his feet," la Signora whimpered. Santa Caterina di Siena refused food for days at a time, until, at the end of her life, she needed nothing but a Communion wafer to sustain her from day to day. "Poor Caterina, one half-hour every other night, that's all she let herself sleep." And she beat herself with chains three times a day—once for herself, once for the living and once for the dead. When Santa Caterina's parents tried to arrange a marriage for her, she shaved off her hair.

If the penance of these saints was so extreme, I asked la Signora, how bad were their sins?

"What sins? They had no sins. They were saints. That was their holiness, to feel guilt even when they were innocent."

From that moment on Sunday when Luca turned away from me, his mouth dripping with water, the voices of Aunt Sofia and my father screamed in my head. *What were you doing in the kitchen, alone, with that boy?* He's the one who started it. He walked in, he touched my neck. *What were you trying to do with him, eh? What did you think would happen?* It was him, it wasn't me. *It's always the girl, always the girl's fault.* But he walked in, he touched—

After Luca and Carlo left, Zia Assunta said she was going to evening Mass. For the first time all summer, I went with her. The pews were packed with old women in black and teenage girls trying out new makeup and new dresses. There were hardly any men in the church. The late-afternoon light floated through the stained-glass windows and turned neon, red and blue. I knelt in the cool church, looked up at the statues of Sant'Antonio, the Sacred Heart of Jesus, San Francesco di Paola and waited for their stone faces to cry.

I remembered one summer in Homefield, I was about thirteen, and a girl who looked not much older than me was coming with her mother every week for a session with my father. Through the back yard hedges, I looked for them on Tuesday afternoons. The girl was a wreck, her hair long and knotted. She never wore shoes. Once she had a thick dirty bandage on her foot. Her frayed bell-bottom jeans dragged on the ground. Her leather vest fringed down to her knees, and thick bands of jewelry clanked all over her. Usually when they arrived, they weren't talking. The mother got out of the car, slammed her door, and a few minutes later, the daughter got out, slammed hers. An hour later, when they left, though, the mother and daughter were sometimes smiling. Once they came out and the mother had her arm around the girl's shoulders. All that forgiveness had taken place in my father's office. It had never happened for me with him.

In church with Zia Assunta I thought of going to confession. It would have been nice to hear an Italian voice telling me, Go, you are forgiven, but I needed more than absolution. Could that priest stop the *Lu*-ca, *Lu*-ca, *Lu*-ca beating through me like an angry pulse? Could he give me back that rush of freedom I'd felt riding on the motorino with Luca, and that power I'd felt when Luca's eyes were on me—could the priest give that back to me? Why had I had all that, and now, why was it gone? I'd been so close to everything I'd been waiting for. What did I do wrong? Could that priest explain to me how it was decided who got what?

The people who have everything don't need to talk. That, I suppose, is why the air seemed thickened with silence or with trivia when Zia Claudia was around. It wasn't that she never spoke—she did. She just never told me the things I needed to know from her, the secrets of happy love. It was like listening to a record set on the wrong speed; you're always waiting for some other sound. We never did have even a moment to talk, the two of us alone, but all during those months in Italy Zia Claudia showed up in my dreams, more than anyone else in the family. Sunday night I dreamed she and Luca were walking on a wall topped with jagged bits of stained glass, but the glass didn't cut their feet. They were laughing, she looked pretty. Then the wall turned into the back of a large couch, and Luca and Claudia were lying on the couch kissing each other passionately while her hand reached over his head for chunks of blue and red glass.

Tuesday afternoon Loredana ran down to the beach, calling me urgently. "Giulia!" She skidded to a stop in the sand next to me, and she told me in a hurried whisper, "What good news I have! Bernardo called for me this afternoon, secretly, at the bar. He is coming to me tonight. We arranged it on the phone. I will tell my father I am going for a walk to get an ice cream, then I go down the other way, into the lido . . ."

"Where?"

"The lido, the small cafe inside the orange groves, and Bernardo will be there waiting for me. It's beautiful, no?" Loredana was radiant.

I suppose you think that's nice, no? That girl going alone, in the dark, to meet that boy in those trees. "Aren't you nervous?"

"Yes, a little, but just this kind of risk I need to make me fall in love again. This is when I am happiest. Ah, I almost forgot . . ." She was sitting on a magazine and a newspaper, and she pulled them out from under her. She flipped through the pages. "I must read you this horoscope of mine. I read it after Bernardo called me and it absolutely made me get goose bumps. It says, 'You will have something today you've wanted a long time. Be secretive. Romance thrives.' Incredible, no?"

"Read mine. Capricorn."

" 'Big changes are coming for you in the future,' " she read. "Oh, Giulia, to my ear this sounds very good."

When Loredana left, I walked and walked. Over the rocks, onto the gypsies' beach, where the sand was dirtier and more littered than on our beach. Watermelon rinds left from the weekend were pressed into the sand and flies hovered over them. I could hope for Luca to come this weekend, maybe even a surprise, a tryst in the lido. I could hope for that, but I wasn't Loredana. I wasn't Claudia. Besides, I'd already promised the saints I would never talk to Luca again. Oh, maybe a word or two to be polite if he showed up at the house. But I would never be alone with him again. Ever.

On Saturday morning I was sitting on my bed writing a letter to Molly when Carlo appeared in the doorway, tall and unshaven, looking tired, like a man who was coming back from the world.

I put my hand over the letter. *"Ciao."*

He came in and sat on the edge of my bed, like a brother. "Did you hear what happened?" he said meaningfully. "Luca's motorino, we were riding it here and it broke down. Four kilometers we had to push it, all the way along the highway. My mother is hysterical. Luca's down on the beach."

"Look at you, you were out all night. You found Loredana and took her dancing, I bet."

"Yes, and now her boyfriend, that gorilla, is after me with a gun."

"Where were you?"

"I told you. Last night, we rode to Luca's parents' house. It was too late to try to come here. This morning, six o'clock, Luca woke me. Giulia, you don't know what I've been through this week with him. We have only three days now until the exams, and all Luca would do is ask questions about you. If he read two pages this week it was a lot."

"What did he ask you? Tell me."

"Did I know if you'd ever come to live in Italy? Would your father like him? I told him, 'Luca, I don't even know if her father will like me.' That was his big worry yesterday."

"Why?"

"Giulia, *cretina.*" Idiot. "He's in love with you."

"Stop it, Carlo. You're making fun of me."

"Giulia," he said seriously now. He took my hand from the letter, squeezed it. "Why do you think this about us, all the time, that we're teasing you? I think you're teasing us, trying to make us look stupid. He's going to fail the exams."

I pulled my hand away from Carlo's. "I don't care," I said in a low voice.

"Ah, so at least now we know how you feel about him. You don't care. Fine, just say so."

"I didn't say I don't care."

He sighed. "Giulia, what do you want Luca to do?"

Something inside me loved this conversation, with *Luca, Luca, Luca* all over the place. "Carlo, he shows up, he disappears. Why doesn't he say these things to me. Why you?"

"It's embarrassing for him here, can't you understand that? Imagine, with all these aunts and uncles and nonnas and cousins. You see how they are. Meanwhile, Luca has no idea what's going on with you. This morning he told me, 'This is it, the last time. If nothing is cleared up today I won't go back. Ever.' " Carlo smiled. "Luca is a little dramatic. But that's nice, no?"

"Carlo, you don't understand."

We were silent for a minute. Words in any language seemed useless.

"He told me about the kitchen last Sunday," Carlo said. "He tried to kiss you, eh?"

"Tried?"

"What happened? He was trying to hitchhike back here

121

last Sunday night to talk to you, but his brother passed him on the road and made him go home."

My eyes watered, Carlo blurred in front of me. "I don't understand you two. Maybe it's a cultural thing, maybe . . ."

"Giulia, what kind of boys are you used to? Maybe you have boys in Ohio who every day push a motorino four kilometers to come see you." How could I ever tell my family in Italy the truth about America? "If you have a boyfriend at home, tell us."

"Just tell me something." My voice was rising. "Does Luca have a *fidanzata* in Montemaggiore?"

"That I can't tell you. For that, you'll have to talk to him yourself." Carlo stood up. "Now I'm finished with you two. I have my own problems. Do you know where Loredana is? Is that gorilla around?"

"She's here. I saw her hanging out clothes."

"So then I'm going. Should I tell Luca you're coming?"

"Yes, I'm coming," and then, because Carlo hadn't told me if Luca had a *fidanzata* or not, I said, "I'm just going to finish this letter first."

Carlo left and slammed the door.

When I got to the beach, Luca was still lying in the sand, his face buried in his arms. I said, "Hello."

For a long moment, he didn't move. I thought of Giulietta, how she went up close whenever someone was napping, to make sure they were still alive. Finally, he spoke. "Tell Carlo we're leaving early this weekend. Maybe tomorrow morning. I have to go visit some relatives." I said nothing. "Tell him we might even leave tonight."

"OK, I'll tell him." I stood up. "I think I'll go help my aunts in the kitchen."

. . . .

I don't know what would have happened if Zio Anto hadn't called Carlo and Luca into the house to help fix the sink in the bathroom upstairs. I imagine Luca would have gone home, pushed off with his motorino without eating dinner and maybe he wouldn't have ever returned.

I went upstairs to my room to change for dinner. I didn't know the men were working there until I passed the bathroom. They were just finishing. As Zio Anto started down the steps, he asked, "Giulia, please, a few bottles of water for the dinner table? I forgot to get them."

"OK, Zio."

And then Luca and I were in the kitchen again, like the week before. All the voices coming from downstairs guaranteed we were alone behind the kitchen door. It was more frightening this time because now we both knew what was going to happen. I had promised the saints, but I forgot about that and concentrated on getting back at Luca. My hands tracked straight down his back, scratching lightly. I forced my leg between his and pushed hard, made him jump. Luca kept trying to look at me, but I was moving too much in his hands. I was like a fish. I sucked in his tongue, his upper lip, his chin. I bit his neck. "Giulia," he said sadly, "you're hurting me."

I had his bottom in my hands, but it felt lifeless, like two rocks I'd picked up on the beach and that meant nothing to me. I was aware of smiling a vindictive smile, but after a few seconds, it felt stupid on my face. Luca's hands were soft on my shoulders. I realized I was the only one playing this game.

"What's wrong, Giulia, what's wrong?"

I started in Italian to say "You did it to me. Last week . . ." but then in English I told him, "You were a real asshole, you know that?"

"Shush," he said, because my voice was rising, then he started to whisper urgently. "Giulia, I'm sorry about last

123

week. I didn't know what to do. All I knew was that I wanted to kiss you."

One of the kids was upstairs, in the bathroom. Luca came closer to me, whispering, pulling us together.

"Luca, you were so . . ." I had no more Italian words. And his hands started to knead my shoulders, and his lips at my ear stopped talking and he kissed me, murmured my name and then whispering again, said, "Do you know how much I think about you?"

"Oh, Luca."

"But you, who knows what you're thinking here all week long? You say nothing. Giulia, last week, I didn't know what else to do, I had to let you know how I feel. Did Carlo tell you? I tried to come back last weekend, but my brother . . . I just wanted to talk with you."

We looked at each other. Eyes again. Finally, like the first days. "So, tell me, what do you think? Do you ever think about me?"

"Yes, Luca." Waves of relief. "I think about you all the time." More relief.

He took my face, rubbed gently under my eyes. "You're so angry," he said.

"I know," I said. "So are you, angry."

"I know."

But now, at least, we were on the same side of anger, and in that moment we moved into some new orbit, a wider orbit, farther from the hot center. Up against the refrigerator door again, we were kissing, but this time it was all slow and soft, and the kissing melted us to the floor, where Luca's shirt fell aside and mine fell open, and when they called us down to dinner, Luca held my head safely against his chest, kissed my hair and yelled down to them, "OK, OK, we'll be right there."

EIGHT

The Happy Days

FROM THAT AFTERNOON when Luca and I arrived at the dinner table together, our relationship was sanctioned by my family. Luca took his place next to the men, and I saw Zia Berta tell Carlino with her eyes to move down a place so I could sit next to Luca.

Luca and Carlo took their exams, did well and came straight to the beach. I saw Luca every day, sometimes all day long. He rarely ate with his family. He was always with us. Usually when I went downstairs for coffee in the morning he was already sitting there, at the big table in the courtyard, tossing a tiny espresso spoon in the air.

I was so happy waking up to those Italian mornings. My first words of the day were Italian. I woke up from Italian dreams. Italian was beginning to taste so good in my mouth. My lazy American tongue was getting crisper, sharper, giving shape to *ti, to, do, ta. Sono innamorata,* I'd tell Luca. I'm in love. We'd begun to say it to each other. *Sono innamoratissima.*

This happiness every day was as predictable as the sun and the heat. I hurried to the beach in the morning, ran into the water and dove and dove, swam out and floated back, and every morning the sea was green and clear and as warm as hugging arms. It was as good as being a child again and waking up every morning and finding my mother.

Now that the waiting for Luca was over I started taking pictures, lots of pictures. The world looked so good. Afternoons, Luca, Carlo and I left the courtyard and let the camera lead us. White sunlight was a constant, so we looked for shade. We wandered far down the beach, much farther than I'd ever gone by myself, to a place where there was a cluster of palms, another place where the wrought-iron balconies of an old hotel spread shadows across the sand. The hotel was abandoned, an old heap, a decomposing skeleton full of the ghosts of other people's long-ago vacations. Once in a while Loredana let us persuade her to come out into the afternoon heat, and the four of us sat on the cracked terrace of the hotel and smoked cigarettes and told stories. For Carlo, I took lots of pictures of Loredana.

They were impressed that my camera had a self-timer and that I knew how to use it. Every time I set up the camera and dashed into a picture myself, Luca pinched me or kissed me or gave me horns over my head. Many of those pictures turned out with a blurred corner of action around Luca. The hardest thing in the world for him was simply to stay still.

One morning a friend of Luca's and Carlo's, Tonio, came by on a motorino. Luca had his motorino. Zia Assunta was at Mass. She was the only one who would try to stop us. We could take off. The boys wanted to show me a beach where there were rocks for diving.

"Like this you never saw in your life," Luca yelled to me in English as I held on to his waist and we took off down the dirt road. My camera hung around my neck. When we reached the highway and were waiting for a break in the traffic, I photographed the billboards, just because they were covered with Italian words—anything to help me grasp that place and that time and the days I was spending with those boys.

We rode on the congested main roads for a while, then turned off onto a stony path that got so small we had to leave the bikes leaning against a sandy slope. We walked along a cliff, sliding on the rocks, down to the beach, a horseshoe of sand wrapped around a green pool. Brown rocks jutted up, broke the surface of the water, which was so calm you could see the base of the rocks below. Yes, perfect for diving. There were only about ten other people on the beach; most of the women were topless.

"Lu-ca, now I know why you brought me here. Diving! I'm sure we came here for the diving."

"Really, really, we did. It was never topless before. Last summer we came, the women were dressed. Tell her, Carlo."

He was staring around him, his towel slipping sadly out of his hand. *"Merda.* We should have brought Loredana."

Tonio was bent over, untying his tennis shoes. He looked up at me and smiled. "What about you, Giulia? Aren't you hot in that bathing suit top?"

"You pig," Luca said and pushed Tonio over into the sand. "Don't talk to her like that. Giulia, he's a pig. Ignore him."

"Don't worry about me. I'm keeping my top on. I don't want to catch a draft."

Tonio kicked Luca back. They wrestled and laughed

halfway to the water's edge. "Giulia," Luca called back, "come on, come dive with us."

I waved. "Go ahead. I'm going to lie up here awhile."

Luca's almost constant presence next to me was like a new layer of skin. Sometimes it was a thrill to move away from him, to watch him from a distance. I stretched out, and the sand was soft and fine as cotton sheets under my stomach, my arms and thighs. The night before, lying on a secluded promontory behind the bait house at the harbor of Montemaggiore al Mare, Luca and I had promised each other that by the full moon of August we would spend a night together, sleeping, somewhere, somehow, one entire night. We didn't talk about making love, just the wonder of waking up together in the morning. As he dove with his friends, I lay there and watched them, watched how Luca reached his arms high when he dove, his curly black head bent down, all his bulk pulled up into his shoulders, his middle scooped out, and there were those hollows in his buttocks where I loved to rest my hands while we kissed.

My thighs pressed into the hot sand, waiting for Luca to come out of the water. When he rose up, Carlo splashed him, then they both dunked Tonio. These Italian boys didn't seem so wicked to me anymore. They really had come here to dive and swim. Luca climbed up the rocks. The sun was full on my back. I spread my arms and felt a line of sweat slip down under my arm and along the side of my breast, like a finger tracing me. My eyes were closed, my head buried in the crook of my arm when Luca came up onto the beach and stood there above me. His feet were white and wrinkled from the water. *"Ciao, Luca."* I reached for the arch of his foot. He lowered himself down in front of me, balanced, his knees spread open. When I looked up he was scratching a mosquito bite high up inside his thigh.

"Luca, really, you shouldn't play with yourself in public." By now we could say anything to each other, really almost anything.

He smiled. His weight shifted, and the muscles glided across his shoulders, like sand shifting in an hourglass. "I'd rather play with you," he said.

We grinned at each other for a long, long minute. I whispered to him, "I like you, Luca. I really like you."

He whispered back to me, "Giulia."

"Oh, Luca, I'm so happy."

Luca, Luca. I loved to say his name, loved the way it brought my voice down low, deep, all the way to the rockiness of the hard *k* sound in the middle, the rise of breath at the end; it felt as if I was calling out for something I'd never known I wanted.

Whenever he said my name, he made it into slow music. At home in Ohio, my family always dug into the *Giu,* made it hard, a call demanding me to come immediately to them, or that growl of frustration, knowing that even when I got to them I couldn't give them everything they missed. With my Italian family, though, my name was interspersed with *Nonna Giulia, Giuliana, Marigiulia, Giulietta* all day long, and what it sounded like to me was *joy, joy, joy.*

"That Luca, I'm going to kill him," Zia Assunta said when she found out we'd ridden the motorinos to the beach. "Giulia, what if something happened? How stubborn you are. But tell me . . ." We were shelling peas for dinner, and she pulled her chair up close next to mine. "Tell me, *bella,* did you have a good time?"

The more I loved Luca, the more I loved my family. It was all one, and I was rid of the need to confess. When I went to church on Sundays with my aunt, I saw weddings everywhere. Nonna Giulia had started crocheting a bedspread, the kind that is given to a girl to keep in her hope chest, in preparation for her marriage. "You see what I'm doing here for you, Americana? You see?"

"Nonna, I won't need that for a while, you know."

"Well, I won't be finished for a while."

But there was every indication that my life was on course, that everything was working out fine. I was living in a happy house.

It wasn't always perfect. One hot afternoon Francesca and Giulietta took all the sheets off the beds and made tents on the balconies while their father snored on a lounge chair just a few feet away. When Zia Claudia found the torn and dirty sheets, she accused Rocco: *"Irresponsabile! Egoista!"*

"Then divorce me," he yelled back at her. "Go ahead."

This seemed to me the cruelest thing he could throw at her, but she came right back, "Don't think I don't think about it. At least once a day."

"Stupidi," Francesca yelled at her parents, "you can't get divorced. You're not married." Oddly, the way she said it, there was some perverse reassurance in this; they *couldn't* get divorced.

"You be quiet! What got into you to take those sheets off the bed?"

Francesca yelled back, "We have to enjoy ourselves, don't we?"

"Rocco, don't you dare blame that little one," Berta joined in. "We can't turn our backs for one minute, can we?"

"I asked you, specifically, to watch them. I asked you."

"She asked you!"

"You're right about that, you're all right. Give me the sheets, I'll bring them to the laundry tomorrow."

"And what do we do tonight? What?"

"All right, then I'll kill myself. That's all that's left."

"Call me when you're ready," Claudia said. "I'll help you," and she walked away.

Fights like this broke through the house at least once a day, cloudbursts out of nowhere. Everyone got involved. Loud voices, red faces. Sometimes doors slammed. But these episodes never seemed to take us to the precipice the way arguments in Homefield did. Cetta and Ben, Sofia and Mike could never have said the words "divorce," "leave"; there was already too much angry separation between them. And also the knowledge of departure was too much with them.

The adults in Homefield were never affectionate with each other, I rarely saw them touch. Leaving for work, they'd give each other cursory kisses in the air, a gesture that seemed more superstitious habit than anything else.

In Italy, though, even stern Zio Vito would kiss his wife's hand and say "One thousand thanks" when she brought him his *caffè*. If Claudia started singing a song, Rocco picked up two lines behind her. Maybe it was their language that helped them. It wasn't the frustrated idiom of immigrants, who know, no matter how much they are loved at home, there is a world beyond that they are not able to latch on to completely. The Italians sounded so graceful with each other, and their language connected them to the world outside.

The morning after the fight about the sheets, I happened to get up early and went out onto the balcony. Below me, in front of the gate, Zia Claudia stood in her robe talking to Rocco, who was sitting in his car. The motor was running, he was leaving for a meeting in the city. She was holding the baby. They were talking about groceries, Claudia was asking Rocco to pick up this and that. He shifted gears, ready to go; then I saw my uncle kiss his fingers and touch them to my aunt's thigh.

· · · ·

131

Luca showed up pouting one night toward the end of July. The moon was nearly full, and Carlo, Luca, Loredana, Marigiulia, Giuliana, Carlino and I were going to go to the cafe in the orange and lemon groves. I remember I was all dressed up, just like an Italian girl. I dressed in the evening now, even to take a walk down our dirt road. Makeup. Jewelry. I was wearing a pair of sandals with three-inch cork platforms. They were new, and I felt very classy in them.

"You never wore those shoes before," Luca said accusingly. "You are too tall with those shoes," which meant that I stood an inch taller than him.

We never argued, things were hardly ever dark between us anymore, but the few times they were, I felt oddly excited: Luca and I were so complete together, there was room for all our moods, for his poutiness or mine; together, we always found our way back home. We were sitting on the Sanmicaelis' stone wall, waiting for the others. I put my hand on his arm. "Don't you like my new sandals?"

He clicked his tongue no at me and ran his fingers up the branches of a fern, pulling off all the leaves.

"What happened, Luca? Did you see Mauro today?"

"Don't say that name to me."

"What did he do?"

"You will only get upset." He stripped another branch and avoided my eyes. "But you should know this."

"What?"

"Mauro is telling my parents it is wrong for you and me to see each other so much. He says it's an impossible relationship, that when the summer is over you'll suffer and I'll never study." I shifted, to look at him better. His anger at Mauro was powerful enough to turn him into a boy, almost ready to cry.

"Ignore him," I whispered. I brought his hand to my

face and smelled the scent of green leaves on his fingers. My father was far away by then, a vague voice in occasional letters. "Can't you just ignore your brother?"

"That's what Renata told me."

"She's much smarter than Mauro."

The others joined us. We took the road along the beach, and ahead of us the matte-white moonlight lay across the water, and behind us, working its way down, there was the apricot-, peach-colored sky of the sunset. We could hear the Italian voices of my cousins just up ahead, and coming through the lemon trees, American rock 'n' roll from the jukebox at the cafe. Everything was there, the sun and the moon, Italy and America.

A path off the dirt road led into the trees. For a long stretch the groves were thick, the passage narrow. We had to walk single file, the long line of us. I was right behind Luca, my hand on the back of his neck so he'd know I was still there. We were all laughing. Luca was happy now, whistling "Sergeant Pepper." We walked toward the lights set in the heart of the groves.

The cafe there was so small and inconsequential it offered only two flavors of ice cream—chocolate and pistachio. But there was a loaded jukebox, and we danced out on the terrace. I kicked off my shoes, and Luca and I, our bodies, melted into each other perfectly, hip to hip, chest to chest, mouth to mouth. I loved the way our hair stayed connected even when we pulled apart. I felt his eyelashes on the side of my face, the scratch of his beard near my neck. Over his shoulder I saw a lizard skitter catty-corner across the white wall of the bar, and I laughed out loud. Crickets trilling like a tambourine jingling slightly. I threw back my head. There were stars, leaves turning over in a languorous breeze, the smell of lemons and the sea. I had a momentary premonition of how utterly unbearable the beauty of the world can be if you are alone. But that night my arms were full. Remember this, I told myself, This is Luca, you're holding Luca. And tomorrow you'll see him again.

"Don't leave me, Luca."

"But you're leaving *me*."

It was a week later. We were on the road around the bend from the house. Luca was sitting on his motorino. I was standing, rubbing my knees against his. It was just past midnight, and we'd been saying good night for an hour and a half. The next morning I was taking the train with my uncles and two of my aunts and Carlo to go to Rome to meet my father. We'd only be gone four or five days, but I didn't want to say goodbye to Luca.

"I'm not leaving you," I said.

"Will I see you when you come back?"

"Luca!" By that time I couldn't imagine life being any different from the way it had been during the past weeks.

"But what about your father?"

"Don't worry. He's going to like you." (What's not to like? Zia Berta had said.) Just like my father, I had that streak of fascism in me. I could make the world be the way I wanted it to be. I was a young photographer, learning how to frame scenes so that I got just what I wanted, nothing more. Leave things out, frame the shot. Make the picture exactly what you want it to be. "My father will be fine about us."

I had my camera with me. I was experimenting with superfast film in the moonlight. I held the camera to my face, framed Luca, the bike. "I'm not leaving you, Luca." I snapped the picture. "I'm taking you with me."

NINE

Like a Dream Came True

THERE IS ONE PHOTOGRAPH from my summer in Italy that was enlarged and developed again and again, until everyone in the family had a copy. Aunt Sofia framed hers and put it in the living room on top of the TV. Cetta's went on the mantel above her fake fireplace. Zia Assunta, Zia Berta and Zia Claudia each gave the photo to the uncles one Christmas. Nonna Giulia hung it on the wall in her kitchen in Cimalta.

Aunt Sofia always referred to my summer in Italy as *"la fine del mondo,"* the end of the world.

"Then why do you have that picture sitting out reminding you? Why did you get copies to send to everyone in Italy?"

"Be-*cause*," she said, shocked I didn't understand. "Because can't you see how happy everyone was that day? After so many years, it was like a dream came true. Look!" She picked it up, dusted off the frame with the hem of her housedress and held the picture up in front of me. "Can't you see what a happy, happy moment it was?"

It was noon and hot in front of the hotel in Rome. My aunts, uncles, Carlo and I had been waiting almost three hours. Anxious, we'd moved from the lobby sofas to the benches outside the hotel. My father's plane had landed at Da Vinci airport on time, 8:00 A.M. We had called the airport and we knew that for sure. Thirty minutes it took in a cab from Fiumicino, forty-five at most. Unless there was trouble getting the suitcases, or getting a cab, or maybe traffic. Some problem.

In his letters, my father had insisted that no one go to the airport to meet him, so now my uncles stood at the curb, vigilant, their hands clasped behind their backs. Zio Anto and Zio Vito in their gray suits. Zio Rocco in shirt-sleeves, his tie stuffed into his shirt pocket. All of them frowning as they searched the traffic racing by. Zio Vito, stiff with his neck brace, turned toward Zio Anto holding out a hand with fingers pinched together, asking, So where is he? Anto answering silently with a shrug of shoulders and dark eyebrows. Rocco pointing his chin toward the traffic. None of them noticing they are being photographed. To keep busy, I was pointing my camera at everything.

It was hot. In the shade of the hotel's awning Zia Assunta and Zia Berta sat on the marble bench, Berta's legs crossed at the ankles, her toeless high heels missing the pavement by an inch or more. Wide leather handbags hung in the crook of my aunts' elbows. When I turned the camera on them, Zia Assunta smiled wide with eyes lost behind dark-tinted glasses. Zia Berta waved a lipstick-tipped cigarette.

A helicopter passed above, its noise louder than the traffic. "Giulia," Carlo called and pointed up. *"Ecco,"* he laughed, meaning There he is. Instead of looking, I took a shot of Carlo, caught the sweat mark under his arm. Then, seeing nothing more to photograph, I glanced into the traffic, looked straight at the window of a speeding taxi and recognized the dark thick eyebrows. No one else had seen him yet and he hadn't seen me. His arm was out the window, gesturing to hold back the passing cars as his taxi lurched across three lanes of traffic. And finally the cab braked at the curb. And finally, after two months, there he was in front of me. "Dad!"

But the others hadn't seen him in twenty years and already they had reached him, grabbed him, were hugging him, kissing him. "Nicola!" they cried. "Nicola!"

Not one free spot on his arm for me to reach out for, so I stood waiting until, finally, my father turned and looked at no one but me. I asked if he'd had a good trip. *"Hai fatto buon viaggio?"* This was my biggest surprise. I was going to speak to him in Italian. Silently, he looked at me for a very long time. My tan was dark and everywhere, no strap marks on my shoulders. My Indian-print halter dress could not have been shorter. Raised sunglasses held back the sun-bleached streaks snaking down the front sides of my hair. Gold loops tugged my earlobes and swayed around my jaw.

I took his hand. *"Benvenuto, Papà."*

"Giulia," he said at last, "your accent is really terrible."

A second later someone shouted, *"Foto, foto,"* and I set up the bellboy with the camera. It always spooked me to think some stranger caught that moment. We are all lined up, arms linked, thrilled at the reunion, smiling. Everyone but Nicola, who doesn't face the camera. He is turned to watch me, and on his face is a look as if something has soured in his mouth. I remember how happy I felt standing there next to Carlo, how proud to show my father that this smart boy and I had become friends. Maybe it was

137

just that buoyant look that stung Nicola, that and the way I had learned to hold on casually to the arm of a boy. But that boy was no one but my cousin.

I don't know why my father ever sent me to Italy if he was so afraid something would happen.

After he arrived in Rome my father said very little to me, but all day he watched. All evening, I felt his eyes. We took a long walk, the family all together. Stepping over litter and fruit peels in the street, my father grimaced. It seemed that, so far, he was as displeased with Italy as he was with me.

I stopped at a newspaper stand. "Wait for me a second," I told the others. "I want to buy postcards." I had promised Luca.

"*I* will get them," my father said, reaching for his wallet. "If they hear you speaking Italian the way you do they will know you are a tourist and charge you double."

I stared at him, forced myself to keep my voice low. "Dad, don't you think it's obvious to them that anyone buying postcards is a tourist, even you?"

He sighed. "They will make a fool of you." He spoke in English, so that the others had no idea what we were saying; all they saw was that I was giving my father a hard time. "But if you insist, go ahead."

It was getting dark, and yellow light from the shops and cafes washed over the black, worn-smooth cobbled streets of Rome. My father held his hand on my neck, a gesture meant to be protective, but I stiffened. As we rounded every corner, I touched the walls to feel the day's heat still caught inside the stones. This place was alive. The hand on my neck was tight, but I stared down at my red-polished toes, my sandals stepping over the cobblestones— ancient, overlapping, half-circle stones that looked like thousands of new moons rising up under my feet.

. . . .

It wasn't until we were on the train leaving Rome two days later that my father began to enjoy Italy. We'd been traveling south a few hours, our train had just met up with the coast, and the sea was almost close enough to touch. I left the compartment where our family was sitting. Carlo got up too. We stood in the aisles with our elbows resting on the ledge of the open window. Sand beaches, rock beaches, turquoise water sped by. Swimmers stood in the shallow water and waved their arms at us, gloating that they were already where they wanted to be.

After a while, my father came and stood behind me. My back tensed. I thought, Oh no. But this time he put a gentle hand on my shoulder, his other hand on Carlo's shoulder. "Now," he said, "I feel I am in Italy." I looked up; he was smiling at me. "It is beautiful here, no? Twenty years since I saw this sea."

For the rest of the ride he stood with us, asking Carlo questions about his plans for medical school, pointing to things out the window to show me. I loved my father when he was like this. This was the father I'd told Luca about that first day. Standing, he was a bit taller than the window and had to bend down to take it all in. He had one arm above his head, his fingers gripping the luggage rack for balance. A big block of sunlight stretched across him, made his watch and belt buckle glint. He was squinting into the sun and looked exhilarated by the speed of the train that was taking him deeper and deeper into the South. All the danger points on my father's face—the eyebrows, his forehead, the dark corners of his mouth—were at ease, not tensed for a fight.

Now's the time to take a picture, I thought. Catch this, catch this. But unfortunately, right then, I was out of film.

. . . .

When we pulled into the station at Pizzo, the sun was setting. We climbed down from the train into the hot orange evening and waiting there to see my father was Nonna Giulia. During the two months I'd known her, she had never once left the house to go to a public place. Not for a walk or to the market or even to church ("God knows where He can find me," she said). Standing on the train platform dressed up in her nicest black, she looked much frailer than she did at home. She was wearing a black pillbox hat with a feather. A stiff leather pocketbook hung from one arm, and Carlino held her by the other.

I'd been a little afraid of the moment when my father would see his mother for the first time in twenty years. But when he saw her, he shouted, "Mamma!" and threw up his arms, cheerful as when he used to see me walking up the hill on my way home from school. She held up her short arms and he bent down low so she could take his face in her hands. They were both laughing. I felt foolish for having to put on sunglasses to hide my wet eyes.

Driving from the train station toward Montemaggiore al Mare, Zio Rocco pointed up to the new highway that cut through the hills. "Nicola, remember how long it used to take to drive over those mountains? Now, it is nothing. Easy." We passed a new circular restaurant built on a cliff, and Rocco said, "Nicola, do you believe it? Last time you were here only goats could eat on these hills."

My father was excited about everything, what he remembered and what was new. "Who would have imagined all this twenty years ago? Look at those olive trees! Look!" He turned to the back seat and cupped Nonna Giulia's hands with his own. "Mamma, those olive trees on the farm. Those olives, those olives, what an aroma they had."

140

"Those olives!" Rocco lifted his hands off the wheel. "She made us crazy with those olives, saving the best for you."

"They're still there, Nicola. The trees are still there," Nonna said. "You can eat your fill of olives while you're here. No matter what your brothers say."

It wasn't until we were home, sitting at the long table in the courtyard (Zia Claudia and the nonnas had prepared "just a little something, because Nicola must be tired"), and the bowls from the spaghettini with calamari sauce had been cleared away and the platters of cold roasted veal with rosemary were being brought out, when Giuliana came out of the kitchen with a small bowl and brought it to my father. That's when it happened. "Zio Nicola, Nonna Giulia fixed these for you. She said they were the best olives. She's been saving them."

It was then that my father looked up, overcome, unable to speak. He stood and went to Nonna, knelt by her chair and really hugged her this time. Nonna's head rested on my father's shoulder.

"You stayed away so long. Why? Why?" Nonna's questions hung unanswered in the silence around table.

Years later when a photography teacher told me, "Passion is specific. The eye is moved by detail, just like the heart is," I remembered that moment when a bowl of olives cracked the hard mask covering my father's twenty-year longing for home and left us all with the question, Why? Why hadn't he come back sooner?

Francesca whispered, "Was it the olives, Mamma? Was it the olives that made Zio Nicola cry?"

"Maybe they don't have olives in America," Daniele whispered to Francesca, and she said yes, probably that was it.

"Well, he traveled far enough this time for his damn olives. This time, Nicola," Zio Rocco said, "you can have my share too. These poor Americans come here starved for good food."

"Rocco's right," Zio Anto said. "The Americans are hungry. Let's eat. Let's eat."

Dinner went on for hours, way past midnight. There were no rules that night. Giulietta, Francesca and Daniele refused to go to bed, wouldn't think of it. Francesca ran through the courtyard in Zia Berta's best high heels. Giulietta was breathlessly telling me what I'd missed while I was in Rome—a fight between Francesca, Daniele and Giulietta and the Signorinelli and Sanmicaeli children. "And then," Giulietta's eyes were big, blinking fast, "then they told us that when we weren't looking they would steal our shoes and give them to the egg-cart lady and she would put the *malocchio* on them, and then they'd bring us back the shoes and when we wore them we'd be cursed. They said that, and then . . ."

And then Luca was standing at the end of the table and Carlo was introducing him to my father. "A friend of mine," I heard Carlo say. ". . . study together in Rome," I heard. My father and Luca were shaking hands. Carlo was offering my father a cigarette. My father pulled out his lighter, but he stopped, looked up, startled. *Oh God, he's figured out already who Luca is.* But he was listening to the sad cawing that had just cut through the laughter. "Giancarlo?" he asked. "Listen, is that the baby?"

"It's the refrigerator, Zio Nicola!" the kids yelled.

"No," he said.

"Yes! Yes! It wants to be fed. It's crying."

We were all laughing when Luca's eyes found me. My father turned to talk to my uncles, and Luca drifted away from him, said hello to my aunts, made his way down to me. He kissed me on both cheeks, a formal gesture: if my father was watching, Luca was still no one but Carlo's friend. Luca was dressed casually, wearing shorts and a loose shirt, but he was clean-shaven and his hair was damp from the shower, and I thought, What if my father notices these small efforts and begins to suspect?

Luca was smiling, but he stepped back from me a bit, waiting for a cue. "How was Rome? Did you enjoy it?" Instinctively, I touched his hand; then, instinctively, I pulled it away, looked around. My father was laughing, still oblivious. I was sitting and Luca was standing in front of me. I wanted to press my face against his belly and cry.

"You're just in time," I said, a bit louder than necessary. I knew I was avoiding Luca's eyes. "I was just going to take some pictures. I've got to go get my camera."

Luca took this as his cue. He said, "Fine," and walked away to find Carlo.

On my way upstairs I passed Zia Berta in the kitchen. She pinched my cheek. Her own cheeks were red from too much champagne. "Where are you going, *bella*?"

"Upstairs. To get my camera."

"Yes, good idea." She winked at me, sure I was going to fix myself up for Luca.

The upstairs rooms were quiet and still. There was enough light from below, I didn't have to switch on a lamp. My hands found my camera by my bed. Then I stepped out on the balcony that hung over the dinner table. I watched. Was this really my family? After a few minutes the scene below seemed to have nothing to do with me. I saw Luca, sitting on a beach chair near Carlo, sulking, wondering where the Giulia was who had left and promised to come back. That Giulia had disappeared and been replaced by some nervous stranger. "Come up here, Luca," I wanted to yell down to him, because the empty rooms were wide open behind me, offering up all their dark cool privacy.

I saw my father at the head of the table. He was asking,

"Where's Giulia?" He said it loudly, full of authority, sure he had the right to demand, to know.

"Getting her camera," Zia Berta told him. "She'll be right down."

"Ah yes, good. We should have some pictures now." Satisfied, he went on talking, sure that his Giulia would materialize soon. I was starting to wish he'd never come to Italy, but seeing the pale bald spot on the top of his head, I almost shouted to him, too, "I'm here."

With my father and Luca both in the courtyard there were so many Giulias, but they negated one another, canceled one another out, until there was no Giulia down there at all. The laughter, the party, the family—none of it was mine. Up on the balcony, though, the darkness was mine, the distance was mine, the camera in my hand was mine. The only Giulia who couldn't vanish was the one who stood back alone and watched.

TEN

Nicola in Italy in August

THE NEXT DAY at the beach, my father ignored Luca and asked me, in English, "That daughter of my friend Rinaldo, she is engaged to that dentist with the beard?"

"Is that what her father told you?"

Loredana and Bernardo were tangled together on a towel.

"Rinaldo is concerned for the girl's studies. He says she is not doing very well. I am surprised Rinaldo let the situation get to this point. He himself was always a very good student."

"She's just not very interested in school, Dad. Not everyone is."

"Having that boyfriend does not help her, I would think. I hope that girl has not become a friend of yours."

For the first time in a month, Luca did not stay with us for dinner that day. But in the late afternoon, when the feast was over, when Zio Vito pushed away from the table and said, "Well, I'm going upstairs to hang myself," and Zio Anto was snoring with his head on the table, and Zio Rocco and my father were asleep on lounge chairs in the shade of the big tree, I went to the beach. I walked into the water to cool off, stood with my back to the house, looked into the blue distance and wondered when and how my father would attack. He had said nothing about Luca yet.

Suddenly there was something dark under the water right in front of me. Luca's head appeared. "Eh," he said, and stepped in close. I turned to look back at the house. "Don't worry," Luca said.

Water covered us up to our necks. His hands looked wavy below the surface of the water, but felt firm and strong when he moved them to my waist. I grabbed his feet with my toes, rubbed my foot up to his knee. I was just learning that summer how bodies greet each other, before words. Carlo and Loredana were kicking sand around and talking at the water's edge. Between us, Luca and I had a little pocket of privacy.

"I missed you," I told him.

"Your father," he said. "He doesn't like me."

"Why do you think he doesn't like you?"

"Either he doesn't like me and he told you to stay away from me, or you're afraid of him. You are strange since you returned from Rome."

"No, I'm not."

"Yes," he said, with his eyes closed. There were moments when Luca seemed older than me. Sometimes it made me feel safe; that moment it did not. "Tell me the truth, are you afraid of your father, Giulia? Is he going to make troubles for us to see each other?"

"I want things to be just like before, Luca." I dipped my

146

finger in the little pool of water caught in his collarbone. "I want to see you all the time." He looked doubtful. "Like before," I added, a little desperate.

Luca said nothing.

"So don't come here if you don't want to see me."

"Giulia, don't do this." Luca's tone warned me, Don't play around here. His grip tightened on my waist. "I was miserable without you these past five days, and even more miserable when I think you're leaving for America in less than a month. And now your father is here. I'm afraid things will have to change."

I looked back at the house. Carlino and Daniele were on a balcony, trying to spit all the way over into the maestro's garden. I circled Luca's thigh with one of my legs. I had to be the leader here. I had to show Luca that in facing my father we were going to be brave and defiant. We were going to be ourselves.

I kissed Luca, but quickly.

"So what should we do?" he asked.

"We should do just what we were doing before. See each other as much as before."

"Yes?" Under the water, his hands slipped down to my hips. He squeezed my bottom.

"Yes," I said. "Only more."

"So, your father doesn't like Luca," Carlo said as soon as Luca and I got to the beach.

"She says he likes me," Luca said flatly.

"It is ridiculous, this thing of the father liking the boyfriend," Loredana announced. "All that pressure, it makes boys so stupid sometimes." She stuck out her lower lip and blew up at her bangs. I could see the tiny heat blisters underneath them. "For dinner today my father brought out a bottle of his homemade wine, which no one will drink. It is terrible. But Bernardo, of course, always trying to please my father, drank and drank and asked for more. And even before the coffee, he fell asleep, right there in his chair. I don't want to be there when he gets sick. Let my mother deal with it. Come on, let's go for a walk. I want to hear everything about your trip to Rome."

We headed down the beach. "So, Giulia, was Carlo a good Cicerone in Rome?" Loredana asked. "All the naked statues, I bet that's what he showed you."

We all laughed. Then Carlo and I laughed harder, since it was true. Walking through Rome, as we'd passed gray stone statues of bearded warriors and white marble heroes and gods, most of them naked and over seven feet tall, Carlo had said to me in a low voice, "Look, there's Luca." As we walked we saw Madonnas painted on walls and frescoed above doors and on murals enshrined with flowers. At every Madonna, I pointed and told Carlo, "Loredana."

"Oh, how I would love to go to Rome." Loredana sighed and took the cigarette from Carlo. "To be anywhere but here."

"In Los Angeles in California," Carlo said decisively. "Everyone says New York, Manhattan, but no. I want Los Angeles."

"Los Angeles? *Stupido!*" Luca told Carlo. "It's the same as Naples—dirty, and everybody's a crook. All of America, really. None of it is any good."

"You told me you love America. You said you were going to visit me." I laced my fingers through his hair. I didn't mean to, but I pulled a little.

"Ow." I let go. "I do not like it anymore. If there was no America you would have no place to go in September. Columbus, that *stronzo*. Leave it to a northern Italian to make all these problems for me."

Loredana shook her hands in front of his face. "What a shame. All that English you studied. For nothing."

148

"No, not for nothing. I will go to Australia. With those long empty roads, no one around but the kangaroos. And a car that will make a hundred eighty kilometers an hour," Luca said. "That's what I want."

"La libertà, come sarebbe bella!" Loredana moaned. Freedom, how beautiful it would be.

After a while, we left the beach, went out to the road and walked, half dazed from the heat, with easy insults bouncing off one another, like bumper cars in slow motion. It was lazy and nice, and we walked close, side by side, our arms brushing, feeling each other's warm breath. In three weeks it would all be over.

Our usual path led us into town, to the cherub-faced water fountain, where we took drinks of overheated water. Slowly, we made our way around the harbor. Loredana picked up two Coca-Colas at a shop where her father had credit. Carlo asked if he could share with her. She said OK, if he promised not to spit into the bottle. I heard her tell Carlo, "Bernardo always does that, spits into the bottle."

"Really? Tell me, what else does Bernardo do?"

Luca and I walked ahead, reached the road lined with weeping willow trees and cypresses that hung low, in a mournful curtsy. As we stepped into the narrow corridor of shade, there was the relief of the cooler air and also that jolt of excitement—a hidden place, an empty room. I reached for Luca, wrapped my fingers around the top of his arm. I squeezed, and he swelled his biceps in response.

I stared at his lowered eyelids, the creases of untanned skin, and there was that light-skinned scar breaking his right eyebrow, and around his mouth, more thin lines. I touched his face. "Your skin," I said, "it's like all that marble I saw in Rome." During the two months I'd known him, Luca had turned beautiful; it was impossible to believe I'd once thought he wasn't attractive. He hadn't shaved that day, but around his mouth was a halo of smooth skin where his beard didn't grow. I stopped walking and looked over his shoulder for Carlo and Loredana. They were gone. Luca and I were face to face. No one was around. I ran my tongue above his upper lip, down below his lower lip. His skin tasted so good I opened my mouth wider, tried to breathe him into me. No matter what my father said or did, there would have to be a few minutes every day when I was alone with this boy. "We saw you all over Rome, Luca," I said, low. "All the statues, they looked like you."

"Is that right?" He laughed.

"Oh, you two," Loredana called from somewhere down the road. "Here they are," as if we were the ones who had ducked behind the trees.

"Someday, maybe in a couple years I'm coming back," I whispered to Luca. "I've decided." I kissed his neck. "Maybe I'll study art in Rome." I licked his shoulder. "I love Rome."

"Ah, so then it is the city." He was talking to me with his lips up against my ear. "It is Rome you are coming back for, not for me."

I opened my mouth and let him feel my teeth against his throat.

When we got back onto the sand, colors were seeping into the air just in front of us. Families were starting to come out of their houses.

We had reached the big rocks that bordered our beach. Bare feet on warm rock, we climbed. Luca and I sang "Yesterday" as loud as we could, and Loredana, who had a nice voice, hummed. Then Carlo said, "Giulia, look, your father."

He was walking toward us, swinging his arms fast, back and forth. I jumped down from a high rock and walked toward him, explaining before he could ask any questions, "We went for a walk. I took pictures."

When I was close enough to him so the others wouldn't hear, he asked me, in English, "Do you know how long you have been gone?"

"You were sleeping, Dad. Back at the house, they knew where I was. We always walk in the afternoon."

"Four hours almost," he said and held four angry fingers in my face.

"Buona sera, professore," Luca said politely.

"Ciao, Zio Nicola. Is everything all right?" Carlo asked.

My father held up a friendly hand. "I would just like to speak with my daughter for a minute."

Luca called out, "Giulia, wait!" And I thought, He's going to save me. But then he just said, "Your camera. You forgot your camera."

"Go get it," my father commanded. When I came back with the camera, he told me, "Now, walk." His footsteps were fast and close behind mine. That angry wrinkle was shivering across his forehead. "I told you this morning not to go with that Loredana. What if someone saw you? What would they think? Two young girls with two boys walking all over?"

"Dad, many people saw us. I'm sure all they thought, if they thought anything, was that we were taking a walk. There's nothing wrong with that."

People under umbrellas nearby were silent, listening. "I believe that I know Italy a little bit better than you do, Giulia, and your behavior today—in fact, since I arrived in Italy—has been unacceptable. Young women do not act this way here. You know very little about this place. I

151

should have known that you would come here and take advan—"

"Ni-cooo-la," Rinaldo was walking down the beach, calling through cupped hands.

My father waved and called back, *"Caro Rinaldo, buona sera."*

"Dad, what you're doing isn't fair—this harassing me in English, then smiling at everybody else in Italian."

Rinaldo was close. My father told me, *"Stupida,* I'm trying to save you embarrassment. Stop making a show out here."

"Me? Listen, you and I have to have a talk," I said, but Rinaldo was there with us now, and my father smiled and held out his hands.

Rinaldo took my father's hands. "Nicola, will you join us for a game of cards on my *terrazza?* Come."

"Of course. Excellent."

Rinaldo pointed with his chin toward the rocks and asked me, "Giulia, why aren't you with the other young people?"

"She's going back to the house," my father said, smiling. "Her aunts need her help in the kitchen. Go now, Giulia. We will talk later."

I smiled back at him the same way he was smiling at me and said, in English, "You're damn right we will."

We didn't talk that day or the next. My father lost himself in the family and avoided me for two days. It was easy among all those people in the house, on the beach. The third morning we crossed paths on the stairwell. I grabbed his arm. "Dad, I want to talk."

"I am very upset with you, Giulia."

"You're upset with *me?*"

"From now on, I want you where I can see you at all times. Is that clear?"

"You said we were going to have a talk. I want to talk."

"I have said what I have to say. No more going off with that Luca, do you hear me?"

But it was completely unnecessary for my father to tell me that. Luca had stopped coming around.

ELEVEN

Nonno Carlo

WHEN MY FATHER CAME to Italy that summer our relatives found he was more wonderful than any of them had imagined. During his twenty-year absence, the reality of him had faded for them. They'd had only the legend, which, like yeast, had become a thing bigger than itself: Nicola, who was so brilliant at school; Nicola, who was the best, the most responsible, who worked so hard, who was the tallest . . .

And then he was finally there with them and they saw what they'd forgotten—how, when he laughed, the sheer joy ate up all the tired wrinkles around his eyes; they forgot the gentle way he leaned his too-tall body forward when he was listening to your stories and, if you made him laugh too hard, the way he'd lift his eyeglasses and wipe away happy tears.

"Zio Ni-co-la, ciao!" the kids yelled, because even after the other adults got tired, Nicola was still willing to lift them and spin them around, get down in the sand and dig

deep moats with them, go into the water, onto the raft, out in the boat. When we took drives at night, the kids all wanted to ride in whichever car Nicola was in.

"*Mannaggia,*" Zio Rocco yelled at his children in mock anger, "did you forget who your father is? Did you forget who bought you those shoes, that bicycle? Was it Zio Nicola or me?"

"What do we do with these kids after you leave, Nicola?" the aunts asked him. "You can't go back now."

With Nicola in the courtyard, everyone felt they'd been glanced at by a god. I remembered from when I was a little girl, that feeling when Nicola noticed you. His name for Giulietta was Giulietta del Mare, Giulietta of the Sea, and she turned pink every time she heard it. She'd been as afraid of the water as she was of everything else. Until Nicola got there she'd refused to swim without inflatable arm bands and a rubber life saver. But Nicola insisted— "In the water, with no paraphernalia!" The ocean looked huge to Giulietta, but Nicola was more powerful. She had no choice, she went in. He made her float on her stomach and kick while he held her. One day he slowly let go and walked beside her as she made her way to shore.

It was only when Daniele hollered, "Giulietta, you're swimming!" that she looked up and saw Nicola's hands on his own waist, not holding hers. She screamed, swallowed water, cried.

"But you were swimming alone! You did it," everyone cheered. "*Brava!*"

"Let's try again," Nicola said. "Come. Right away. I'll be right here next to you." She was still crying, but she ballooned her cheeks and held her breath as he had taught her. She started kicking, then she was moving forward. Every day she swam farther. "*Bravissima!*" Nicola cheered loud, clapping his hands over his head, way above her, somewhere up in the middle of the sky.

155

I had gone to Italy and immediately surrendered. But my father, Nicola, the Italian, arrived and insisted on maintaining his American ways. He always cleared his own dishes from the table, even though the aunts yelled at him to stop. And he introduced a purely American idea: "Everything that is good can be made better, perfect." Within a week he had silenced our nights, got the irritating bell off the end of the toilet chain—everyone else had tried and given up. He didn't find a cure for Giancarlo's colic, but he did guarantee that in a month it would be gone.

Nicola figured out a way for him and his brothers to haul the larger refrigerator downstairs to the kitchen where all the cooking was done. The women were thrilled, but Nicola wasn't content yet. The smaller refrigerator, relieved of its burden, didn't cry as much as before, but it still hummed during the night. "This must be fixed! Let's call the owner to replace it. Let's call today."

My uncles started laughing. My aunts even started laughing. They laughed so hard they couldn't speak, and Marigiulia had to explain. "Zio Nicola, it's August. Don Marco, the owner, he's on vacation. He can't be reached."

"And even if he could be reached," Giuliana added, "a new refrigerator in August is impossible. Who would deliver it?"

Anto clamped his hands on Nicola's shoulders and shook him. "You're in Calabria, Nicola. Remember? This isn't Milano. This isn't America." Sometimes Nicola was too much, but that only made them laugh and love him more.

"You see, your brother isn't like you," Zia Assunta told Zio Anto. "He can't ignore what a mess this house is."

Anto told her, "Nicola just proves my point. All this house needs is a little work—very little—and it would be in perfect shape. I say we rent it again for next year."

"Well, then you'd better learn to cook this winter, because next summer I won't be with you."

The arguments about the house ran in circles until Nicola suggested that all four brothers go in together to buy a beach house.

"Does this mean you'll come back every summer, Nicola?"

"Well, not every summer, but I'll come by for a swim now and then. Sure."

The next day Zio Anto called a friend of his in town who knew about beach property. He set up an appointment for all the brothers to go look at houses the following week.

"Next week?" Zio Vito complained. "Not sooner?"

I think for all of them, there was a feeling of having waited and waited for someone, and now Nicola was there and he was it. For the four brothers, it was almost like having their father among them again.

My grandfather, Carlo, had gone to America when he was a young man, worked in the steel mills, made some money, and after a few years he'd gone back home to Cimalta with a great plan: even though he was a peasant with nothing but a small plot of land and a few olive trees, he was going to make all his sons doctors.

His friends told him, "Carlo, you're crazy to make your sons better than yourself." His enemies said, "He'll never do it."

But Carlo was a determined man, and when his first son, Nicola, was ten years old, he told him, "Because you are smart, because you are my first son, because I love you, you are going away to Montemaggiore to study. This is an honor. You will be the best in your class. Someday you will be a doctor."

The pronouncement was dizzying, almost too much

sweet wine for a boy, especially one so skinny, so scrawny and so often sick with colds that his mother made him wear a small pouch of salt around his neck. This had been advised by the old women of Cimalta, for protection against the *malocchio,* that potent green glance of envy that could leave an unprotected person headachy, queasy, unwell or just plain unlucky. It was most often jealous or malicious people who passed on the *malocchio,* but it was possible, though not common, that a look of excessive love could have the same effect. Nicola, the women believed, was *addocchiato*—or cursed—by his own father, who loved him too much.

It was an early morning in October when his father and his uncle Torquato packed the donkey with cheese and salami and olives, enough food for a few months, then lifted Nicola up onto the *ciucciu*'s back. The boy was so small he could sit huddled between the bundles. His mother reached up and kissed him many times goodbye.

In Montemaggiore, Nicola was brought to the home of a widow and her three children. He saw the little attic room he would share with the woman's sons. His father helped him make his bed with the blankets from home— they had the color and feel of hay. Then, a few hours later, Nicola's father and uncle left to go back to Cimalta.

By the time Carlo and Torquato reached home that first night, Nicola was lost in the dark of his new room, strange bed, faraway city. There were no telephones. And the mail was so slow that by the time a reassuring letter arrived, the sharpest stab of homesickness had numbed. That first night, all Nicola had for comfort was the promise his father had given him—that he would have a fine future as a doctor one day, if he studied hard.

Nicola got the highest grades. *Scuola media. Liceo classico.* He completed two years' exams in one year. His father was proud but not surprised. Everything was going according to plan.

Until Nicola went to Naples for medical school and was drafted into Mussolini's army. Carlo told Nicola to forget medical school and come home. Mussolini had already ruined his farm and his village, and Mussolini wasn't going to get his son. But there was no choice. As the oldest in the family, Nicola had to serve. "The only way for me to finish medical school, Papà, is to be in the army."

But then Carlo got a letter saying that Nicola had orders to go to the port of Brindisi to board a ship headed for Africa. As soon as he read this news, Carlo took off, traveled by donkey, by train and by foot, and was already in Brindisi when Nicola got there. Carlo knew someone who could speak to someone who could speak to someone who could keep Nicola off that boat. Nicola was on the boat, ready to sail when he was told he'd been reassigned, to a medical unit in Rome. The next day, while Nicola was on his way to Rome and Carlo was making his way back to Cimalta, the ship sank.

"Dad," I said, my child voice hushed, incredulous when he first told me this story at the dinner table, "your father saved your life."

"More than once," he told me. "More than once."

The father Nicola worshiped was a man who had been to America and back. Nicola, his brothers and Sofia had grown up hearing Carlo's stories of all the exotic places he'd seen: *Clevalanda, Pittsaburgho, San Diego.* Many men of Cimalta had gone to America, but Carlo was one of the few who had seen the Pacific Ocean, had actually walked into it. The other side of the world.

"Papà," his children asked, mesmerized, "tell us, the Pacific, how is it?"

"Wet," he told them solemnly, "it is wet."

Years later, when the war was over, Carlo still flirted with the idea of America. He spoke of it only with his sons and the men of the village who sat out on his wide porch in the evening to talk, as if America were a woman Carlo had once known. Nicola had graduated and was home that summer for a rest; he and his father had decided that in September Nicola would go to Rome to specialize. Anything was possible now. The war was over and Carlo's sons were on their way. Now, Carlo said, he might go back to America. "For a visit. I'm curious to see how they've changed things over there."

It was the evening of one of those long generous days of early summer; the men were gathered, talking. Carlo and Nicola sitting on the top step, next to each other. Young Rocco, the clown, was sitting on the stone wall, telling a joke about a drunk Sicilian who tries to get his donkey onto a ship headed for New York. Everyone was laughing, and Sofia and her friends were down below playing a game, and crickets were trilling, and the church bell was striking eight o'clock, and suddenly, Nicola felt his father heavy against his arm.

I was always grateful that my mother had at least given me warning—she was sick, for months, for years. But a single moment divided Nicola's life: he had his father with him, right next to him, then the clock clicked forward one minute—in Italy, in America, all over the world—and his father was gone.

Nicola couldn't go to Rome now, he couldn't go anywhere. He set up an office at home and became the doctor for Cimalta, San Giovanni and a few other nearby towns. He had to make sure there was money for his brothers to graduate, to fulfill the plan. Sofia had to make a good marriage. His mother had to be taken care of.

One miserable day in late summer, a day when everything was exaggerated by the heat, when the shadow of a butterfly looked like a vulture's, and each minute lasted long enough for the change of several seasons, a messenger came to Nicola to say that a woman in San Giovanni was having a difficult birth. Quick. Premature labor. Nicola was a good doctor. He forgot he was depressed. He rushed.

A few hours later, the baby came into the world small and alive. Nicola was washing his hands, ready to head home, when they said, *"Dottore,* please, if we got someone to work the switchboard would you wait, just to tell Pippo, the husband in Milano, that everything is all right?" Nicola nodded, thinking to himself that his obligation to these villages would never end. The messenger rushed to the other side of town, where, he'd heard, there was an American girl visiting who might be able to place a long-distance call.

Maggie was sitting in her grandmother's kitchen, small and dark like all the kitchens in San Giovanni. She was wishing she was back at her job at the phone company in Ohio, where, on a day hot like this, she and her friends would eat their sandwiches sitting out on a park bench, glancing at the handsome men in suits who walked by. Instead, she was stuck here in this Calabrian heat, forcing a smile at the circle of visitors, trying desperately to catch her mother's eye to let her know that no, she would never marry this village man who'd been brought to meet her. He was missing a front tooth.

Why had her parents made her come here? Why in summer? San Giovanni, like most of southern Italy, was desolate in the years just after the war. So little running water she could only wash her hair once a week. Nothing to do, not even a movie. Just these visits with relatives. Dazed from the heat and too many glasses of liqueur and cups of *caffè,* Maggie tried to listen to the heavy Calabrian dialect, which she could understand until a story started flying; then she was lost. She was itching to go take off her skirt and change into some nice wide shorts, or at least peddle pushers and a cool halter top. As it was, all the visitors were staring at her sleeveless white blouse and her bare arms. And on top of everything was the terror that her father might decide this man would be a good husband for her.

And then all of a sudden, like some kind of miracle, a village boy came running to the door, saying they needed somebody at the telephone switchboard. Quick!

Before Maggie knew what was happening, her mother and father and grandmother were rushing her to the switchboard, which was in the pharmacy. While she worked the wires, her mother sat next to her to translate. Her father stood at the door, ready to explain to anybody who came by that it was an emergency, which was the only reason his wife and daughter were working. He was afraid it didn't look right—*brutta figura*—that his women were out in town like that. And then that same young boy ran into the office and said, "Hold the line, hold the line. The doctor's coming." And in rushed this young Dottore Nicola from Cimalta.

After the call, Nicola looked over the Americani—a middle-aged, well-dressed couple and the daughter dressed like a girl in a magazine. Nicola couldn't resist the chance to maybe hear the names *Clevalanda, Filadelfia,* those places his father had loved, so he asked Ben, "Where in America are you from?"

"From Ohio. We come from the state of Ohio. I am Benedetto Florio. This is my wife Cetta, my daughter Margherita."

Nicola asked, "Perhaps you are from Clevalanda in Ohio?"

"Yes, Clevalanda! Really, Homafielda, near Clevalanda."

"But I think I have heard of this Homafielda. Many years ago my father lived for a while near Clevalanda."

"Yeah? What's your name?" Ben asked.

"I'm Nicola Di Cuore. My father, Carlo—"

"Carlo Di Cuore! You're not the son of Carlo Di Cuore?"

"I am."

"Dio mio!" Cetta gasped. "Carlo Di Cuore! I remember that man like it was yesterday he was sitting in my kitchen."

Children from the village stood with their faces pressed against the pharmacy window to see the Americana who knew how to work the telephone switchboard. Nicola sent the kids to the bar to bring some cups of *caffè*. He wanted to find out everything about his father's life in America.

"Your father was foreman in a mill, the boss," Ben told him, "did you know that? Difficult job."

"How did he do a job like that? He spoke no English."

"Your father knew English, he got by. Your father always knew everything he had to know."

"What I remember," Cetta said, "was when he went to the farms outside of Clevalanda and brought back baskets of peaches and plums—"

"He picked the fruit just like here in Calabria. Your father always had that in his head, to come back here."

"And he would give that fruit to everyone, all the *paesani.*"

"I told him many times, 'Stay in Ohio, Carlo. You make a good living. Write to your wife, tell her to bring your children, you can make your life here.' But he said no. He said, 'If God wanted me in America he would have

163

planted me in America.' Carlo always was the man who knew what he wanted.

For Nicola, these were precious secrets about his father's other life. And the American girl sitting beside her parents was so young and pretty, slim and well dressed. She was silent, but her eyes weren't lowered like the village girls'. She smiled and looked at him with unafraid American eyes. And she seemed so cheerful. Since his father had died, Nicola had felt swallowed by those sad poor villages. That afternoon, when he found Margherita at the telephone switchboard, he was sure his father was saving his life again.

Once you have known the love of such a powerful father, you can never be rid of the need for him. And if he is gone from you forever, and you can't find him anywhere, you have no choice but to become that man yourself.

TWELVE

The Third Full Moon

WHEN LUCA HAD BEEN GONE from our house for two days, Zia Berta came into the bathroom while I was brushing my teeth. She closed the door and leaned against it so no one else could come in and so I couldn't get out. "Giulia, listen, where is Luca? Has something happened? Was there an argument?"

I was furious, especially with her. She, more than anyone, had coaxed me to believe that something was possible with Luca, that my father would like him, that I should never wait when I finally found what I wanted. I looked at her, my mouth foaming with toothpaste. "How should I know where Luca is?"

"Well, for heaven's sake, before, he was here all the time. You two were always together. Now, nothing."

I spit, rinsed, starting brushing again.

She sighed. "Are you okay? You're not too upset about this?"

"Upset? Why would I be upset?"

"Do you know when he will be back?"

"I'm not his mother."

She watched me a long time. "Don't brush your teeth so many times, *cara*. It's bad for the enamel." She slipped a cigarette into the pocket of my bathrobe and turned to leave.

"Zia," I said sharply. It was time, finally, to ask her what I'd wanted to ask all summer. "All those years you were engaged, what did you do?"

"I sat with my mother and embroidered," she said, and shrugged. "What else could I do?"

Four days I hadn't seen Luca. I found myself stooping in front of the tiny refrigerator and holding cold nectarines and plums to my cheek just to feel the cool skin.

With Luca gone, Carlo was gone too. "Carlo hasn't been home for four nights in a row," I announced at supper. Those boys had so much freedom; what did they do with it? "Isn't anyone worried about Carlo?"

"Who knows where he is," Zio Anto said, smiling, proud that his son was out in the world.

"He'll be back. When he gets hungry, Carlo will return," my father said from the head of the table. He reached for the bottle of wine and filled his wineglass (since he had arrived, the aunts had begun using good crystal for the men). "No one will be waiting for Carlo when he is in Rome at the university. Better he learn now how to get by on his own."

My wine was in a tumbler decorated with Donald Duck stencils. I took a sip to calm myself and said, "So then you think it's good that Carlo is going to Rome to study, that he'll be away from his family."

"Away from his family," la Signora whimpered and

pulled her shawl tight around herself. "But what can we do? He has to study. God help him there in Rome."

"Dad, answer me. You do think it's good for Carlo to study away from home, is that right?"

"Yes. Apparently, Rome is the best university for him."

"Then why can't I go to college in New York?"

He was slicing his meat with his right hand, bringing his fork up to his mouth with his left, that European maneuvering that had always made my friends stare when they came to dinner in Homefield. I could hear our neighbors at supper, the clank of their forks and knives, all of them slicing with their right hand, just like my father. Here, he was in step. Everything around him backed him up.

"Now she wants New York!" Zio Vito scolded me. "Giulia, *tu vuoi mangiare tutto il mondo*. You want too much."

"Dad, answer me. Why is it OK for Carlo to go to Rome?"

He wiped his mouth and when he lowered his napkin, his lips were curled and showing his teeth. "You understand nothing, do you?" he said in English. "You are a young woman, do you understand that? And your cousin is a man. Must everything be spelled for you?"

"Don't *do* that. You're too smart for that."

Everyone looked up. *"Mamma mia, che gridate Americane!"* Francesca giggled. What American screams!

"Shh," her mother told her.

"Come on now, Giulia, eat." Zia Berta said, trying to pass me a plate of grilled eggplant.

I wouldn't take it. "Do you know what my father just said to me?" I told them in Italian. "He said that since I'm a woman I can't leave home, I can't be trusted, I have to be watched, guarded . . ."

Zio Rocco looked up from his plate. "Ahh, so this is the

argument. This! I thought it was about university, but . . ."

Zio Anto tried to calm me, tried to hand me a plate of cheese. "It is this world your father doesn't trust, Giulia, not you. Not you."

"This is interesting to me," Rocco continued, rubbing his beard. "I have had students with these problems. But it's always the ones from the country, with the fathers from the old days. Nicola, in America they don't think with this old head, do they?"

My father yelled at Rocco, "New York City she wants. This is not a discussion of equality, of education. This is a discussion of a girl going to live alone in a city of criminals." He pushed his plate back. "Giulia, you have been brainwashed with cheap ideas of instant freedom. Sure, go to the ends of the earth and you think you will be free. Freedom is in education, in disciplined hard work and learning. You are an intelligent girl with ideas that lack—"

"Lack what?" I stood up, rocked the bench. La Signora faltered. *"O Dio,"* she gasped. "Tell me, come on, lack what?" I challenged him in English. "Your own brother can't believe you think the way you do."

"Sure, to your face, they smile. What can they say? They see you are an undisciplined girl. I am sure they are disappointed, as I am, to see how you behave."

Daniele asked Carlino, "What are they saying?"

"Boo."

"Dad, they trust me. They did from the start."

"And I see your boyfriend, too, has disappeared. That Luca."

He'd said it—Luca—and everyone got silent. He said what I'd been afraid to think: Luca had left me. *You have to trust your family. Your family loves you. Nobody cares like your family about what happens in your life.* My fingernails clawed the palms of my hands. *Don't cry. Do not* cry. *Don't give him that.* "Yeah, he's gone. Pleased, aren't you?"

"Giulia, it hurts me very much to see you unhappy as you have been this past week. Everyone is tired of seeing you mooning about. I point out the fact of this boy's disappearance so that in the future you will learn to control yourself. To not jump first and think later."

"Why would he come here after it was clear you didn't like him? I'll never forgive you for this."

"Giulia," my father said, his eyebrows strenuously arched, telling me he was blameless, "don't make a fool of yourself. If this boy had any interest, then where is he?"

I heard Zio Vito telling the kids, "Do you see how your cousin talks to her father? Do you see how the Americans behave?"

"Did you hear how he was talking to me? No one pays attention to that."

"You are the only one talking," my father said in Italian and turned away from me, toward the others. He rolled his eyes and told them, in dialect, "She talks and talks and doesn't even hear herself talking."

He laughed, so they all laughed with him. That's when I picked up my glass of wine, gripped it tight above my head. I aimed at his face, but I couldn't do it. The glass flew across the courtyard, and it broke against the wall.

I ran to the gate. Carlino chased me.

"Hey, is everything all right?" Signore Sanmicaeli looked over his wall.

"Giulia," Zia Berta screamed. "Carlino, grab her, stop her." He caught my arm and I pulled away. I ran and ran.

For the first time in days I was out in the dark, on the road, I was away from my father. I wanted to run straight to Luca, but I didn't know where he was.

"Giu-lia."

I was on the beach, running. Carlino still chased me. I

169

turned over the green boat, pushed it into the water, jumped in. It was a race. I pulled the throttle and took off.

"Giulia!" It was my father's voice, far off.

"Fuck you," I said sharply to the horizon, but it was blotted out by the night.

The moon was full, the water flat. Soon I was beyond their voices. I stopped the engine and floated. My jeans dripped water onto the floor of the boat. My feet rested in the puddle, which was warmer than the night-chilled sides of the boat.

It was the August moon. Luca and I had said that during this moon we were going to spend the whole night together. *Somewhere,* we had told each other, *somehow.* Never. Too late. This moon was my father's. *Zio Nicola's moon.*

The sky was high and deep and overstuffed with stars, like a clear May night when I was nine years old, camping with my Girl Scout troop. We all wanted to work on our astronomy badge. My mother was one of the troop leaders and she told us to roll out our sleeping bags in a circle around the fire. She didn't know the first thing about constellations, so she said we should lie on our backs very still and watch the sky. "Look for pictures, girls. What do you see, anything yet?"

"Mrs. Di Cuore, where's the Big Dipper?"

"Oh, that's an old one. Let's find something new. Hey, I think I see a big bowl of fruit."

"Where? Where?"

We all went over to where she lay, pointing. Since she was my mother I could lie down right next to her. Her clothes gave off the scent of wood-fire smoke. Her hair smelled of Breck. "Where, Mom?" I whispered.

She took my finger and stretched out my arm with her arm alongside it. She used my finger to point. "See, there's the basket, that round bunch of stars. Then that bright one up there starts the stem of grapes. Do you see it?"

"Yeah, I think I do."

"What should we call that constellation, Mrs. Di Cuore?"

"You girls name it, anything you want."

A year later she was sick, in the hospital. My father brought me in to see her as often as possible. No matter how weak she was, she sat up and smiled. It wasn't enough. She was my mother, she was right there, and I was standing next to her, but she had tubes bandaged into the crook of her elbows and her wrists. I didn't want to hug her, not when she was like that. "Come here, you," she said, smiling. She moved her arms aside so I could wrap my arms around her waist and she could kiss the top of my head. I wanted to cry but I couldn't let myself. What's happening? I wanted to ask her. When is this going to stop? Her questions always swallowed mine up.

"Sweetie, tell me, how was your math test? How was Girl Scouts this week? Which badges are you going to work on next? How about sewing? Gramma Cetta sure could help you with that, huh? Just think, pretty soon it'll be spring again and your troop will be going on camping trips."

"Mom, I don't want to go if you're not going."

"Oh, come on. You're one of the older girls now. It would sure be good if you went and helped the younger ones. And soon you'll be a Cadet. I think it'll be fun, don't you? You'll go on longer camping trips. Think you'll like to be a camp counselor when you're big?"

Some days I felt so annoyed with her good cheer. Then one day I went to her room and her face stayed solemn. She told me, "I have to tell you something, Giulia. And this is very important." Her voice had no strength, and in place of that constant note of cheer there was urgency.

"Margherita, rest," my father said softly.

"No," she said, then coughed for a long minute. "No. You be quiet," she told him when she could speak again. She never talked back to him, so I knew it was time to panic. Her face was whiter than the hospital linens. She held on to my hands. "I want to tell you this and I want you to remember it: you will be happy again, honey. I know you're sad now," she said, and I felt such relief. Finally, I could start crying. My mother was dry-eyed. "We all are sad right now. It's a real unhappy time for us, but it's not always going to be like this. You believe me? It's the truth." She was having such a hard time breathing. "Always think ahead. You're going to grow up, be a big girl. Do big-girl things. You'll have fun. Listen to me." She ran her hand over my wet face. "Listen, you will be happy again. No matter how sad you feel, just say that to your-self: *Things will work out, I'll be happy again.* Say it, Giulia. *I will be happy.*"

Now, years later, in Italy, sitting in that cold boat, I looked out into the Italian night. "Mom," I pleaded si-lently, "Mom, where are you?"

"So what do we do now with this situation?" Zio Vito was whispering.

"Don't look at *me*," Zia Berta said. "I didn't encourage anything. I did nothing."

"You didn't really *dis*courage her, though, did you?"

Zia Assunta: "Shush, both of you. If Nicola comes back, he'll hear us." All my aunts and uncles were in the kitchen for a conference. My father had the kids down on the beach to play soccer. I was on the balcony above. The transom over the kitchen door was open; I heard every-thing. "What time did she get in last night? She was out in that boat for hours."

"And Nicola?"

"Nothing. He went to bed. This morning he didn't say a thing. And if he says anything, we'll tell him . . ."

"We'll tell him the truth. Luca is Carlo's friend. He's been coming around for years. Giulia arrived. It just happened."

"Happened?" la Signora piped in. "What do you think happened? *O Dio!*"

"Mamma, please, no hysterics."

"It is Giulia's fault," Zio Vito said decisively, in a stage whisper. "She should not have put us in the middle."

"In the middle how?"

"We were responsible for her."

"Oh, come on," Zia Claudia said, "she's going to university in September, no? She flew here by herself, no? Is it possible in American she never met boys? Where are we, in the Middle Ages?"

"I still say she knew her father would be opposed."

"Opposed to what? There are no plans yet, no proposals, no propositions, no declarations."

"It is in God's hands. Marriage, babies, families—all this is in the hands of God."

"Mamma!"

Zio Anto said, "But stop with the marriages! It was school they were arguing about. University."

"It was *not* school," his wife told him. "They could have been speaking Chinese for all I know, but I heard it just like you did—it is Luca that is making Nicola crazy."

"Nicola was always crazy," Rocco said. "Don't you remember what he did to me? Nothing good enough, nothing right . . ."

"Rocco," Claudia warned him, and he stopped.

"The only thing we know for sure is that he is upset. Maybe it is something between them, something that has nothing to do with us or Luca. What do we know?"

"But this is what confuses me," Zio Anto said. "Nicola

173

is the expert, he advises families all the time. How could he have these problems with his own daughter?"

"The shoemaker's children are always without shoes."

Six days passed. Afternoons, I lay on the beach and thought about Luca. I pressed myself against the hot sand, but I felt nothing. Lifeless breasts, lifeless flesh. It's over, I decided. Forget about Luca, look out for yourself.

Finally, Carlo came home. He said he could stay only half an hour and asked his mother to iron a clean shirt for him. He was going to the country with Luca's family.

"Go," Zia Assunta yelled as he took a quick shower and packed some clothes. "Go, but remember where your family is. Do you think someday we can see you for more than twenty minutes?"

"Mamma, I'm not going to war. I'll be back. Relax." He kissed her twice on both cheeks.

Just as he was leaving, I caught up with him at the gate. "Where've you been?" I whispered, letting him know I was angry.

He winked at me. "Wish me luck," he whispered back. "I've met a girl who's helping me forget Loredana." When I didn't smile, he said, "Luca—he says to tell you he misses you."

"Where is he? Why hasn't he been here? What's going on?"

"Buon viaggio, Signor Carlo," my father called down from a balcony just above us. "So I hear you're going to the country."

"Yes, Zio Nicola."

"Well, enjoy yourself," my father said pleasantly, a man talking to a man. "Have a good time."

"Thank you, Zio." Carlo closed the gate. *"Ar-*

rivederci," he called to us as he rode off on Luca's motorino.

When my father came down a few minutes later, I was still standing at the gate, stunned. He crouched down beside the herb garden and started pulling weeds. "If this patch is cleaned out, we could have several more rows of basil." When I said nothing, he told me, "So, Miss Giulia, your aunts tell me there is a necklace you saw in town that you like. Shall we go shopping this evening?"

"Shopping? Dad, a necklace is the last thing in the world I want from you."

I started to walk away, but he called me back. He was holding up a shard of glass he'd just found in the garden. My broken wineglass. "Here," he said, "I believe this is yours. Are you proud of yourself?"

It was almost impossible for me to live in that house with him anymore. Zia Berta caught me in the hallway. She whispered into my ear, "I saw, I heard him yell at you about the glass. I know. He's wrong. Still, you have to let it go. Let it go before something happens."

But I wanted something to happen.

The next morning I woke up and everyone was in the courtyard watching Nonna Giulia kill a chicken. "Come, Giulia, watch!" Daniele said. "This, you've never seen before." They were in a circle around Nonna, who had a fat brown-feathered chicken vised between her knees, her black skirt riding up her white thighs. With one hand, Nonna held the chicken's wings together, but they were strong and fighting her.

Carlino reached over. "Nonna, here, let me help you."

"Out of my way," she told him. "I have a knife in my hands."

Nonna fought and got the wings pinned together; she

175

stuffed them under her right arm. With her right hand, she grabbed the chicken's head and held it still while the knife in her left hand plunged deep into the chicken's neck. The bird's cry was so furious I stepped back inside the kitchen door. Nonna didn't flinch. Brown blood spurted out.

Francesca squealed, *"O che bello!"* Beautiful! She laughed at Daniele, who had his face hidden against his mother's hip. "You're just like Giulietta," Francesca teased him. "Scared as that pathetic chicken."

"Did you hear your daughter?" my father teased Rocco, "she doesn't sound like the child of a veterinarian." Rocco didn't laugh. "Two veterinarians, I should say." Rocco still didn't laugh.

Nonna's knife sliced the neck open and left it hanging there by a shred of skin. Then she had to hold tight, her fingers lost in the blood-matted feathers, while the bird's body twitched fast, then slower, then fast again, almost spinning a full turn and sending a spray of blood across the sandstone of the courtyard. Nonna gripped more firmly and aimed the open neck downward, and the rest of the blood plopped, plopped, dripped into the tub at her feet, where it almost instantly congealed.

"Brava, Nonna!" Francesca was clapping her hands. Carlino was whistling.

Giulietta hung over the balcony and screamed, "You're all pigs to be killing a chicken in the middle of the house."

Zia Claudia was holding the burlap bag with a second chicken in it. She told Giulietta, *"Cara,* it's OK. Nonna Giulia does it fast, quick. The poor chicken feels very little, really."

"But all this blood . . ."

"Giulietta," I said. "Go inside." I was already picking around inside the burlap bag, trying to figure out how to get the chicken out. A thick stench rose up out of the bag. But then I caught the scent of a match as my father lit a cigarette. He was right behind me. I made myself lean deeper in to get the chicken.

"Giulia," my father commanded, "away. That chicken will bite you."

"Nonna," I said, "show me how you did it."

Zia Berta whined, "Oh, that nice nightgown, you'll ruin it."

Nonna Giulia grabbed my arm with the same strong grip that had choked the first chicken. "Americana, what do you think you're doing?"

The chicken's fat black eye looked up at me, it nipped at my finger. "Ow." I pulled my hand back, the bag fell open, a panicked flap of wings.

"The chicken! She's loose!"

It flew up, wings beat under my chin, but the foot caught on the burlap and Nonna pulled the chicken back down.

"Nonna!" I was almost crying. "Please, show me what to do."

"No, Giulia." My father stood in front of me now. All I saw was his hand, his thumb flicking his cigarette hard. "No," he said.

"Yes," I said.

"She won't cut herself, Zio Nicola," Francesca told him. "Go ahead, Giulia. *Brava!*"

The chicken was fighting me hard. The pin-sharp point of its beak brought up dots of blood on my hand. Nonna put her arms around me from behind and helped me grab the chicken's wings. She pushed them up under my arm. She was breathing hard. *"Testa tosta,"* she called me. You hard-headed one.

"I got it, Nonna."

She held the chicken's head still. "Cut here," she scolded me. "The neck. Quick."

I jabbed the knife into the neck. *Oh, yes, finally, it feels*

177

good. A thick squirt of blood ran down the front of my nightgown, the chicken almost flew away from my knife. *"Hold* it, Giulia," Nonna yelled into my neck.

"Hold it," they all yelled.

I heard his voice, calm, loud, deep and in English rising through all the noise. "Cut deep, Giulia," my father told me. "If you are going to do it, do it right. You must cut deep or it will never die."

THIRTEEN

The Truth, Nice and Clear

WITH NONNA GIULIA'S HELP I dug the knife deep, slit the neck, killed the chicken. There was a moment—when I felt its fury flying through my hands—that I felt better than I had in days; then, when it hung there heavy and limp, I felt worse. My aunts took the dead chicken from me, and bloody feathers stuck to my palm.

At dinner, after everyone but Giulietta and me had eaten the chickens, Rocco tapped his glass for attention. We all thought he wanted to tell a joke, but he said, "Claudia and I have been talking. We have an idea to propose."

"Tell us."

"We would like to invite Giulia to come to live with us in Naples this next year. She could take classes at the university. Art, Italian, whatever she likes. Then, next June, July, when her Italian is perfect and she knows all the paintings in all the museums, we'll send her home. Giulia, what do you think?"

"What a beautiful idea," Zia Berta said.

"Thank you," my father said, "but no."

"We didn't hear yet what Giulia thinks," Zia Claudia said.

"Impossible," my father said.

"Do you think I could answer a question for myself?"

"Listen, we made some phone calls, Nicola. I talked with our professor friends. They said it is no problem for her to enroll. If she's serious about this photography, she needs to study art, no? Better than the art in Italy you're not going to find."

"Rocco, Claudia, thank you for your efforts, but you shouldn't have. Giulia will be in America for school, either at St. Helena's or, if she changes her mind at the last minute, at home, where she belongs. Rocco, please, don't feed the dog at the table while we're eating."

Rocco picked another piece of chicken off his plate and held out his hand for Topo, who licked his fingers. Rocco patted him and said, "So, really, Nicola, you don't trust us to take care of Giulia."

"Rocco, it's not that."

"What then?"

"It's because Mamma and Papà aren't married."

"Francesca!"

"Don't yell at her. The child just spoke the truth. That is exactly what Nicola is thinking."

"I am absolutely *not* thinking that. Thank you for your invitation, but it is not appropriate for Giulia."

Nicola stood and left the table. The others, one by one, got up to clear away the dishes. Only Rocco and I were left there with his bright idea. He shook the last drops of water from the green bottle into his mouth. "Don't you worry, Giulia. You'll be in Italy next year, count on it."

· · · ·

Be careful what you pray for, Cetta had always told me. For years, I'd prayed for someone to help defend me against my father, to help win him over to my side. Some saint had listened. What had I done?

Rocco was different during the next few days. After dinner, he'd stare into his empty coffee cup, poking his small spoon at the coffee grounds. In the afternoon, he lay on the lounge chair under the wide shade tree, but behind his sunglasses his eyes were open, watching, alert.

It was deep into August now, and the heat was unbearable; so was the tension in the courtyard, but the kids were happy. The adults, trying to avoid each other, were available to play all the time. Nobody talked about universities or politics or much of anything during our long meals. We helped the kids memorize their multiplication tables and fanned them with our oversized cloth napkins. Peeling a small cucumber one afternoon after dinner, my father called, "Franceschina, come here." When Francesca, wearing nothing but her flowered bathing suit bottoms and a string of pink rosary beads around her neck, ran over and stood in front of him, he said in a thundering voice that made her squeal, "For the Principessa Francesca, the best-dressed member of this household, I award you with this." He cut off the tip of the cucumber and stuck it on her forehead.

"Ah, *fresca!*" Her eyes closed, she smiled.

"Giulietta," my father commanded.

"Si, Zio?" She ran over to him.

"For Giulietta del Mare, for excellence in nautical skills, for bravery in confronting the perils of the sea, I award you with this." He cut off the other end of the cucumber and stuck it on her forehead.

"Oooo," she said as the cool compress touched her, and

181

she blushed at the honor of being called fearless. From across the courtyard, Zio Rocco watched.

My father sliced a long strip of cucumber skin and called Daniele to him. "For the Noble General Daniele, for heroic guardianship of his younger cousins." He gave Daniele a cool green strip across his forehead.

"Daniele, you look like an Indian," Giulietta said.

"Make me an Indian, too, Zio Nicola," Francesca pleaded. "Here, give me a strip on my cheek."

"Giulia?" he offered me a green strip.

I clicked my tongue sharply to say no; I didn't look at him, but I remembered how good it felt, one thin slice of cucumber skin on a hot face, sucking all the heat away. I watched my little cousins stand before him, wiggling, delighted that for that one moment, they were the only thing he saw. I remembered how that felt too, a moment of grace in which you felt you were perfect. His hand, holding the knife, offered me a strip of cucumber. "Are you sure, Giulia?"

"I told you, no, thanks."

He peeled a second cucumber and put the tip on his own forehead, way up high near his pointed hairline. He handed out cooling strips of green skin to Anto and Vito and Berta, and they happily decorated themselves.

"Professoressa," my father said, offering a slice to Zia Claudia.

Zio Rocco's voice ripped through the still air, "You can call her Claudia. Her name is Claudia."

We were all relieved when Renata showed up. As she came through the gate, all the men stood. They shook her hand. She was wearing a sundress that covered her long legs down past her knees. No jewelry, no makeup. She looked serious, dependable and, in spite of her dowdy dress, beautiful; she looked like the kind of woman any good man would want to marry.

"What a pleasure, *signorina*," my father said, smiling. She'd come to our beach with her mother now and then, and my father was always happy to see her. He offered to peel another cucumber, so she could cool off, too.

"Thank you, but no," she said. She was a little down, she told us as Zia Assunta brought her a *caffè*, because Mauro had been called away to fill in at a hospital up in the country near his grandfather's farm. It seemed he would be gone for a week, maybe longer. Renata was taking a walk to distract herself. She came by, she said, to see if I'd like to keep her company.

"Go, Giulia, go," Zia Assunta said. "If your father says it's all right, why don't you go."

They all looked at him, and he said, "She may go."

Renata and I set out walking leisurely. I hoped we'd walk a long way so that eventually we might get around to talking about Luca. I kept thinking, Renata please talk to me, don't make me ask. But when we were just out of sight of my family's house, she said, "Come on, Giulia, faster." She grabbed my arm and we were almost running. "There's not much time."

"Where are we going, Renata?"

"Just hurry," she pleaded.

At the bend in the road, by the path leading into the orange groves, Renata stopped me. A long maroon motorcycle was leaning against a tree. *"Ah, bravo,"* she said when she saw the bike.

"What, Renata?"

She pulled me into the groves. "Come on." There was the cool shade and the scent of citrus. I wanted to stop a second, but Renata kept pulling me. I smelled cigarette smoke. Then I saw Luca, leaning against a tree.

Renata got to him before I did. "Half an hour, Luca," she said in a low voice. "More than that and it means trouble for us all." And she left.

Luca.

He tossed the cigarette and put his hand on my face. I took a step toward him, then away. He looked past me to see if anyone was around, then he touched my face again, I touched his chest. We both looked around us. No one. We hugged hard. He bit my ear. "Where've you been?" I hissed at him. "I want to kill you. Where've you been?"

"I'll explain everything," he said, and took my hand and led me down an aisle lined with orange trees. "Let's walk."

I kept looking over my shoulder. No one was around. We passed an old gardener with a bucket and shovel, we dropped hands, but the gardener didn't care about us.

Luca finally told me, "I've heard, Giulia, what's going on at your house."

I looked at him, still ready to hate him.

"Loredana told Bernardo," he said. "Bernardo told my brother."

"What?"

"That day on the rocks, after your father came to get you. You had an argument on the beach. And then one night at supper you argued. Loredana's sisters heard you. Later, Rinaldo heard from your Zio Vito that your father was angry about me. My brother told me that unless I want to cause big problems for you I better stay away. 'Apparently the father doesn't like you,' Mauro said to me."

"Mauro? You listened to Mauro?"

"I told him, 'The father doesn't know me.' Mauro told me, 'Keep it that way.'"

"You believed Mauro?"

"Of course not. I was ready to kill him. We also had a

big fight at my house. I think he is jealous because my parents gave me the motorcycle."

"That huge motorcycle is yours?"

"A gift, from my parents for my exams. But—forget that. I asked Renata—I had to beg her, she hates to go against Mauro—I asked her to go by your house one day and investigate a bit. She told me she sat and talked with you, your aunts, your father."

"And what did she report?"

"That you were not like before, that you were very upset. That obviously between you and your father there was some war."

"So that's why you stayed away? You didn't even come to say goodbye. I'm leaving here in two weeks, Luca, and you took off for the mountains."

"No, no. We never went to the mountains. I made Carlo say that. If your father thought I was far away I thought it would be easier for you to leave your house." He smiled. "Clever, no? I've been planning this meeting for a week."

"Where's Carlo?"

"Ah. Useless. He's at my house, following around some fourteen-year-old girl in a leopard-skin bathing suit. He says if he doesn't look at her face, she's Loredana."

We both laughed.

"You missed me?" he asked.

I punched him, harder than I intended, in the stomach.

"Aiya," he said. He pinned my hands behind my back and kissed my shoulder. We were lost in the maze of orange trees now, oranges nesting within shiny green leaves for as far as we could see. The air shook with the sound of afternoon crickets. I rubbed my face against his neck and breathed deep. "Luca, don't ever leave me again."

"I never left you."

We stood looking at each other, touched foreheads,

leaned closer and touched noses. Resting my chin on his shoulder, I thought, again, how perfectly we fit together. We were so evenly matched that as we stood there, our ears were right next to each other, and we pressed them together, half expecting to hear the ocean between us.

"La verità, bella e chiara!" The truth, nice and clear. That's the first thing Renata and I heard as we rushed down the dirt road back home. It was Zio Rocco yelling. "Now, Nicola, it's time to speak the truth."

We found the kids standing in the road, in front of the gate, with Zia Assunta, Giuliana and Marigiulia. They were all wringing their hands like people at an emergency, waiting for an ambulance to arrive.

"Rocco, you are purposefully misunderstanding me."

"I understand *too* much, Nicola, *too* clearly. I understand that you don't trust us to watch your daughter. I understand that you have not once sat to converse with Claudia since you got here."

"Rocco," Claudia said, "drop it. Don't start."

"No. I will not drop it. Nicola, I understand that you never sent us a gift or congratulations when our children were born. I understand all of this."

"Rocco, you're taking this the wrong way."

"I take it the way I see it. Claudia, we're leaving. Pack everything. Get the children."

Giulietta ran through the gate into the courtyard. "Don't leave me. Mamma, don't leave me."

Francesca grabbed Zia Assunta's legs and screamed, "Don't make me go. I don't want to go."

"Rocco," Berta said, "don't exaggerate."

"Claudia, talk to him," Vito ordered.

"We're going, Claudia. Pack everything. Now."

"Don't do it, Rocco," my father said. I'd never heard him like this. "I beg you," he said, and I thought, Rocco's gone too far, he's got to stop, he can't make my father this upset. "Do not make the children leave. If you want, I will go to a hotel." He turned to Nonna Giulia. "Mamma, talk to him."

"You heard Rocco. He wants to go."

"Claudia, get that dog in the car. Pack everything."

Within an hour, Rocco was loading his car. His brothers tried to take the suitcases out of the trunk.

The rest of us stood at the gate, watching, crying. Even Zia Claudia said, "Rocco, reconsider."

As they drove away, Francesca stuck her head out the back window and yelled, "I don't want to leave you." Her forehead was still crossed with a strip of cucumber.

FOURTEEN

Look into My Eyes

AFTER IT HAD HAPPENED, it didn't seem that anything could save our family. It was as if Rocco had thrown open the gate of the courtyard when he took his family away and now any danger could walk right in on us.

Without Giancarlo crying at night, nobody could sleep. Daniele, who'd been so capable around his little cousins, suddenly turned helpless. "Mamma, *where's* the pump for the raft?"

"How should I know?"

At dinner, Zia Assunta and Zia Berta would leave the table to get something in the kitchen, then forget what they'd gone to find.

My father, Zio Anto and Zio Vito would try to begin conversations, grab anything off the front page of the newspaper, then they'd lose track in midsentence of what they wanted to say.

La Signora couldn't find her rosary beads. She made us all pray to Sant'Antonio, patron saint of lost objects, until we found them—they were at the bottom of a closet, where Francesca had left them after playing dress-up.

Every time my father came back to the house from the beach, he asked, "No word from them yet?"

"It's not your fault, Nicola," Nonna Giulia told him. "Rocco feels bad about the whole thing with Claudia. Really, it bothers him a lot that they haven't been able to get married."

"I see that. Now, I see that. But I thought he was just being irresponsible, rebellious. I never imagined Rocco could change so much during these years."

"Many things changed during the years you were away, Nicola."

This was news. My father chewed it over, late at night. I found him awake downstairs, sitting at the table, alone with an ashtray, smoking. "Dad?" I walked up behind him, startled him. "Are you all right?"

"Fine, yes. Everything is fine. But something told me you were not asleep. I knew you were awake." Through the crowd in the house, through the quiet of the night, my father and I still kept track of each other.

"I was worried about you." Then, to remind us both that I was still angry, I said, "You're smoking too much."

"You are worrying too much. Go, Giulia. Go to bed now. I am fine, everything is fine."

"Good night, Dad," I said, and then, because now in the afternoons I was meeting Luca in the groves, because now I had managed to grab back a piece of my life, I kissed my father on his bald spot. *"Buona notte."*

Hours later, when I finally heard him make his way up the stairs to go to bed, I cursed Rocco. How could anyone leave my father? How could anyone make my father so sad?

· · · ·

189

Not every day, but frequently (so I had to be ready all the time), Renata showed up, usually toward the end of dinner, and everyone was happy to see her, grateful for the distraction. She arrived looking sorrowful, missing Mauro, asking me if I wanted to go for a walk. And every day Zia Assunta asked Marigiulia and Giuliana, "Why don't you girls go with them? Get out. Do something." I held my breath. Renata and I exchanged glances. Fortunately, though, my cousins had no interest in wandering around in the heat.

Renata and I left. Casually, we walked past the neighbors' houses. Then, around the corner, we took off to find Luca in the orange trees. The walk was less than a quarter mile, but it was filled with dangers for us. Once, Professoressa Signorinelli drove by and asked, "Where are you *signorine* off to in such a hurry?" The train to Messina passed us every afternoon. Bored by the long train trip, young passengers hung from the train windows and called out to us. Once a boy threw a bottle and it crashed at my feet. I got a small cut, but Renata and I kept walking. Just before the bend in the road, a German shepherd from a nearby farm always came charging. I was terrified of the dog, but Renata's Roman voice filled with authority and she ordered, *"A casa! Subito!"* Go home, now! And that sent the dog cowering. One day, though, the German shepherd stood at the side of the road and howled, throwing up his head. We could hear other dogs nearby.

"O Dio mio," Renata said, "don't tell me. Listen to those animals. Don't tell me there's going to be an earthquake."

"An earthquake?"

"Always before an earthquake the animals act up like this. Listen to them. Giulia, if the ground starts to shake, leave Luca and run. That's all I need is for you two to be found together in the middle of an earthquake. If that happens, I just hope the ground opens up under my feet and swallows me."

I smiled at Renata. She was the smartest woman I'd ever met. She could charm my father, settle wild dogs, read the air for natural disaster. "You're wonderful, Renata. What would Luca and I do without you?"

She held up her big manicured hand to silence me. "Please," she said, and laughed. "Just make sure Mauro never finds out. First your father will kill me, then Mauro will do the job again." She pulled my arm through hers and we walked, shoulder to shoulder, laughing. We always laughed a bit too loud. Early on, we'd recognized something in each other—the way, I suppose, strangers with similar diseases know what they share. "Is it these southern men, Giulia, who make us crazy, or were we crazy to begin with?" Renata and I loved to laugh together. "Listen to what Mauro told me last week, his latest excuse for why we can't get married soon. Did I tell you?"

"No, come on," I urged her. "Tell me." It seemed we never had our fill of talking about the men who were ruining our lives.

Yet even as we laughed, I knew we were betraying ourselves. Something serious was at stake. "This sneaking to see Luca is good practice for me, isn't it?" Renata told me, "for when I become a mother. Oh, imagine that Mauro—what he'll put me through, just like your father."

Renata. Her name meant "reborn." Women like her were born over and over, again and again.

"In two weeks you're leaving," Luca said accusingly, scooping up a handful of gravel from the path in the orange groves, rubbing the pebbles fast between his palms. "All we have is this one hour in the afternoon. We're losing time together, Giulia."

191

"Luca, we're here now." My fingers went up inside the sleeves of his T-shirt. Our skin had turned almost the same dark color.

"And this sneaking, I don't like it. Why is it a crime that I love you?"

"That's not the crime. The crime is that *I* love *you*. That's what my father can't stand."

"How can we go on this way?" he demanded. "You and I should not be crawling around like this, like lizards."

"Luca, we're not lizards." I backed him against a tree. "We're more like snakes," I said and flicked my tongue into his mouth. And finally he relaxed, loosened his fist, let the gravel rain onto our feet. We stayed under the tree until it was time to go.

For me, each afternoon I took the road to the citrus trees was like traveling a little farther away from home. There was an Italian song popular that summer; it played everywhere I went, and it wasn't until I'd been hearing it for weeks that I realized how very corny the song was—if it had been in English I would have switched off the radio immediately—but in Italian I loved it. In the song, a woman with a deep, sure voice sang to her lover, *"You don't know what I'm capable of."* She dared him, *"Look into my eyes. Tell me if there's anyone who can separate us."* The guitars played behind her voice in long, stretched-out chords of longing. As Renata and I rushed down the dirt road toward Luca, the song played through my head. *Luca, look into my eyes. You don't know what I'm capable of.*

I'd begun to feel powerful when I had my hands on him, but I worried about Luca. "This sneaking," he told me, "it makes me feel small, like a boy." I wasn't sure how much more he could stand. Luca was looking at me with an angry, sharp-green, intelligent gaze. "Take me for a ride," I told him. "Now, on the motorcycle."

Fed up, he closed his eyes and turned his face away. *"Che gazzo stai dicendo?"* This basically meant, What the fuck are you talking about?

"I mean it." Like a gambler on a lucky streak, I couldn't resist the urge to push the limits. I wanted to show Luca I trusted him, and prove to myself that I trusted him. So, together, we walked out to the road, to his motorcycle, which was large as a small love seat and glinting at us in the sun. The seat was black leather and hot. We threw our legs over it and sat down slowly. Still, the leather burned. "Let's go."

And then our feet were off the ground and my arms around his waist and my chest pressed against his back and my face in his long black curls, and we were speeding through the empty piazza, down the road, chopping through the air, pushing the heat away.

"Excuse me, *signori,*" the child called through the gate into the courtyard. "There was a phone call, at the bar."

"Rocco!" my father said happily, standing, ready to go return the call right away. "It was from Professore Rocco, no?"

"No. It was a man from the city, he called to say he has some houses on a beach for you to look at tomorrow. He left a number. Here it is." She held a paper through the bars of the gate.

"Would you like to come in and have fruit with us, *cara?*" Zia Assunta asked her.

"No, thank you. I have to get back to the bar."

"Then here. Daniele, bring her these peaches. Thank you, *cara,* for the message."

Renata was sitting with us, but no one tried to disguise the sad silence around the table.

"So, my friend found us a house," Zio Anto said, disappointed.

"Nicola, do you still want to look at the houses?"

"Sure. Go, look," Nonna Giulia said. "When Rocco comes back, you'll have some things to show him."

More silence.

Renata finally spoke up. "Well, listen, this is perfect timing. We've been wanting to invite Giulia to dinner, my mother and I. We're leaving soon. Giulia, how about coming to dinner while your father is looking at the houses?" With her eyebrows raised, she smiled at everyone. "My mother would like it very much. What do you say, Giulia?"

"Probably these days, I should stay here. In case—"

My father, remembering it was his job to pretend nothing was wrong, turned to me. "Why? There is no reason. It would be very nice for you to have dinner with Renata. Why don't you go?"

The next morning, not long after my father and uncles left, Renata came to get me to have dinner at her house. My aunts, pleased to have an afternoon with so few mouths to feed, stood at the gate and waved goodbye.

Renata led me through the piazza and onto the road lined with weeping willows. We couldn't see the beach and not a soul was on the road. Except Luca. He was sitting on his motorcycle, behind a tree, waiting.

"So far so good," he said as he stood and made room for me on the seat of the bike. I gathered my skirt and sat down.

Renata told us, "Four o'clock and no later, you hear? And Luca, slow. Slow!"

We both kissed her goodbye, then Luca and I took off on the motorcycle, up into the traffic of the main road, heading south toward his family's home on the beach.

· · · ·

"Quando si mangia si combatta con la morte," my uncles often said, or loosely translated, Eating is a deadly serious matter. Where food was involved, Luca was just like my uncles.

We were in his mother's kitchen. A pot of water for pasta was boiling on the stove. Luca was making dinner for us.

"Luca, you don't have to do that."

"Well, Renata told you that you were invited for dinner, no? Could we send you home hungry?"

I moved up behind him, wrapped my arms around his waist and slipped my hand up inside his T-shirt. His middle was hard and flat and sweaty. The kitchen was hot. He was starting to relax into my arms. Then he glanced at the clock, tensed, and said, "But it's dinnertime. Come on, we have to eat." He pulled away.

We'd never been in a house alone before. "Luca, what's wrong? Don't you want to kiss me?"

He was washing a handful of tomatoes under the spigot; confused, he turned and looked at me. "But of course I want to kiss you. I like very much kissing you, but it's one o'clock. We have to eat, no?"

How Italian he was.

I watched as he peeled tomatoes and chopped them, tore basil leaves, pitted black olives, stirred everything in olive oil and sautéed garlic to make sauce for our pasta. Salting, spicing, tasting, Luca knew what he was doing.

The kitchen was huge, with three windows that opened onto a balcony and took in the entire harbor of Montemaggiore al Mare. The house was up on a hill with wooden steps leading down to a stone beach. It was big and modern. Spreading this way and that, on three different floors, were white, low-ceilinged rooms, with sparse, modern gray and white blocks of furniture. A rambling overgrown garden surrounded the house; red roses spilled in through the living-room and kitchen windows and added the only disorder.

The house was as close as I ever got to meeting Luca's mother. Years earlier, she had spent one whole summer decorating it, Luca said; after that she just came for a week in July and another week in August. There was no excess, no doilies, no froufrou. Luca's mother was from a wealthy Palermo family. On the coffee table was a brightly painted piece of Sicilian pottery. On the kitchen walls, some bright ceramic plates, wildly painted quasi-abstract images of peasant and country life. These were the only items of any personal significance. There were no photographs anywhere. She was a pediatrician, devoted to her work. Luca's father was a surgeon, devoted to his. Luca had told me he had perfect parents: they left him alone. Mauro, Luca's worst family problem, was usually not around. In essence, Luca was a free agent.

In the kitchen, he was completely competent, his own mother and his own father. He winked at me. "I will be a good husband, no?" Just like my aunts always did, Luca held out a string of pasta on a wooden spoon for me to taste. "What do you think, is it ready yet?"

"Luca, where did you learn how to do all this?" The table was set. I could tell he had swept the floor because the sun lit up one thin strip of dust that he had missed. Everything else was spotless. "Who taught you?"

"I was in love with our maid when I was a little boy. I spent whole days with her. She taught me everything."

"She was like a grandmother?"

"No, just the opposite. She was very young, in her twenties, with beautiful long legs," he said. He kissed me on the forehead. "Come, sit down, let's eat. The pasta is ready."

We sat at one end of a long table. The white marble top was decorated with our two bowls of pasta, our two

196

glasses of red wine, our striped cloth napkins and the green water bottle. I had never eaten a meal alone with a boy. Sitting there with Luca felt like the most intimate thing we had ever done together. We ate and he told me about the languages he wanted to study in Rome. "English, of course. Then also German, because if I work for an importing firm I need to talk to Germans, and their accent is very bad with Italian. And then Russian."

"Why Russian?"

"Russians like to eat. I will be the first to export all the pasta of Italy to the Communists. They will love it. Yes, in my fourth year I will learn Russian."

"When I get to college," I told him, "my first project is going to be all black and white photography. All shadows. No color."

We talked without stopping in that empty, echoing house, as if we'd needed all that privacy to talk about these things.

"Sweet Baby James" was playing on a tape deck in the hallway. There was a certain lilt to James Taylor's voice that made me miss American things I'd never known. The pasta was good and I asked for more, and Luca told me, *"Brava."*

When he came back to the table with my bowl, I said, "Tell me about Renata. Why is she doing this for us?"

"Because she is a good woman. And because she's mad at my brother."

"Yeah? How do you know?"

"In her situation, who wouldn't be mad at him? He doesn't treat her well. He takes advantage. She was only fifteen when they met. Mauro was her first *fidanzato,* and her only one. For some reason I cannot comprehend, she adores him. Every once in a while he sets a date to get married, then he changes it. He wants her and he wants his life with no responsibilities, no children, no house."

197

"So why doesn't she leave him?"

He raised his eyebrows. "Who knows? She convinced herself she loves him. Renata has had a hard life. She never knew her father—he died before she was born. She and her mother stuck very close. Renata runs that family business all on her own, and she has to deal with all types. Suppliers, service people—all of them men trying to rip her off. She is the strongest woman I know, and yet she hangs on my stupid brother." Luca tipped his chair onto its back legs and got cigarettes off the counter, tossed the pack a few times. "Even my mother prays for Renata that she'll meet another man."

He offered me a cigarette. I shook my head no. He offered me a *caffè,* and I said, "Yes, perfect."

His brown solid body moved gracefully around the white kitchen. I studied him. He reached into the refrigerator and found the coffee without looking. Quickly, he assembled the pieces of the small *caffettiera* and filled it with ground coffee, and I watched his back widen as he twisted the coffeepot shut tight. Is this how people decide to get married, I wondered, just by realizing they could spend the rest of their life watching the other person move through the house?

He felt my eyes on him. "Giuu-lia," he sang. "So quiet?"

"I'm just thinking."

"Yes?"

"Just that I like talking to you more than anyone I've ever known."

When he turned he was smiling. *"Si?"* he said, then in English, "I like talking by you also."

"Talking *to* you," I corrected him.

He came back to the table and sat down, rested the high arch of his foot on the rung of my chair. "To you, for you, by you, about you, all this things I like." His hand reached over, picked mine up off the table. He lifted my index finger and stroked it with his thumb. Lifted another finger and stroked. He could never sit still.

I pushed the black tangle of curls back from his face. After two and a half months in Italy, I still felt there was something ungraspable about Luca. His light eyes, even when he looked straight at me, had the distant solemn quality you see in formal black and white or brown-toned photos of men from the 1920s, '30s, '40s. He was sitting there in white tennis shorts and a white T-shirt that had Bob Dylan's face stenciled on it, but Luca looked like a man from a different age. Like my father, he seemed to cover centuries.

"Giulia, you were courageous to come here today."

"You were courageous to invite me."

"Your father. Tell me, why do you think he left Italy?"

"Because of my mother."

"She didn't like Italy?"

"No, she would have lived here. They did live in Italy for about a year after they got married, but then she got sick. He took her to America so she could see her doctors. They were planning to come back as soon as she was better."

"But they didn't."

"I guess she was pretty sick. Then my father started studying to be a psychiatrist, and that took a couple of years. And then"—I held up my arms—"I was born."

"And he never came back until now, this month?"

"Never." During the early days in Homefield I'd once overheard Cetta and Sofia talking about my father, that he was thinking of returning to Italy for good, as soon as I got over the shock of losing my mother. They said that's why he was renting the convent rather than finding something more permanent.

"Your mother, she was beautiful?"

"I think so."

"Beautiful enough for him to leave his country and his family?"

I looked him over for a long moment. "You're never going to come to visit me in America, are you?"

"For us, it is very different. America is closer to Italy now. But when your father went there, America was the other side of the moon. Who knows why he did it."

"Why don't you believe my mother was a good enough reason?" I had no idea what I wanted from Luca, but I couldn't bear any hint that he wasn't ready to give me everything.

"Tell me the story. How did they meet?"

"Sort of the same way we did."

"*Sì?*"

"My mother was in Italy with her parents. She was only twenty. Did you know she had a job? She was different from the other Italian girls. I'm sure my father had never met another girl like her. Anyway, they were in their village, San Giovanni, for a visit. My grandmother wanted to see her mother."

"And your grandfather wanted an Italian husband for his daughter."

"How did you know that?"

"You think your mother was the only one? This story is classic. Don't look at me angry like that." He leaned over and pushed the hair out of my eyes. "Did she have this hair like yours, with the blond and dark all mixed up?"

I wouldn't answer.

"Come on," he said softly. "And did she speak Italian?"

"Just a little."

"And your father, did he speak English?"

"No."

He leaned back in his chair. "So then, what was it? No

language together. Don't tell me it was sex, not in those days."

I started to laugh. "You know what convinced my mother?"

"Tell me."

"Well, she did think he was nice-looking. But when they invited my father for dinner, my mother saw he had nice table manners and that's how she knew she could marry him."

"Psh, good thing it wasn't your Uncle Rocco. He would have never passed that test of the table manners." We laughed. "And me?" he asked. "Do I pass this test?"

"Brilliantly."

"Americans, they eat like barbarians, no?"

"Cannibals actually." I leaned over and bit his arm. The scent of his flesh was like home, warm as toast.

He pulled me onto his lap.

"Luca, I'm too heavy."

"A little heavier than when you arrived. You were too skinny then. Do you remember, Giulia, the first day, how nervous you were on my motorino?"

"I wasn't nervous."

"No? No?" He imitated my stiff posture. "Now you aren't nervous with me?"

"No, I am *still* not nervous with you."

"Giulia," he murmured. That voice. "Remember how we talked, that we were going to lie all one night together? Let's go now, for a while."

"To your room?"

"Come, it's down here." He led me by the hand.

The shutters were pulled halfway down, the bedroom dark, but I recognized some of Carlo's clothes hanging on the back of a chair. "Luca," I whispered, "does Carlo know I'm here?"

"Don't worry. He won't be back this afternoon. He's with his new girlfriend."

Two neatly made narrow beds were side by side. I sat down on the bed by the door, but Luca said, "Not that one, that's Mauro's. This over here is mine."

I walked over, sat on Luca's bed. I lay back on the pillow and Luca lay beside me. He leaned on one elbow while his hand stroked my hair, my wrist.

"Is this okay here?" he asked me.

"Yes. Are you okay?"

My hand moved up the curving valley of his spine. The full spread of my fingers could fit across his shoulders four times. The music down the hall was slow and sad. His fingers stroked my neck and pushed aside my bra straps. After a while he lifted my skirt.

We felt our way deeper inside clothes, struggling to touch skin. We needed more skin, as if skin was air. Hands swimming over flesh. The cool stretch of skin across his bottom, where he wasn't tan—even my hand could feel how white and untouched he was there. Naked, I felt so much larger than him—breasts and hips and a wider waist, but then he loomed above me a second, his chest spread, and his shoulders and arms took me all in.

The slowness made it too exciting, but slow as they could, my hands moved from hollow to curve over the hardness and softness of his body—*a man's body*—while his hands on me brushed and stroked and pressed and rubbed, and it was like moving through a dream of your own house but suddenly there are new rooms, whole new places you'd never known about before. His leg wrapped around mine, and his penis pressed hard against my thigh. I wasn't afraid. I touched, and my breath caught when I felt how smooth his skin was at the tip, smooth but firm as a tongue. I couldn't stop rubbing. He watched me watching as a pearl of liquid poised there.

"Oh, Luca."

I opened my hand and his hard flesh filled my palm. I felt my legs opening against his thigh. When I looked up, though, his face was tight. He pushed my hand away.

"Why?" I whispered.

Gently, he pulled me down next to him so my head rested on his shoulder. "Luca?" I said. But his arm was covering his eyes.

He wouldn't say anything, and I heard a thousand other voices: *Don't let them say Professor Di Cuore's daughter grew up to be a wild thing. It's always the girl's fault. Do you have any idea how much you do not know about this place?*

"Luca, please, say something. Tell me what's wrong." When he still said nothing, I told him, "Maybe I should leave."

His legs gripped my thigh. "No."

He moved his arm away and finally I saw his face. I started to cry. "You're mad. What's wrong, Luca?"

"This isn't right. I love you," he said, and though he was still dark and furious, relief shuddered through me. "Giulia, don't you understand? It took us so long to get to this point, and now you're leaving. You shouldn't be leaving me." I was still crying. "Giulia." He turned onto his side to face me. Our knees were touching, our eyes locked. "Giulia," he whispered, "I want you to be mine."

I told him, "I am." But what was he asking?

"I don't want you to go back to that fucking America."

"We have time yet, Luca. There's time."

"Giulia, there are only twelve days. Twelve days and twelve nights."

"We have less than twelve days, Luca. I have to go to the village this weekend. To Cimalta, for the feast."

"*Oh, cazzu,*" he swore. "Tell them no, you won't go."

"I have to go."

He sighed and pulled me to him. We held on tight. My eyes were closed, and so, for me, the words he said next were surrounded by complete darkness: "Giulia, I want you to come to live with me in Rome."

"What?"

"You don't want to go to that college he's sending you to. You should come with me." My hand was pressing hard on his chest. He could tell I was afraid. He softened. "Giulia, we're in love. We should be together," he said, but it was too late. I'd already heard that other thing in his voice: *I want you to* . . .

"Giulia, you said your father went to America because he loved your mother."

"Oh, Luca, he did, but . . ."

"What?" he challenged me.

I'd been so fearless all day—riding with Luca on the motorcycle, on the highway where we could have been seen. Having dinner alone in the house—if my father found out, I'd have to admit it had all been planned. I'd even been ready to make love with Luca. Now he wanted more. What was he asking me to do? *Una selva oscura.*

"Giulia, come on. Look at me."

"No."

I was trying hard to remember those lines of Dante that Luca had recited the first day, when we got to the park. The two of us alone, for the first time. Something about finding yourself in *una selva oscura*—a dark forest—and the straight path in front of you has vanished.

That night in the courtyard my father and my uncles talked about the beach house they had seen. I listened, but with my heart beating too fast and somewhere up in my throat. I had traveled so far from my father that day, was there any way I could ever make my way back to him?

But then he turned from the others and said to me,

"And, oh Giulia! what a view we saw today from the balcony of this house." His arm swept over his head. "I thought of you with your camera. You would love this house, up in the hills a bit, and the whole southern coast we saw!" He rested his hand on my head, just a moment, and it felt like absolution. I had told Luca I would think about Rome. But, of course, I would never go with him. I would tell him no as soon as I got back from Cimalta. "And how was it for you today, your dinner with Renata's family?"

"Yes, tell us," my aunts asked. "What pasta did they serve?"

"I'll tell you later. Let's hear more about the house."

Before I went to bed, my father asked, in English, "So, Giulia, you enjoyed your day with Renata?"

"Yeah, it was great."

"Good. Good. She is a very nice young woman. I can hear also that your Italian is improving a bit."

The anger between us hadn't disappeared, but for the time being it had settled, like sediment to the bottom of a bottle of wine.

FIFTEEN

In Cimalta

CIMALTA, or *cima alta,* means high peak, and most of our trip to the village was on narrow, winding, climbing roads. I was in Zio Anto's car with Zia Assunta, Giuliana and Marigiulia.

"We never made this trip so fast," Zia Assunta complained.

"Usually, Giulia, we have to stop for Giulietta and Francesca. They get so carsick on this trip. Every twenty minutes they need to stop."

"They are experts, those two. For staying clean while throwing up, they are the best."

Zia Assunta stared out the window. "And that baby, ooph, how I miss him. What a mess we found ourselves in this summer with that Rocco."

"It's my father's fault," I said.

"No, Giulia, Rocco was always crazy. Laughing, laughing, and then out of nowhere, he explodes. What a shame this had to happen when Nicola came all this way."

Everyone still wanted to protect him. And I have to admit that when we got to the intersection of two gravel roads and I saw the bent pole with the rusty sign CIMALTA, I stuck my head out the window and shouted to my father, who was in Zio Vito's car behind us, "Dad, look!" He was already waving and pointing the sign out to me. "Giulia, do you see! Take a picture! Take a picture!"

Our cars continued uphill through thick-leafed trees, sun-spotted fresh green. We rolled the windows down all the way, and Zia Assunta didn't say anything about the draft. The air was cool and full of the scent of moist earth. We passed a man slowly pedaling an eggcart and a woman walking with a knotted-up bundle balanced on her head. Zio Anto honked at them and yelled, "Walk, walk. It's good for you. Your old lungs are in better shape than mine."

The couple stopped, recognized Zio Anto, laughed and waved. "Lazy," they shouted. "Always lazy, you city people!"

Zio pulled his head back into the car and told me, *"Paesani nostri."* Our relatives.

"Get ready," Marigiulia warned me. "Up here everyone is our relative."

The road took a few more sharp turns; then we were at the cemetery, which I knew marked the beginning of Cimalta. I looked back at my father again. His arm was out the window, his hand spread open; he was so happy to be there he wanted to feel the air.

The road dipped and brought us into the skinny streets of town. Our cars almost scraped the walls at some points. Faces appeared in the open windows as we drove past. People stepped through the hanging fly-strands in their doorways to see who was arriving. It was a village full of eyes. Old women in aprons sitting on straw-bottomed chairs and old men in black felt hats sitting on stoops shielded their eyes from the sun and stared. A few recognized Zio Anto. *"O Anto, ciao!"* Then someone saw my father, "Ni-*cooo*-la! *Nicola dell'America!"*

"Oh oh, here it starts," Zia Assunta said. We looked back and saw that Zio Vito's car was stopped and surrounded. My father was grabbing hands through the car window. People were reaching into the car to kiss him.

Zio Anto kept shifting gears, moving our car along. *"Attenzione!"* he shouted out the window. "Later, we'll see you in the piazza. We have children here who need to use the bathroom."

"Oh, Papà! Don't tell them that."

"Excuse me, but if we stop to even say hello to one person, do you know when we'll get to Nonna Giulia's house? Next month."

"Fine, but you can tell them *you* have to go to the bathroom. Why always is it us?"

"Anto, they're right. The girls are really too big now."

"Mamma mia, how sensitive everyone is all of a sudden."

The streets snaked. The walls of the houses were old and cracked and worn, just as in Rome. But in Rome, the ancient coexisted with the contemporary; Cimalta was a peasant village set completely in peasant time. Most of the people staring and waving at us were old, dressed in black. Small children clung to their long skirts and trousers.

Nonna Giulia's house was built on the highest tip of Cimalta. Squeezing through the streets toward the house, our car climbed as far as it could. Zio Vito's car pulled up a few minutes after us. The last bit of road, we had to walk.

"Girls, remember," Zia Berta whispered, "nothing about Rocco. If someone asks . . ."

"We know. Work. They had to leave early to go to work."

We carried our suitcases and jugs of water up the hill. A steep flight of stone steps led to the big, open porch of the house. Relatives and neighbors were waiting there to help us. "Nicola!" they shouted, and *"Giulia di Nicola! Ciao, bambini!"* Kisses on both cheeks. A red-faced woman took my chin in her hands, met my eyes and asked me, in dialect, in a deep voice, "Do you know who I am? Can you guess?"

Her teeth were brown-tinged and gave her the antique look of an old tinted photograph. A black mole balanced on her upper lip. She was like no one I'd ever met before. Yet there was something familiar. Her voice.

"Are you related to Comare Roseanna in Homefield?" I asked.

"Braaa-va," she screamed and laughed a laugh I'd known all my life. She clamped my face to hers. Her skin was as rippled as wet sand after the tide goes out. *"Brava!* So I look like my sister, eh? But no, Roseanna is Americana, all with nice dresses and jewelry. I see in the pictures."

In fact, Roseanna did appear at Mass every Sunday "all done," as Cetta said. Roseanna had her short thinning gray hair teased and sprayed into a nimbus around her scalp; her winter coat had a mink collar and cuffs. She called me Julie, and always left a pink-lipstick kiss on my cheek. The only thing that connected Roseanna to her sister, rooted her in this place, was her voice when she spoke the dialect, that rushed incomprehensible murmur with the power to take away the Evil Eye. Roseanna did it over the telephone, her kitchen wall phone—yellow to match the teapots on her wallpaper—probably while sitting on a stool at her Formica counter, sipping Sanka from a mug. How much distance people can cover in one life-

209

time. Roseanna's sister was still holding my face. "Nicola, you see how intelligent your daughter is. She knew me right away."

An old man took my hand. Two of his fingers had no fingernails. He was missing a thumb. "And me? You can't guess who I am," he dared me, "can you?"

With him it was the eyes. Sparkling shades of hazel, like tiger's-eye beads, circled with thick black eyelashes. "You're Luigi Parone's brother, aren't you?"

"Exactly, exactly!" He kissed my hand and wouldn't let go. "And here, meet my daughter and my granddaughter, my grandson. Tell them," he said, "tell them about my brother in America. A big car he has, no? Oldsomobila. See," he told his grandchildren, "from forty years ago, still I remember the English. So many words—washinga machina, Woolaworth. I remember the clothes—jacketa, underapants."

"Listen! How he knows English!" His family winked at me with Luigi Parone's big eyes.

I wanted to photograph everyone. They took me in and hugged me, sure that they'd known me all my life. The older relatives told me over and over again, blessing themselves, "You have your mother's face, God rest her soul." Though I knew this wasn't really true—my mother's looks had been softer, prettier; I had Cetta's wide peasant face—I was happy that so many people remembered her.

"You're all your mother, all over your face," they told me.

And my father added, "But she's smart like me."

An hour passed before we made it up the steps. When we got to the top, Nonna Giulia was leaning out the kitchen window, waiting for us. My father reached in for her hand. "See," he told me, "this is where I'd find my mother every time I came home."

"You've kept me standing here for twenty years, Nicola. How do you explain that?"

Anto and Vito were already inside, taking off their shirts, changing into shorts. My father hesitated at the door a moment, laughing. "I cannot believe we are really here."

"Come on, Dad," I said, "let's see how it looks." Together, we went down the dark hallway into the past.

Walking through Nonna Giulia's house for the first time felt like going back to a place I knew very well. There was the small added-on bedroom. When my father and his brothers were young, when they were all wound up and wrestling with each other, Nonna Giulia used to lock them in that bedroom and tell them, "In there if you want to fight, and I'm not going to open up until I see the blood coming out from under the door."

In the back of the house was the big main room with the long wooden table where my parents had sat with my mother's Italian-English dictionary trying to talk to each other and to make plans.

The best room was in the center of the house. It was small but full of light and had two high balconies. It had been my father's first medical office. Years later, it was where Aunt Sofia first saw Uncle Mike, the American soldier who took her away. This was also the room where San Francesco had appeared.

Daniele was sitting in a straight-backed chair, and I tipped him backward and kissed the top of his head. There was a split second of pure happiness, when I thought how much I loved my family, and next a second of regret when I thought how much easier it all would have been that summer if there were no Luca to worry about. "So this is it, isn't it," I asked, "where San Francesco sat when he came to talk to Nonno Carlo?"

211

Daniele jumped up off the chair and ran to his mother. "Oh, Mamma! That story! It scares me more than watching the chicken get its neck slit open."

Carlino teased him, "You have to sleep in this room tonight, Daniele, all by yourself. And San Francesco might come back for a visit."

"Never," Nonna Giulia reassured him. "San Francesco here to see you? You little devils? Why would he waste his time?"

By late Friday afternoon, the feast was filling the town. The small streets were clogged with cars; license plates from far away: northern Italy, Germany, France, all the places where the young people of Cimalta had gone away to work. The houses were so close together we could hear the neighbors setting the table for dinner. We could smell their pasta sauce—"too much onion," Zio Vito complained. "Those people across the back alley always used too much onion. One of their sons wanted Sofia."

There was hammering as men erected arches of red and blue lights up and down the streets. Then all the noise was broken by a steady slow-beating drum. Everyone got quiet. The drumming came closer, sounded more urgent, pulled us all out to the balconies.

"*I ciaramejari,*" my father yelled when he saw them. "*I ciaramejari.*"

Just as the drumming passed under our window, the high-pitched whine of a bagpipe came in, then a whistling flute. *I ciaramejari* were three solemn old musicians wearing wide-brimmed hats dark as the pigskin the bagpipe was made of. The drummer wore his drum low on his leg and limped along straight-legged.

And running behind the old musicians, leading a pack of kids, was Francesca. Giulietta was right behind her.

212

"Francesca!" Daniele yelled down into the street. "Giulietta! Wait for me!"

Zia Berta grabbed him by the sleeve. Daniele pleaded, "Mamma, let me go."

"Let him go down there with them," Nonna Giulia said and leaned so far over the balcony to look that Marigiulia grabbed her sleeve. "Bring those girls back here, Daniele."

A young boy poked his head in the kitchen window and said, *"Ambasciatore!"* He'd been sent as an ambassador, a messenger. He announced, "Professore Rocco and his family sent me to tell you they are coming."

"When?"

"As soon as they can climb the hill."

"They'll need help," my father said. "They've got the baby, they'll need help." He and Anto and Vito rushed out the door.

Assunta looked at Berta and blessed herself. *"O Dio,* what if they fight now for sure. Did you hear Nicola coughing? What if one of them has some kind of attack?"

Berta brushed past her. "Assunta, everything is always opera for you."

"But without the music," Marigiulia said and walked with Berta out to the porch to wait. "Mamma, why would they fight now, when Zio Rocco came to visit?" The rest of us followed them outside.

Finally Rocco came up the stairs, waving at us but he wasn't smiling. "We're here for half an hour, that's all. The kids were crying that they wanted to come to the feast. I promised them an ice cream, then we're leaving." He kissed all the women and girls, but he was stiff; as he moved from one to the other, we each touched his arm, but he was already walking away.

Claudia looked exhausted.

Berta was polite enough not to notice. *"Carissimi!"* she smiled. "Where are you staying?"

213

Behind Rocco's back, Claudia puffed out her cheeks to let us know their place was a disaster, but Rocco said, "A terrific house, we found it right on the water. Small, but beautiful."

"In the middle of August you found such a nice house?"

"We were lucky." He headed inside. "Where's Mamma? Mamma, where are you? Do you have any fresh figs for me?"

I took the baby from Claudia. "Here, let me help you." Zia Assunta, Zia Berta and Giuliana came over and we all breathed in the scent of Giancarlo's neck. "We missed you," we cooed at him.

"We missed you," we told Zia Claudia.

"You have no idea. He's been impossible to live with."

"The baby?"

"No! Rocco."

And still she stayed with him. What went on between people in love?

"Shh, listen," Giuliana said and moved closer to the door. The men and Nonna Giulia were in the studio. We heard Rocco first: "I have nothing more to say."

We heard the strains of my father's apology. I couldn't hear the exact words, but it sounded like all his apologies —it offered forgiveness, but admitted no guilt.

"I'm sorry, Nicola," Rocco answered, "if I could feel differently, I would. For me, right now, it's better not to be here."

Nonna said something we couldn't make out.

Rocco snorted, "It's my vacation, too, no? Do I need to raise my blood pressure on my vacation?"

Vito pleaded, "But Rocco, reconsider. For this little thing, this invitation for Giulia to go to Naples. Is it worth it?"

"For this little thing? This little thing? What kind of a fool do you take me for?"

"We don't—"

"Rocco, Rocco," my father said, "this explosion came so fast, from nowhere. Are there things you want to talk to me about?"

"Are you trying to psychoanalyze me, Nicola? Very well. I went to medical school, too. I learned a little of your psychiatry myself. Let's start with childhood—that is what you do, isn't it? OK, childhood, when you made me sit for hours and study. We can start with you telling me I'd never amount to anything. Or we can start with you never saying to me, 'Good, you did well.' Then we can continue with your never congratulating me for the birth of my children. The way you never address Claudia by her name. And then we can conclude this session with you insulting us, making it clear you feel your daughter would not be in good hands staying with us."

He was yelling now, and the baby was crying. My aunts and cousins and I paced on the porch, found each other's eyes, then looked away.

We heard my father's deep sigh; it carried all the way out from the center of the house.

"What do you want me to do, Rocco?" my father said. "Tell me, please. What can I do?"

Rocco laughed a laugh that meant nothing good. "You're doing the same thing again, Nicola. You want to fix everything, do everything. It's not all in your hands."

"So then, what do you want?" Zio Vito insisted.

"I want to visit with Mamma a few more minutes, have an ice cream, get my children and go back to my house at the beach."

Anto couldn't let go: "I don't suppose you're interested to know that we went to see a few houses for sale on the beach. We saw one we thought you'd like."

"Not this year."

"Next year?"

"Next year, we'll see. For this year, these few weeks we have left, my family and I want to be alone, to spend some time alone together."

"Oh, Rocco," Zio Vito said, "now you sound more American than the Americans."

Rocco was the first to come outside. He was walking like my father, with his hands in his pockets, his shoulders hunched. "Time for ice cream," he announced. He sent the neighbor boy down to the bar to bring up *granita di limone* for everyone. All the uncles tried to pay, but Rocco's voice cut through and said, *"I will pay,"* and the others stepped aside. He sent Giuliana and Marigiulia down to find the kids. The *granita* arrived on a tray from the bar and melted faster than we could eat it.

It was time for them to go, but before he left, Zio Rocco whispered to me, "If you decide, you know you are always welcome at our house. Any time, Giulia."

"Thanks, Zio." I couldn't tell if he was wiser than me, stronger in his crusade. Or was he just meaner, actually walking away from my father?

Rocco and Claudia kissed everyone goodbye and we all hugged Giulietta, Francesca and Giancarlo. We stood on the porch and waved until they were over the hill. Then we rushed into the studio, out onto the balcony and waited for their car to reach the opening in the road where we could see it again. Without looking up at us, Rocco honked the horn. The girls waved their arms out the windows and shouted, *"Ciao, arrivederci!"*

"Oh," Zia Assunta whined, "why wouldn't he let those kids stay longer."

"At least they didn't bring that dog," Nonna Giulia said.

"Well, he came to visit," my father said. "That is what

is important. To see him and to know that they all are
healthy, and everything is fine."

During the next three days, we went through the rituals of
the feast. On Friday and Saturday nights we dressed up
and carried chairs down to the piazza to watch the movie,
which was projected onto the big white side wall of the
church. The sound came from a speaker in a window
somewhere behind us. The dialogue was almost a full minute ahead of the action, so that at one point the leading
man told the heroine, "I must leave you," before she even
appeared at the door.

My aunts had told me to save my best dress for Sunday
morning to go to church, which was so hot, the benches so
packed, that two women fainted and had to be carried
out. After Mass, everyone pushed into the piazza, and the
statue of San Francesco di Paola was carried out of the
church. Rising life-size above the crowd, in black hood
and heavy black robes, he was more haunting than in the
pictures on the calendar that hung in our cantina. The face
of the statue was painted with lifelike detail, but had the
eerie over-made-up look of an actor seen close up. A gold
halo floated in the air above his head. I couldn't see how
the gold wire was connected, so the statue really did look
like something that had been to heaven and come back.
The power was in the eyes, which rolled up to the sky. To
me, the rolled-up eyes looked too pained to care about us
gathered below, and I could not—as my father, Nonna
Giulia and my aunts and uncles did—see a friend in the
statue.

Scarier than the rolling eyes was the tightening crowd of
worshipers. As soon as the statue appeared in the piazza,
the drumbeat began, loud, echoing off the stone walls
around us; the air was shaking. And then the trumpets
began, then the whole band, sounding like a collective

wail. People got down on both knees and blessed themselves. Others rushed forward to touch the gilded base of the statue, to try to kiss its chipped toes.

"San Francesco's coming through. Let him pass," men ordered the crowd.

Four men and two women were below the statue, supporting the platform on their shoulders. One of the women was old, in bare feet. "Dad, that woman, she's going to collapse under there. Someone's got to stop her."

Like everyone else, my father's eyes had a funereal glaze. "Oh no, she will not. San Francesco will help her. He sees her faith."

By now it was almost noon and the sun was baking the town. I saw people take off their shoes and walk barefoot over the hot stone streets. I noticed others putting on heavy brown or black robes, like the saint's. The sun glinted off the thick collection of gold chains hanging from the saint's neck. Ex-votos from the faithful. Arms, legs, babies, hearts made of gold. One of our relatives, a young woman from the family of cousins with the beautiful eyes, gripped my arm tight with a sweaty hand. "Giulia, up there on San Francesco, there's a gold medallion for your mother. Did you know that?" She blessed herself, kissed the cross at the end of her rosary beads, held it up to the saint. "Your grandmother Cetta had the medallion made after one of your mother's illnesses. See if you can find it. It's big, it's round and gold. Do you see?"

"I'll look for it," I said and let the crowd take me away from her. The looming statue with its rolling eyes, the crying cousins, the music, the heat. I was being tugged and pulled, inside and out. I put on my sunglasses and looked straight ahead. What was this impulse to humiliate yourself, to throw yourself at the feet of a clay statue? I thought of Cetta, so panicked about my sick mother that she had turned her prayers into gold. If she had been able to come to Italy during those months my mother was sick, Cetta would have walked barefoot and fought to carry the statue. She would have taken the heaviest part. Aunt Sofia would have too. Probably even my father. They never talked about it, but I knew their desperation. And me, I would have carried the statue myself, with no help, I would have worn black robes, walked for miles in heat or cold to make my mother get well. The winter I was ten I cried so hard in bed at night that in the morning, big wads of damp Kleenex made bumps under my pillow. I flushed them down the toilet so no one would know. But here, people were crying in the streets.

The procession bottlenecked as we moved out of the piazza. Faces and bodies pushed close. Mists of sweat everywhere. There were arguments about who would get a chance to carry the statue next. Somebody was crying loud. When children got tired, fathers picked them up and kept walking. Pregnant women refused to go home and rest.

By the second hour, we were only halfway through the tiny village. The crowd was thinning, slowing down, falling back from the statue. The band had begun playing jumpy marches. Men in the crowd started lighting cigarettes.

We came to a fork in the road near the cemetery, and a fight erupted between the Monsignore, who was trying to lead the procession back to the piazza, and the police chief, who was trying to detour the procession past his mother's house. He was in full uniform that day and feeling proud.

The Monsignore yelled, *"Carabiniere,* you've watched this procession all your life. You know the road it follows."

"That is the problem, Monsignore," the police chief

shouted back. "The problem with this town is we need a new direction. We need new leadership."

The police chief's sister was trying to calm him down. "Forget it. Let Monsignore take the procession where he wants. Mamma won't mind. Stop. Don't do this."

People were laughing now, shaking their heads, saying, "Leave it to the police chief. He does something like this every year." It had been two and a half hours. The mood of the crowd now was that relief you feel as you walk out of the confessional.

A little girl overheard me ask my father, "What happens now?" and she told me, "San Francesco, *poverino,* he's tired. We're taking him back to his church."

When the saint was back on his niche near the altar, where he would stay until next year's procession, a hundred candles were lit in front of him. Some people stayed in the pews to pray. Most went home to eat.

At our house, my aunts boiled a huge pot of pasta on the small burner of the stove. During dinner, we all had to take turns standing alongside the table swinging a dish towel around to keep the flies away from the food.

It was late Sunday night. The fireworks had just ended. We'd all stood together on the balcony and watched. Now my father and I were the only ones left in the studio. He was sitting at his old desk, looking through the drawers. I was standing on the balcony, and the village fanned out in front of me.

At night, Cimalta was a still, small, precious thing; from a good lookout point, you could see its outermost boundaries. For my father and me, the village was the furthest point back into our past. This was the first home, the real one; everyplace else felt like an imitation, a way station, an experiment. Tomorrow or the next day I'd see Luca, and he'd ask me, again, "Giulia, Rome?" And what would

I tell him? Probably no, but if I didn't go to Rome with Luca, I would go somewhere else. Or maybe I would go to Rome. Either way, it wouldn't matter. In my deepest heart I knew Rocco was wrong. You should never leave your family. It's wrong to leave home.

My father called out to me, "Come here, Giulia, you will like to see this."

I turned to look and in that first second's glance at him sitting in that Italian room, wearing a madras cotton shirt and whistling "Seventy-six Trombones," I saw that my father was not an Italian. To assimilate means to shed layers, to stop being one thing, to become another. What had we become? "Look at what I found here."

He had pulled out the deep bottom drawer and lifted it onto the desk. The drawer was filled with old photographs. I caught a few as they spilled out.

"Dad, look at all this." Faded black-and-whites, brown-tone wedding portraits, Kodak color prints.

"I wondered where these pictures had ended up all these years."

"Dad, look at *this.*" It was a black and white picture of my mother standing on the terrace I'd just been on.

My father glanced at the picture and for a second I wished I'd kept it to myself. What if it upset him? But he smiled and said, "Hey hey," and took the photograph out of my hand to look at it better. He seemed delighted to have run into her here.

It's a hot day in the picture and she's wearing white Bermuda shorts and a black and white striped shirt tied up tight around her tiny waist. With an ache, I realized she *was* prettier than me, thinner. My mother's hands are plunged deep into her pockets. Her sunglasses have pointed-tip frames. A thick wave of her blond-brown hair is blowing across her forehead. She looks like a movie star standing on the deck of a ship. Though her eyes are hidden by the dark glasses, her face is happy, the cheekbones high. Her lips are dark—lipsticked—and shaping some word. She's talking to the photographer.

"Who took this picture, Dad?"

"I believe I did."

As my father and I dug through the drawer, we found a whole series of photographs taken one afternoon on the terrace: Cetta, in a dark flowered dress, standing between my mother and Ben, who is in a suit, a vest and tie. My mother is in a white dotted dress with a matching scarf wrapped around her hair. Another picture with Cetta, Nonna Giulia and my mother, standing close together, smiling, happy. Then, an uncentered picture of my mother and father, their faces close. She'd taken the sunglasses off, pushed her hair away, and you see her full face: she is completely happy.

The sun was bright and clear that day; the black and white contrasts sharp. On the back of the photographs, written in my mother's crisp Catholic-school script, was the date: Sunday, July 15, 1951. I showed the pictures to my father. "You took a lot of pictures that day, Dad. How come? Some feast or something?"

He looked at it and took time to light a cigarette and exhale. Then he told me, "That was the day your mother and I were engaged."

July 15. They had met in May. They'd known each other only two months, one month less than I'd known Luca. *If I did go to Rome with Luca, what would happen?*

The drawer seemed bottomless as a well. We dug deeper into the old pictures, and the images moved back and forth in time. My father before he met my mother, on the beach with friends, all of them thin and boyish in swimming trunks, making a human pyramid. Years later, another world; my father sitting proudly in his first car, a big-finned American monstrosity with fat rounded bumpers. When he found the picture he took off his glasses and laughed. "This car, this car, it was a very ugly shade of green. The dealer gave it to me for a good price just to get it out of his lot, but, oh, I felt like Rockefeller in that car. And here, look at this, Zio Anto in his first car. I wonder how he felt in that matchbox?" A Cinquecento, a car so tiny that with his arm sticking out the window, Zio could almost touch the ground.

I looked closely at the photos of Easters, New Year's Eves, and found the two young girls who would eventually become my aunts. Pictures taken over years of long engagements. Exchanging Christmas gifts, summer after summer in groups at the beach. Young Assunta and Berta hardly ever hold the arms of their *fidanzati,* rather they pull Sofia, the little sister, into the picture as a prop. Then, finally, triumphantly, Piazza San Marco in Venice, Piazza Navona in Rome: honeymoon photos of young wives dressed in traveling suits and spike heels, smiling indulgently at pigeons swooping down at bread crumbs cupped in their gloved hands.

Then us, the children. Our baptisms, first communions. My American cousins and I dressed as hobos for Halloween. The Italian kids in beautiful costumes for Carnevale: bullfighters, little queens. My kindergarten and third-grade class pictures: Bucky Henning smiling a mouthful of braces; Molly's face puckered up as she tries not to giggle; my teacher, Mrs. Graves, dressed in British tweeds, with her bifocals hanging from her neck. All of them there in the desk drawer in Cimalta, a place they would never come to and probably never imagine.

My father and I pulled out handfuls of photographs. Wordlessly, unaware of what we were doing, we took all the pictures of my mother and spread them on the desk. My father was thrilled every time he came across her face. "Margherita, I mean Giulia, look at this." He had not called me Margherita in years; that night, though, he started talking to her again. "Our first apartment in Cincinnati," he said and showed me a black and white snapshot of a small room, so clean but so sparsely furnished that tears choked me. There were no people in the picture, but the room was ready for guests. The bed pushed into the corner. In the center, a card table covered with a white tablecloth that was not quite long enough to hide the flimsy fold-down legs. Dishes, glasses and silverware laid out, a centerpiece of carnations. Folding chairs set up. "Our first Easter, our first party, really. Oh, your mother, she cooked and prepared for three or four days."

It was there, in that picture of table and chairs, that I found my mother. She was always preparing for something, but it never really came to her.

He reached for the picture, but I ignored his hand. "Dad, why didn't you ever let Mom go back to work at the phone company? She loved that job."

"Oh, come! A telephone operator? Is that a good job for the wife of a doctor? Besides, your mother did not want to work."

More than once she'd asked me, "What would you think if Mommy took a job? Just something part-time, to get me out of the house."

"What would you do with the money?"

"Take you to the movies. How's that?"

"That'd be good, Mom. When are you going to do it?"

"It's just a crazy thought, Giulia. Daddy doesn't need to hear about this, you hear me? I'm just thinking out loud."

As far as I knew she never tried to get a job. Instead, she moved through the house like some kind of storm, organizing all the closets—piling towels up according to size, arranging her skirts and dresses according to color, labeling all our shoeboxes, all the boxes in the basement and up in the attic.

And then there were the days when I'd find her lying on the couch, her arm thrown over her face. Was she sleeping? I'd move in close. "Mom?"

"What, Giulia?"

"Are you OK?"

"I'm fine. Go play."

"Mom, did you get a job yet?"

"Giulia, forget that stupid idea. You hear me?"

She never drove the car except once a year, when my father went away to a psychiatrists' convention. He didn't let her drive, he said she wasn't experienced enough. But when he was gone, she wrote down the mileage (she knew how to change the odometer), then she and I took off. We picked up one or two of her friends to go get hamburgers and then see a matinee. They laughed together: "Oh, Maggie, if Nicola finds out . . ." I sat in the back seat and ate potato chips, which were never allowed when my father was home. I pretended I was a teenager hanging out with some friends. She glanced back and warned me: "This is girl stuff, Giulia. You understand? If Daddy asks, none of this happened." During our last few escapades I was already starting to wonder why we couldn't just tell him what we wanted to do. Sometimes it was as if my mother and I were the children united against one parent.

That night in Cimalta I started thinking about my parents' marriage, how my mother played it like a game. Was this any way for a grown woman to be married? And I realized that in this, my mother had lied to me. She'd made me believe that hiding, sneaking, scheming was all part of the fun of marriage, and that there was no price in anger or resentment or loss of love. Would this game have been as easy for her in its second or third decade? Would she have finally confronted him? Would my parents have eventually got divorced? *Probably it would be a disaster if I ever went to Rome with Luca.*

But then my father was holding out a picture. "Giulia, look here," and there was my mother lifting me, a baby in baptism clothes, her face turned away from the camera so she could smile at me. "And here, Giulia, look." And there she was again and again. My mother holding out our birthday cakes, blowing out the candles on her own cake, pulling Christmas tree decorations from her well-marked boxes. In Homefield we had so few framed pictures of her. The image of her face fit too perfectly an aching gulf that yawned between my father and me nearly all the time, a cold void we usually tried to fill with words, with arguments. But that night, we saw her moving again, we could hear her laughing. I remembered her body, how sure and capable it felt next to me as she ran alongside me, teaching me how to ride a bike. "Bal-ance, bal-ance. Eyes straight ahead." She was so much with us in the studio in Cimalta that we both ignored the fact that on the other side of this night she'd be gone.

When the desk was covered with all the pictures of my mother, we stopped and looked into her young eager face. Even in those taken during her last summer she had the advantage of youth over the other aunts and uncles. She was no older than Zia Claudia. Now, I was closer to her age than my father was.

"My God," my father said. "I do not think I ever realized how really young your mother was when we married."

"She was twenty, about two years older than I am now."

He went over to the balcony to stamp out his cigarette butt. "You are right," he said absently.

"Are you afraid I'm going to run off and leave you and get married? Is that your secret fear?"

"You are not going to shock me by becoming a psychiatrist, are you?"

"Dad, answer me."

He tapped a fresh cigarette out of his pack and raised his eyebrows comically. In dialect he told me, "The sooner you're off my back the better."

"I'm asking you a serious question."

"When you have a serious marriage proposal we will talk." We had reached the bottom of the drawer and he was stuffing the photos into two large envelopes—one for each of us. I wanted to argue, to tell him, No, we're not done here yet, you can't just put these pictures away. But then my father asked, "Would you like to take a walk?" and completely surprised me.

The night before, I had wanted to go out late with my camera, and he had said, "Are you crazy? At this hour? Where do you think you are? People do not roam these streets at night. After eleven everyone is home, in bed."

"But it's a village—it's safe."

"That is not the point. People will talk."

"They will," Zio Vito said.

"So let them. I don't care what they say about me."

"But I do," my father said. "No, it is time for bed."

That night after we put the pictures away, he told me, "Come, let's take a walk. Bring your camera, if you would like."

The town slept so soundly, all the windows locked against the wicked night air. My father and I walked, and our footsteps claimed the streets, echoed off the cobblestones. Heading down the sloping road from Nonna Giulia's house, we could see the clay-pipe roofs of the village, all slanting in different directions, at various heights. The sky was clear, and there were stars.

In the direction of the piazza, the dome of the church rose up. Night pigeons swooped around it, small patches of dark moving against the lighter dark of the sky.

"Dad, stop a minute," I said. "I want to get this." I took out my wide-angle lens, screwed it on. He stood smoking, waiting while I photographed.

"What are you getting? The dome?"

"And the birds."

"Ah, yes, very good."

When I was done we walked on. My father held back his head and exhaled extravagantly into the night. After a while he asked me, "Tell me, Giulia, what is it you like about taking pictures?"

"Power," I said, squinting my eyes and looking tough, but he was waiting. It seemed he really wanted to know. "Well, it's like I'm making a moment last, and later I can study it. I know it's a total illusion, but I feel like with pictures I'll never miss anything or forget anything."

"Illusion is probably an important factor in any creative vision."

"What do you mean?"

"With creative work, one is doing something never done before, stepping out into an area of risk where there are no guarantees. Internally, we do what we can to compensate for our fears. An illusion can be a very useful tool in making it possible for an artist to persevere."

I took his arm. "Stop lecturing. What does that mean for real people?"

"I am thinking of my father. He had the idea of educating all his sons. This was his vision. Until it was realized, though, his idea was in many ways an illusion—what made him think it was possible? There was war, poverty, no change from the past, except that things seemed to be getting worse. Until I graduated there was no proof that my father's vision was not a crazy man's idea."

We were on the road that led toward the cemetery. "Dad, what do you think your father would have said about your going to America?"

228

"He would have said, Do the best you can, do what is best for you and your wife." We had reached the open field where the soccer games were held. I became aware of the big slow presence of cows grazing not far from the edge of the road. " 'Wherever you go, be the best'—that is what my father always said."

"Do you think he'd have liked my photography?"

"He would be very proud of all his grandchildren."

"Dad, I bet Nonno Carlo would say that if I got into a college like Barnard, then I should—"

It was a night for miracles; my father didn't yell. "There is a word for you, Miss Giulia, you know that?"

"What?"

"Incor*ri*gible." I didn't correct his pronunciation. "You really want college in New York City, don't you?"

"Yes. Yes."

He sighed. "I do not understand it, Giulia, but if, for you, it is so important—"

"It is, Dad."

"Then I suggest you go for this first year to St. Helena's, take your basic courses, adjust yourself to college-level studies, and if all goes well, perhaps we will consider another college for next year."

"But, Dad, I think I could still get in to start Barnard this September."

"Next year," he told me, just as Zio Rocco had told us, *Next year.* "So tell me, what would you do if you went to this liberal no-good college?" He was smiling, and he wasn't saying no.

"I'd take art classes. I'd try to get an internship at a museum or a gallery." I slipped my arm through my father's, and he was looking at me. My father was listening to me, and we kept walking. "Dad, you know, sometimes I think I could live the rest of my life here."

"There is still much of Italy you have not seen. Venice, I

would like to show you. And then Tuscany, Umbria. *Mamma mia,* places so beautiful, so green you would not believe. I remember . . ." and there we were again, slipping into the Italy of my father's words and promises. He told me about a time during the war, he was on a train, going south, and the Allies were coming north. *"Un tempo da pazzi,"* a time of crazy people, my father told me, shaking his hand in the air, as Italians do to show that a situation is beyond control. The commanding officers said, "You're on your own." So my father jumped off the train, with other helpless soldiers, and they found themselves in a field. "I think we were just outside of Rome, but who knew? We were in a vineyard, and I have never felt so lost or afraid in my life," my father admitted to me. "But then I looked and it was beautiful, this place. Grapevines forever. You must see that someday. It is really something."

"But tell me, what happened to you and your friends?"

"Three days I think we spent in those fields. We lived on the grapes. One friend, he was Vittorio, like my brother—he kept count. 'OK, that was just another liter of wine we ate. That makes twenty liters we've stolen from this poor farmer.' During the day we slept. At night, when we could not be seen, we walked."

"Who were you hiding from?"

"Everyone. If the Italians saw us, they would say we were traitors. If the Americans found us, they might say we were the enemy. There was no TV then. Who knew what was going on?"

"Weren't you scared?"

"Of course, it was an exciting time. A time . . ."

Another of those times that felt more real to me than anything I lived myself.

"Dad, I'd love to see these places."

"Yes, yes. We will go. Bring your camera. I will take you."

At the heart of our life was—had always been—a whirlpool of confounded love, its dizzying motion fueled by words, words of promise that suspended us as gently as white parachutes, soothing words, angry words, accusing words that ricocheted. Words that denied everything and said don't you dare. Expansive words of encouragement and snickered words that teased, but also words of warning marked off routinely and predictably, like the beads of a rosary. Words I misused and others my father mispronounced. Multitudes of words, like the grains of sand on the beach, stars in a night sky, so many words but never a last word. The arguments went nowhere, could go nowhere. They just circled and circled and ended where they had begun, so that finally ending they were once more beginning. This hot, never-ending spin of emotion was dazzling, compelling, but it left me powerless, straitjacketed by the terrible, wondrous assurance that at the end of every battle to free myself from my father I would find him there again with his all-embracing love.

The next morning I woke up from a dream in which I was furious at Zia Claudia. She was walking in a place where the air felt dry—even in my sleep I could feel the thirst in my palms. I was chasing Claudia, yelling, accusing her, "You made a pact." Those words kept repeating, "You made a pact." In two weeks, I was going to be at St. Helena's. The summer was almost over, and I still had nothing in my hands I really wanted.

As everyone prepared to leave Cimalta, my father called me into his room. He was packing his suitcase. "Giulia, I must apologize to you."

It's about time, I thought to myself. "Yeah?" I said.

231

"Just now, when I looked in my suitcase I found this package. It is from your friend Molly. She asked me to bring it to you, but I had so many gifts for people in this suitcase it must have slipped to the bottom and got lost. I am very sorry I did not remember sooner."

The package fit in the palm of my hand. It was soft, all padded inside, and wrapped with paper that was covered with big peace signs. Seeing it, I missed Molly. My name was written in fat bubble handwriting, a big circle dotted each *i*. I tore away the wrapping paper, but underneath, the package was wrapped again and taped tightly. There was a note in a sealed envelope. I opened it. In big emphatic handwriting, underlined in red, Molly had written, OPEN THIS ONLY WHEN YOU ARE ALONE. DO YOU HEAR ME? ALONE. ALONE. ALONE.

"So what does Molly have to say?" my father asked.

"I'm still opening it, Dad." I headed for the bathroom. "Thanks a lot for bringing it."

I sat on the bathroom floor with my back against the door. Now my heart was beating fast. If Molly had planted marijuana on my father, I was going to kill her. But the package rattled as I opened it. I was afraid something had broken. I tore away the second layer of paper. There was tissue paper, then some layers of Kleenex, and finally I found a round pink packet the size of a compact. Was it makeup? Acne medicine? I lifted the pink plastic lid, and arranged in a small circle perfect as the full moon was a month's worth of birth control pills. Another note was taped to the bottom of the packet:

Dear Giulia,
So, here's enough to get you started. Read the
directions. One a day for seven days, and you're set.
They're easy as anything. I should know. Guess what
I've been doing this summer? So now's as good a time

as any to tell you—especially since you've landed that hot Italian—I've been *seeing* someone new. Keith and I broke up. Well, it's not just someone. It's Morrisey. Yeah, well, go ahead, hate me. I know I'm an asshole friend. But you were gone and he was here. But don't sweat it, he's kind of a jerk. More on that when you get home. Just don't hate me, OK?

The pills? Cindi and I went to this free women's clinic in Cleveland and when we told them we were going away to college, they gave us a whole artillery of birth control. I'm not kidding. Our purses were *packed*. It was such a riot. You should have been there. But what I really want to tell you, Di Cuore, is HAVE FUN. Don't miss your chance with this Italian (even if he's got a weird name. Luc*a*? Are you sure he's a guy?). I miss you and I'll be waiting at the airport to hear all about it.

Love ya, M.

Daniele was knocking on the door. "Giulia, hurry. Emergency."

"One minute, Dan-i-e-le." I sang his name. My mother had left me when I was ten, but not before she taught me some things. I swallowed the first pill immediately. *Daddy doesn't need to know about this, you hear?* I had no idea what would happen when I got back to Luca, but there were more possibilities now. I wrapped the packet up in Molly's paper and buttoned the gift into my skirt pocket.

Later, in the car, when we were beyond the borders of Cimalta and everyone was silent, my father turned to me in the back seat and asked, "So, how did you like the film Molly sent?"

"Huh?"

"Molly was very concerned about the film getting ruined. 'Do not put it in the sun. Do not do this, do not do

233

that.' I told her, 'Molly, I am sure Giulia can buy film in Italy if she needs it.' But Molly wanted to make sure you had enough. She is very complimentary of your photography, you know?"

"Yeah," I said. Molly was fearless. "She's a good friend."

"I just do not understand how I did not see her package in my suitcase sooner. It is strange. I know I emptied that suitcase when I first arrived, but I never saw the package until we were in Cimalta."

Daniele and Carlino looked at each other, eyes wide. "Zio Nicola?" Daniele said quietly, cautiously.

"Sì, bello?"

"Zio, maybe it was San Francesco."

"Yes," Carlino said solemnly. "It was him. San Francesco put the package there."

SIXTEEN

Leaving

ON THE DRIVE back from Cimalta we stopped in Montemaggiore to pick up the mail. We were getting into the elevator of the apartment building when the *portiera* came out of her apartment waving a telegram. It was for my father. "Thank God you came," she said. "For three days this telegram has been staring at me and—please, just open it."

We all watched my father's eyes widen and his face drop as he read.

"Nicola! What is it?"

He shook his head.

"Nicola!" everyone screamed. "Who is it from?"

"The airlines. Giulia, there is a problem with our plane tickets."

The *portiera* threw up her hands. "For this you are upset? For this I've been trembling? Thank God it's nothing bad."

On the way upstairs in the elevator a woman I'd never

seen before asked us, "Did you get your telegram? Is everything all right?"

"Yes, *signora,* thank you."

As Zio Anto unlocked the door, his next-door neighbor stuck his head out the door. "Anto, a telegram came for your brother."

"Thank you. We got it."

"Nothing bad, I hope."

"Nothing unmanageable."

Before he even took off his jacket, my father was on the telephone to the airlines. They told him our flight was canceled because of a one-day airport strike scheduled for our day of departure. Passengers had been alerted and asked to call in to rebook as soon as possible. By the time my father called, the only two seats available were on two different flights leaving a week apart.

My father spoke with several different managers—to some in Italian, to others in English—but it ended with him saying, "No, I cannot reschedule. No, I cannot leave my daughter in Italy for one week without me. Where are we, the Soviet Union? This sort of thing would not be tolerated in America," and he slammed down the phone. "Anto, do you know any travel agents in Montemaggiore?"

"Of course, but you've already talked with the airlines in Rome. The travel agents can't tell you anything Rome didn't tell you."

"Well, we have to try. Wait here, Giulia," my father told me, and he stomped out the door with my uncle to go do what had to be done.

Two hours later, they came back, defeated. "I am sorry, Giulia. There is nothing to be done. We will have to leave on different flights. I must take the earlier flight. I have to get back for my classes to begin and you do not start school for a few weeks."

"When do you leave, Dad?"

"Saturday."

"And I leave the next Saturday?"

"Yes."

Zia Assunta's arm was tight around my shoulders. "Eh, well, at least we won't be losing you both at the same time."

"Really, this is perfect," Zio Anto said. "Carlo was planning to leave for Rome that Friday. He and Giulia can go together on the train. That way, Giulia won't have to travel alone, and Carlo can make sure she gets her plane all right."

"He can help her with her suitcases," my aunt said. "Yes, it's perfect."

My father wasn't convinced. "Carlo is traveling alone, without Luca?"

"Luca is leaving sooner, with Renata and Mauro."

Later, my father warned me, "I do not like this situation, I do not like it at all. But I hope you will be able to behave yourself."

"Trust me, Dad. Trust me."

Back at the beach a few days later, going for the newspapers (Zio Anto read the Christian Democrat newspaper, Zio Vito read the Socialist newspaper, and neither would buy a paper for the other, so Nicola went out every morning and bought newspapers for everyone), my father and I were alone and he confided, "I do not know how my brothers live here—strikes, no organization, disorder. How do they stay in a house with no telephone?"

"But there's the phone at the bar," I said. After I'd spent three months in Calabria, this sounded logical to me.

"Do you think that is professional, especially for doctors? How would you like if your physician had no phone."

"But don't you think there's something kind of nice about the kids from the bar running over with phone messages, and the *portiera* and the neighbors getting all worried about your telegram? It's like you're not alone, there're people looking out for you. It's more human or humane or something. I like it here."

"Human, humane. You are talking about abstracts that have very little to do with the reality of getting from day to day. If I buy an airplane ticket I want to know I can fly. If I need my doctor I want to know I can reach him."

"But Dad, there's something about living in Italy—I think it's better than home in a lot of ways." I was in the ridiculous situation of defending Italy to my father.

Two days before my father was scheduled to leave, Don Marco, the owner of our beach house, came by. He was an elderly man in a light-colored suit, a straw hat, dark-tinted glasses. His cheeks were dappled with liver spots. He carried an umbrella, which he used as a cane. When my uncles introduced Don Marco, my father didn't stand up, he just extended his hand for a curt handshake and said, "So, finally, the elusive Don Marco appears. Now, at the end of the season, when our problems with this house are just about over."

"Problems? What problems?" Don Marco made a face that said he was scandalized. "Problems in this house? No!"

"Sit down," my father told him. "Have a *caffè*. Take a piece of paper and I will give you a list."

"Thank you for your invitation, but, unfortunately, I have little time. My nephew is right outside in the car waiting for me. We were driving around these parts and I thought I should drop in to tell you that if you are interested for next summer—"

"Many changes must take place here before next summer," my father said.

"Tell him, Nicola, tell him," Zia Assunta said.

"The women," Zio Anto said apologetically, "a few small things in the kitchen get them upset, but next summer, of course we'd like the house next summer."

"Anto, no!"

"Well, decide among yourselves," Don Marco said. "If you are interested I will give you the name of the new owner. I am selling the house. I wasn't looking, but a banker from Cosenza made an offer."

Zio Vito came in closer around Don Marco. "An offer?"

"Can we ask you, what did he offer you?"

"Twenty million lire."

Zia Assunta whispered to Zia Berta, "Crazy people. Twenty million for this dump."

"Don Marco, we will offer you twenty-three," my father said.

"Nicola!" the women screamed.

"Rocco loves this house." My father was holding up his hands, defending himself. "You all love it."

Don Marco clenched his hands together like a priest and begged my aunts and uncles and father, "Please, before you start war with each other, I can't consider another offer. This banker and I, we have an agreement, no contracts, but a verbal agreement. It would be hard to refuse him. He saw the house last May and has been after me all summer to negotiate."

"We will give you twenty-four," my father said. "Part of it in American cash."

Don Marco's face widened as he considered new possibilities.

Carlino came out of the house and stepped into the

loaded silence in the courtyard. "What happened?" he asked his mother.

"Your Zio Nicola just went crazy."

"Come on, come on, Don Marco, make it twenty-four million five, and that's it," Zio Vito grabbed the old man's arm and shook his hand to close up the deal. "It's a good offer and you know it. Use the extra to take your banker friend to dinner. You'll find him another house."

Zio Anto put his hand on Don Marco's shoulder, "If there *is* a banker friend, eh, Don Marco? Eh?" My father, Zio Anto and Zio Vito grinned at him. "You were trying to scare us?"

"Sus-pi-cious," Don Marco said, and laughed. "The guilty are always suspicious."

"But we have to do this thing fast," my father said. "I leave the day after tomorrow."

"As you like, Professore. I am at your service." Don Marco bowed.

"What made you decide?" I asked my father later. "A couple weeks ago you said you'd never buy this house. You said it would be buying a bunch of problems."

"Giulia, do you see this location? Right on the beach? Seaside property is always valuable. I see you know very little about real estate."

The next morning Don Marco returned with his lawyer. The papers included all four brothers' names, checks were handed over, and for the first time in his life my father owned property—one-fourth of a house on the beach in Italy.

That night the men were sitting at the table playing Briscola. Zio Vito got up to get a glass of water, and my father, shuffling the cards, said, "Vito, while you're in the kitchen, would you get me a beer?" How natural it must have felt for him to be with his brothers, to be able to make that simple request of Vito. And how precious all of it would seem to him the next week when he was gone.

During my father's last days in Italy, Luca and I continued to meet in the orange and lemon groves. Mostly, we argued about Rome. There was no way to turn. I knew I couldn't go with him, but when his hands were on me, I couldn't imagine leaving. How do you stop your heart from wanting what it wants? One afternoon we stayed longer than usual and I rushed home. Zio Rocco's car was parked in front of the house and my father was at the gate, smiling. "We were waiting for you! Hurry, you are the only one missing."

"We came to say goodbye to your father," Zio Rocco explained when he saw me. "We're staying only a minute."

But the aunts were already bringing out *pasta aglio e olio*. They had squid frying on the stove, the way Rocco liked it. They wanted Nicola to have one more supper with everyone all together.

At the end of the meal, while the others waited for the fruit, I got my camera and went up to the balcony that hung over the courtyard. With a wide-angle lens I could catch the whole stretch of the table with its uneven terrain of plates, and bowls, and glasses, and green and brown bottles. I saw the four bald spots on the tops of the heads of the four brothers. Zia Assunta and la Signora, each with a mountain of hair on top of her head. Zia Berta, with her dark glasses up, talking to Zia Claudia. Giuliana and Mariagiulia huddled together whispering, Giulietta and Daniele sparring with their forks. There was Carlino's feathery hair I loved to play with. Nonna Giulia holding Giancarlo on her lap.

Francesca looked up, her smart little face. "Hey every-

241

one," she yelled, "look up, look up!" And I caught them, all their surprised faces. A moment later, when they were smiling up at me, I snapped the shutter again.

The next morning, our caravan of cars drove solemnly through the predawn dark to the airport at Lamezia for my father to get the flight to Rome. They all cried as they hugged him goodbye, but I was sure that as soon as my father left, the happy days would return to our beach house.

Then I was watching him walk through the gate toward the plane. He was halfway there, and I called him back. "Dad!" I shouted, my American voice breaking through the Italian dawn. "Dad, come here." As he came rushing back, the others wiped their eyes and asked, "What happened?"

"What?" he asked when he got back to the gate. He noticed I was crying and he reached through the fence, put his hand on my face. "Giulia, what's wrong?"

"Nothing," I told him. "I just wanted to hug you again."

Oddly, that day never did brighten. For the first time all summer, there were clouds over the beach and enough wind to whip the water into froth. Unsure of what else to do, I went swimming, as usual, but the waves were huge, the tops of them rising up past my face, and they kept coming, wild, like animals. Just when the waves reached me, I closed my eyes, lost track of how tall they were. Then it wasn't water anymore, just something that was happening to me—grabbing me, falling over me, taking me with it. I was gone, there was nothing but the waves, their power and motion and pull and rhythm.

· · · ·

242

In the days after my father left, Luca showed up early in the morning, he was with me in the afternoon and at night. My aunts and uncles were busy preparing to leave the house. No one had the energy or the desire to be as vigilant over me as my father had been. Luca and I had been given an extra week; it was a miracle. We walked on the beach, wherever we wanted; once we rode his motorcycle to his parents' house but Mauro was there, so we left and rode up into the hills for hours. Anytime we were alone, I cried.

"Come to Rome with me," Luca coaxed. "Come."

"Don't say that. You know I don't want to leave you."

"Then don't leave. You're leaving for what? For St. Helena?"

"Oh, Luca, you know I have to go back."

When we had only two days left, Luca said to me, "I want us to spend a night together before you leave."

"How, Luca? It's impossible." I started to cry again. "We'll never be able to spend a night together, never have the chance to sleep next to each other, never have the chance—"

"Stop it, Giulia. Tonight, come to the beach."

"We'll never see each other again after I leave."

"I'll meet you outside your house. Late. Three o'clock this morning."

"Impossible."

"Bring a sweater, sometimes it's cold."

"We'll never—"

"Don't sleep. Watch your clock. Come down to the courtyard at three and I'll be waiting."

The marble hallways echoed with my family's snoring as I slipped through the house. There were twelve of us all together; I knew someone had to be awake and listening,

243

but I was ready. If anyone stopped me I would say I wanted to sit out and breathe the air so that later at St. Helena's I could remember these Italian nights. I wouldn't be lying.

Passing through the kitchen, I picked up a slice of bread to feed the stray cats wandering in the dark. The kitchen door opened soundlessly. Softly, in bare feet, I crossed the courtyard. I could already see Luca's face outside the gate. The moon was more than half full, and bright. We didn't say a word as I climbed over the gate. His face below me was upturned and smiling, and I thought, If I could ever have what I want, it would be him. We never spoke until we got to the beach, then we crossed over the rocks— "Careful, watch your feet"—and then the houses were behind us, and finally we could hold on to each other.

We were both wearing sweaters. "This is how it would be in winter, if we were together."

"Oh Luca, I'll never see you in your coat and your hat and gloves. I'll never see you in your winter clothes."

"What is worse is we may never see each other again out of our clothes," he said mournfully and made me laugh.

We walked all the way to the old hotel, that skeleton of old vacations. We sat and shared a cigarette, but the sand was cool and damp, so I got up to put my feet in the water, which was warmer than the air. Luca came and stood behind me; his hands held my breasts.

"Will we write letters?" he asked me.

"I don't know if I can write Italian."

The water sloshed up to our knees. We walked farther in, then a wave came over us and left us almost completely wet. The warm water felt so good. I pulled away from Luca and tugged off my sweater, threw it up onto the sand, then pulled off my T-shirt. Luca pulled off his. My shorts came off. Then his. My underwear. His. I dove into the water and Luca followed. I swam and swam until he yelled to me to stop, then he caught up with me and I held on to his shoulders and we floated toward the shore together.

Luca sat in the shallow water and leaned back, stretched out his legs, to keep himself under the warm water. I stayed covered with water too, lying on my stomach next to him, watching moonlight drip down his face. We kissed, then he pulled me closer, so I was floating right above him. I felt my legs opening, making room for his hands, inviting him. I dug my knees into the wet sand, and on either side of Luca's face my hands clutched wet sand. I pushed myself up and my breasts rose and hung in the moonlight, and Luca's mouth followed them, up and up, and my legs wrapped around his. And his fingers were inside me, and I was all water, inside and out. I felt him against my thigh and I felt myself lifting and moving above him, against him, and a wave washing over us, and his mouth on my breast, and I reached down for him. He was throbbing and I covered him with my own throbbing, and as soon as he was inside me he fell back.

"Giulia, is this all right?"

My eyes were open. I was ready. (When I'd told Renata I was taking the pills Molly sent, she laughed and said, "Americana, I think you've become a real Italian girl this summer.") "It's all right, Luca."

"Yes?" he said, as he moved deeper, and I moved with him and together we pressed down into the warm wet bed of sand, and waves covered us like blankets, again and again, over and over. "Luca," I whispered. "Luca." Luca a thousand times.

Afterward, with his hands on my bottom, he said, *"Sei mia. Tutta mia."* You're all mine.

. . . .

By the time we headed back, the sky was light enough to see the fishermen's boats sailing into the harbor. I kissed Luca and he ran his hand up inside my sweater, then he left. He couldn't come closer, in case anyone was watching. As I walked toward home, the sea was still dark but the mountains behind the house were taking shape. Color was creeping into the sky. The blue shutters were all pulled shut. Our big white house was tranquil, silent, and I thought, All summer long, how many dreams had been dreamt in that house.

Up in the room of the Giulias, I took off my damp clothes and slid under the sheets. The other Giulias were sleeping. I fell asleep, too, and dreamed I was in the piazza in Cimalta. It was an afternoon during San Francesco's feast, and the chairs were lined up, ready for the movies. Only a few old women were sitting here and there. I sat in a chair, in a row by myself. Then I looked behind me and saw my mother sitting a few rows back. She was young and healthy, as in the photographs my father and I had found. How lucky, I thought in the dream, I've been wanting to ask her some questions. I went and sat next to her. "Mom, can you see me?" I asked. "I mean, every day, as I'm going about my days, can you see what I'm doing?"

She shook her head no, and I was disappointed and kept asking, "You mean you can't see me at all?" and she shook her head again, no. She wouldn't talk, and I very much wanted to hear her say something. "Mom, not at all, you can't see me at all?"

And finally she said, slowly, as if in saying even a word she was giving something away, "When I see you"—her voice was very slow—"I see you as you were as a little girl. Standing on your head, doing spins on the floor."

"You can't leave now," Luca whispered to me later that day as my aunts were clearing away the dinner dishes.

246

Nonna Giulia was at the head of the table listening to Daniele recite his prayers, and la Signora was at the other end of the table saying her after-dinner rosary. Luca and I were alone at the middle of the table. He was tossing a peach up and down, his nervous habit.

"Don't make me cry in front of them, Luca. You know I don't want to go."

He said nothing, just let my protest linger and echo stupidly in the air. Then he leaned toward me. "Giulia, maybe you don't want to come with me, maybe you don't want Rome. That hurts me, but it's OK. Still, you know, someday you're going to have to say no to your father."

I grabbed the peach from Luca.

He took it back and began peeling. It was a ripe peach, parts of its skin deep red, scarlet, maroon, like velvet swatches in Cetta's sewing drawer. I wished Cetta could have met him. *If you miss one bus, you'll catch the next. But when do you stop? When do you know?* Luca pierced the skin and slid the knife just underneath. He moved his knife along so gently, he wasn't cutting, just lifting the skin from the fruit. He had doctor's hands, like my father's and my uncles'. The peel hanging from the peach was cut so fine it was almost translucent. "What do you want to do, Giulia?" he said without looking at me.

"It doesn't matter what I want. I can never do what I want," I whispered.

"But why?" he whispered back. "You have every possibility." Then his eyes were on me and I had that feeling, like that first morning, that I could do anything. "You say you love Rome. You say you love me. You say you hate St. Helena's. This is your chance, Giulia."

"Where would we live?"

"In the same apartment where Carlo and I are going to live. There's room."

"What will we use for money?" I asked, and when the

words were out, I realized that this time I had said *will* and not *would*.

"We'll manage with whatever my parents send for me."

"I could sell my plane ticket."

He smiled at me. "So you are coming?"

I said nothing. I watched the knife moving around the peach, his hands so steady. I could say yes to Luca and change my life completely, or I could say no. Would it be reasonable to say no, or was it smart to say yes? If he peels that peach without breaking the skin, I told myself, then I'll go to Rome with him.

There was juice on his wrist. The peach had a difficult shape, a deep dent, a welt, a seam.

"Eh, Giulia, si o no?"

I watched and he kept cutting and when the peach skin fell to the plate in a single spiral, I told Luca, *"Vengo."* I'll come.

It was my last night at the beach. "Giulia," Zia Assunta said as we finished supper. "You've got to start packing."

I couldn't move.

"Go, Giulia, get started."

"Oh, Marigiù, Giuliana, please come sit with me. I can't pack alone." We went up to the room of the Giulias and piled everything onto my narrow bed.

"You'll never fit it all into two suitcases," Marigiulia warned me.

"I have to. I have to. I can't leave anything behind."

"OK, OK, don't cry. Come on, we'll help you. But where did you get all this stuff?"

My aunts had given me a white tablecloth with eyelet insets, a setting for sixteen. I lined the bottom of the suitcase with the cloth and used the embroidered napkins to wrap the porcelain ashtrays and saucers, mementos I'd snatched from cafes up and down the Calabrian coast. My

uncles had given me a tripod. I stuffed that and my platform shoes deep in the bottom. "Save these, Americana,
for your hope chest," la Signora had said when she gave
me the table scarves she'd crocheted for me; I used them to
wrap the Sicilian pottery and demitasse cups and saucers
and the serving tray the relatives in Cimalta had given me.
I piled on the gifts I'd got for everyone in Homefield: ma-
terial for Cetta and Aunt Sofia, statues from the shrine of
San Francesco, bikinis for Lina and Molly, fistfuls of Vesuvius for Carl and Skip. A bag of colored beach glass. "Oh,
I forgot about this." Early on, my aunts had bought me a
fringed shawl at the market. When I put it on, Giulietta
had told me, *"O Giulia, con questo farai molte con-
quiste."* With this you'll make many conquests. I had got
so much in Italy, but still there was that desperate feeling
that something crucial was just out of reach.

"What is *this?*" Giuliana demanded, holding out a
dried-up peach pit on her hand.

"I need that." Two nights before, Luca had held it in his
mouth.

"You're hopeless," the girls told me.

Nonna Giulia appeared in the doorway, panting. She
had never been on the second floor of the house. She could
kill a chicken, but climbing one flight of steps left her
winded. "Two hours you've been up here and there's no
progress. Americana, how will the airplane get off the
ground with all this junk? Are you trying to take half of
Calabria with you?"

"No. I want all of it."

She pulled a chair over with her foot and sat down.
"Leave a space to pack this." She held out a thick package
and pulled away the tissue wrapper. "See? Look, you like
it?" It was a bedspread, hundreds of palm-size crocheted
circles all joined together. "For you, Americana." For my
hope chest.

"How did you finish the whole thing?" Marigiulia and Giuliana unfolded it and spread it out in my lap.

"How do you think? I stayed up late all week so Giulia could take it with her. Don't worry, I'm making more for the two of you and for Lina."

"I thought we weren't supposed to get them until we got engaged."

"Ah, who knows when we'll see the Americana again. At least I know, wherever she ends up, she's ready."

The bedspread was white and soft and so extensive, it was like holding a wave of seawater in my arms.

"Oh, Giulia, don't cry. Come on, let's find room in that suitcase."

"No, I want this in my backpack, so I'll have it near me." I unzipped the pack and envelopes of photographs fell out.

"Oh, oh, oh, I see you've been stealing from my house." Nonna caught a handful of pictures I'd taken from the desk in Cimalta.

"I just took the ones of my mother." Nonna Giulia was holding up a picture, and Giuliana and Marigiulia came over to look. "It's OK, Nonna, isn't it?"

"I remember Margherita wearing these white short pants. She was the first girl to wear pants in Cimalta. Did you know that? Nicola wanted her to put those trousers back in the suitcase, and she started crying. But I told her, 'Margherita, if you're going to marry Nicola you can't listen to every little thing he says.' "

Nonna handed me the picture and started folding up the bedspread. "I'm telling you the same thing, Americana. I saw you this summer—you let your father get your stomach tied in knots. You've got to decide—either do what he wants and be happy, or do what you want and be happy." She got the package into the backpack and zipped it shut. "You're at an age—all of you Giulias are—when you should begin to know your own head. Life is difficult, but you can't drag the cross to Calvary every time you have to make a decision." She pushed me gently aside and started unpacking the mess I'd made. "Or every time you have to pack a suitcase. See? You have to roll the clothes up tight, like this."

Giuliana leaned over and kissed Nonna on the forehead. "It takes a peasant to pack a suitcase."

"How can you go anywhere in life? All this screaming about schools and universities, but you kids aren't going to get very far if you don't know how to pack a suitcase."

Giuliana, Marigiulia and I sat cross-legged on the beds and watched her. "Nonna, when we were in Cimalta, I wanted to ask you to show me something, but there was so much going on. That barrel in the basement where Nonno Carlo found the money that San Francesco left. Did you ever know exactly how much he found under there?"

She was filling the toe of a sneaker with seashells. "You don't believe that story, do you?"

"I don't know. Everyone else in the family does. I want to believe it."

"Well, you don't have to believe it, because the story is not true." Marigiulia and Giuliana stared at her, and she told them, "It's not true. San Francesco didn't put that money there. My mother put it there, right after I got married. My father gave Carlo and me the barrel of olives for our wedding. But my mother, and who knows why, came to me a few weeks afterward and said, 'Here, keep this money in a safe place. Tell no one, not your husband, not your father.'"

I laughed, "In case you wanted to take off?"

"People didn't leave their husbands then. We didn't have that stupidity. My mother knew Carlo was a good man. And he was, your grandfather. But my mother had

251

been through one war. She said you never know what's going to happen in life. She wanted the money to give me peace of mind, I guess."

"You never told Nonno Carlo?"

"I completely forgot the money was there. I swear, I forgot. It was a miracle that Carlo tilted the barrel that day—see, now, *that's* the work of San Francesco. It was only when I saw the money that I remembered my mother giving it to me."

Marigiulia came closer. "But Nonna, you never told anyone, not our fathers, not Zia Sofia, no one?"

"No one."

"Then why us?"

She sighed. "I thought it would help you to know, you girls. Life can be so difficult. At least in my time a woman knew a man would take care of her. Even in Sofia's time. A nice American soldier came and took her and made her a home. But, you girls, I want you to know there's nothing wrong with looking out for yourself. Keep your eyes open. You understand?"

I smiled at her. "You mean we shouldn't wait for a saint to leave us piles of money."

"But Nonna, even if we don't tell anyone else, shouldn't we tell poor Daniele? That story of San Francesco coming to sit on Nonno Carlo's chair and talking to him, it keeps Daniele awake at night, really it does. Tell him the truth."

"Oh no, Giuliana, that is the truth," Nonna said, and her face was completely serious. "The saint visited. That part of the story is absolutely true. I swear it."

The next morning at the train station, Zio Anto took my face in his hands and kissed me. Zio Vito said, "Americana, good luck." My aunts gave Carlo and me big bags of *panini* and fruit and water for our lunch. La Signora tucked rosary beads into my hand. The kids had turned shy, as if I were a stranger again. Only Nonna Giulia was smiling. "Americana," she said, "Giulia, you have a good head. Make sure you use it."

Just when it was time for Carlo and me to board, a ten-minute delay was announced. Grateful, I closed my eyes. *Please God, what I want is to stay with my family and never leave. It is wrong to leave your family.* But then the bell was ringing and the men were grabbing my suitcases, rushing me up the high steps onto the train, and I was trying to kiss every one of them again. And then I was on the train, reaching out the window for their hands. And then we were moving, and I sat in the seat across from Carlo and felt the train gaining speed.

Yawning, Carlo said, "Americana, for a week now you've been crying."

"But I don't know when I'll see them again."

"Me, I couldn't wait to leave."

The train tracks were alongside the beach, and I ran across the aisle to look out the windows at the sea. It stretched out in front of me and was the deep color of lapis lazuli. A motorboat was racing over the waves, leaving behind a white tail of foam whipping like a comet. I leaned far out the window, into the Italian summer, and recited, like an incantation, like a prayer with the power to bring me back, the names of that string of beach towns that lay along the coast: Tropea, Briatico, Capo Vaticano, Amantea, Fuscaldo, Guardia Piemontese.

Then we were in a tunnel, the beach gone, and I went back to the compartment. Carlo seemed to be sound asleep. The night before, he hadn't slept at all. I knew that. In the dim light of 4:45 in the morning, I had heard stones tapping the shutters of my bedroom. I jumped out of bed, stepped out onto the balcony. I was expecting it to be Luca, but it was Carlo, hanging from the top of the gate, waving his arms at me. His bright white teeth gleamed as he told me with a thousand gestures but not one word that just minutes earlier he had crawled out of the window of Loredana's bedroom.

Now he muttered across to me, "So the plan is all set, right? There's nothing for me to do until we get to the station at Paola and meet Luca?"

"Yes."

"Good. Wake me when we get there."

I guess I fell asleep too, because the next thing I heard was the conductor announcing *"Paola. Stazione Paola."*

"Carlo, wake up. We're here."

Luca was supposed to be at the station with his motorcycle, I was going to meet up with him so he wouldn't have to ride all the way to Rome by himself. But Luca was nowhere in sight. Carlo wouldn't let me get off the train. "I can't let you go by yourself. What if Luca doesn't show up?"

"He'll be here, Carlo. He's late. I've got to wait."

The bell was ringing for the train to leave when we spotted Luca running down the train platform. "Giulia!" he was calling.

"LU-ca." The aisles were packed with people getting on the train, but from the old women in the markets, I had learned how to shove my way through a crowd. I got to Luca on the platform. Carlo was lowering my two suitcases through the window when Luca said, "Wait! I just realized, we can't take these on the motorcycle." None of us had thought that far ahead. "Carlo, please, you've got to take the suitcases to Rome." As we pushed the bags back up through the window the train was pulling away, Luca was running with the train, heaving up the last suitcase. Just in time, Carlo pulled it in.

And then it was just Luca and me.

·   ·   ·   ·

We rode the motorcycle all the way to Rome. Later, I remembered very little of that trip. Just hours of being pressed against Luca's back, my hands feeling his stomach moving in and out as he breathed, watching the median strip of pink oleanders on the autostrada race past us. Both of us were wearing helmets, the hard plastic separating us, making it difficult to talk. We saw mountains, bridges over valleys, tiered fields of grapes. All I heard was the wind racing and trucks passing and Luca calling out the names of cities as we drove by the exits: *Salerno, Napoli,* and finally, after ten hours, *Roma Centro.*

Luca and Carlo's apartment was a place Renata had found for them. It was near the Campo dei Fiori, back in the side streets. To get to the entrance, we had to walk through a small alley sliced between two ancient buildings. We climbed four flights of dark stone steps. I saw very little that first night. Just a big cool room with a single bed, a cot, a small table, a few chairs. As soon as I fell across the bed Luca reached for me, ran his hands over my hips. "Don't you dare," I told him, "don't you dare even think about touching me. Do you know how I hurt?"

I think he said something like "Americana, we did it. We're in Rome," but I was already on the brink of deep sleep.

We woke the next morning, early, when Carlo pushed open the door and knocked over a chair. From the doorway, he threw one suitcase into the room, then he threw in three more. *"La dolce vita,"* he yelled at us.

"Carlo, you're making so much noise."

"You get used to it if you spend the night in the train station."

"Ah! We were supposed to meet you! Carlo, we completely forgot."

"I had no key. I had no address for the apartment.

Good thing I remembered the name of Renata's bar. I had to wait until this morning when she opened so I could get the key. All night in the train station. Do you know how many prostitutes had their eye on these American suitcases?"

"*Mamma mia,* Carlo, we're sorry."

"Sorry means nothing. Move over and let me sleep."

We gave Carlo the bed, and Luca and I curled onto the cot and slept until noon. When we woke, Carlo was still out cold. Luca and I went down into the neighborhood to get food. Later, when Carlo woke up, three *panini* of prosciutto and provolone and two chilled beers were waiting for him. Halfway through the first *panino,* Carlo had forgiven us.

And the three of us began our days in Rome.

SEVENTEEN

La Guerra È Finita

IT WAS ONLY when I stopped to think about it that it seemed fantastic. Otherwise, my life in Rome with Luca felt completely natural. The small one-room apartment Renata had found for the boys was too small for three of us, so after a week Carlo moved to a place nearby. He was sharing an apartment with the cousin of a student he had just met and fallen in love with; she was from Venice and her name was Loredana.

Luca and I had a wide view that took in our neighbors' vine-covered balconies, the domes of two nearby churches and a slice of the Pantheon's roof. Inside, our walls were ugly, dirty beige, stained, cracked, so I covered them with my photographs of Rome; then the city surrounded us inside and out. We pushed together the bed and the cot and covered them with big sheets. We had a table and three straight-back chairs and one spongy armchair. We had a miniature refrigerator. We had a hot plate with two burners and one tiny burner for the Italian coffeepot. We brushed our teeth at the kitchen sink, and that's where we washed out our clothes (so we could save the money Luca's mother sent him to have his laundry done), and that's where Luca shaved while I sat on a stool watching. The toilet was in a room as small as a closet. To get to our shower, we crossed an outdoor walkway lined with potted geraniums, and we stamped our feet hard so the waterbugs would skitter away.

Above the stove, a spot where Aunt Sofia would have hung a plaque of the Madonna, I hung a photo of Zia Berta I'd taken at the beach house: she was standing in front of the herb garden, first thing in the morning, still in her robe. Her eyes sleepy, but concentrating, as she decided what dinner would be that day. She was bent over, pulling green sprigs here and there; she was saying, "A little of this and a bit of this," as if it had all come to her in a dream.

Luca and I woke when we heard the church bells across the street, gonging together, then separately, then almost together. When Luca didn't have early classes, we went for breakfast at Renata's bar, rushing to get there before 9:20, when the bakery man brought in the second delivery of hot *cornetti.* Renata's windows faced the Campo dei Fiori, which filled every morning with the fruit and vegetable market. Yawning, Luca and I leaned over Renata's counter and watched the vendors bicker and shout. "Look at those fools, one of these days they're going to kill each other and I'll have a front-row seat." Every morning she treated us to our *caffè,* however we wanted it: *caffè con latte, latte macchiato, cappuccino, doppio caffè, caffè freddo, caffè caldo, caffè* in a glass or a cup.

From Renata's, Luca and I went out to the market to buy our food. We were frugal with our money, sometimes buying only three or four tomatoes or a handful of green beans, such a small amount that the vendors told us it wasn't even worth their time to weigh it. *"Ragazzi,"* they yelled at us, *"la guerra è finita."* The war is over.

From the market, we went to pick up Carlo, and together, the three of us wandered until noon, when the neighborhood streets filled with the scent of dinner cooking in the homes above. If the aroma spilling down from a window was particularly wonderful, Carlo and Luca would call up, "Signora, won't you invite us for dinner?" Once an old woman did invite us up and fed us homemade tortellini.

Usually at dinnertime, we went home with whatever we had bought—purple or white eggplants, long-stemmed artichokes, flat beans, round beans, white or purple beans, peas, magenta beets still powdered with soil, tomatoes, potatoes, olives and onions. Parsley, basil, escarole, spinach, and other green leafy vegetables I'd never heard of or seen. Together, the three of us would experiment, every day a different concoction to mix with our pasta. Then, on the days when the hot water was used up, we boiled a big pot of water to wash the dishes.

This was my life—the full sweeping expanse of it was all mine, not just moments pulled from my father's teeth.

The days of September were warm, like leftover summer, like some new season that didn't have a name. It wasn't the ominous autumn of Homefield, that feeling that soon you'd have to turn inward, that some small death was on its way. Even Indian summer in Ohio was no relief—rose petals smelling sickeningly sweet all over our back yard. But in Rome, even late at night, our windows were open. Car alarms and cat fights. I wore a short denim skirt most of the time, and tank tops. Into October Luca wore white tennis shorts, no shirt. How hot it was up in our slant-ceilinged room, but our tile floor turned cool in the evenings and felt so good. The bottoms of our feet were always dirty.

Luca and I couldn't bear to leave each other, so while he studied I sat a few feet away from his desk, trying to read the Italian newspapers, which always put me to sleep. After a little doze, I'd wake up and there he'd be, his never-ending shoulders and his wide, dark back curving, tensing, sighing while he concentrated. At one or two in the morning, we'd make love. Then, famished, we'd bring out olives, hard cheese and bread. Sometimes we roasted hot peppers or fried eggs. We'd follow each other around the apartment telling long elaborate stories, in two different languages.

Rome was, for all three of us—Luca, Carlo and me— the place where, for the first time, we were completely on our own. More than anything else, we were proud of the keys to our apartments, which Luca and Carlo tossed back and forth to each other while we hung out in the Campo with other students in the evening. They all spoke those fast streetwise dialects, and I listened, studied them, and tried to learn. Sometimes, across the crowd, I'd look at Luca and realize that if I didn't know him already, I'd pick him out over and over again.

Every time someone new joined the crowd in the Campo, our friends asked us to tell the story of how we had come to Rome, how I got off the train and climbed onto Luca's motorcycle.

"So, are you here forever?" they asked me. I shrugged. (All I knew was that I believed so completely in our happiness I imagined nothing would ever change, and I'd become completely careless with my U.S. passport. It showed up every few days in all kinds of places—in a pile of dirty clothes, under the hotplate, stuck deep in a book.)

"And your father?" everyone asked me.

"He's getting used to my being here," I said, which

wasn't true yet, but I was determined that with time it would be true.

When I had called my father from Rome and told him I hadn't taken the plane, he said, "Get on a flight tomorrow."

"Dad, please. I've thought about this a lot and I just think—well, I'm happy here. I wouldn't be happy at St. Helena's. It feels like a prison sentence, Dad. College shouldn't feel like that."

"But it is the school *you* chose." He sounded so baffled, lost, and that old urge was there—to melt for him, feel sorry, give him what he wanted.

"Look," I said firmly, but my throat hurt from the effort of holding back tears. "Dad, this is what I want. There's a lot for me to learn here. My Italian's getting better. I'm taking tons of pictures. Dad, there's no place better in the world for me to be."

"There is a flight tomorrow afternoon. Do you know how to call the airlines?"

"I'm staying."

"Giulia, do not make me fly over there to get you."

"Then what are you going to do? Beat me up?"

Silence. I could almost hear the ocean waves cracking between us.

"Dad, listen, I'm in a safe place. It's clean, it's cheap and I'm going to start a job next week, and—"

"What does that Luca have to do with this?"

Molly would have told me to lie, and I almost did, but I just told him, "I'm living with Luca."

I was waiting for animals to start barking and howling, for the walls to start trembling, some sign that the earth was ready to open and swallow me up, but he quietly said, "You have a choice, Giulia. You can come back home within twenty-four hours, or—"

"Dad, I'm not going to make that choice. It's not fair."

"Then I prefer that we do not speak. I have no interest in a daughter who has so compromised herself."

"You don't mean that, Dad. I love you, you're my father."

"That is right. And because I am your father I am giving you a choice."

"So I'm your daughter and do what you want, or I do what I want and that's it, huh? Well, I'm not going to give this up. I'm staying whether you like it or not. Dad, why? Why can't you just let go a little bit?"

"Let go? That is what you want? From now on, Giulia, you are completely free," he said, and hung up.

When I called back he wouldn't answer. I panicked and dialed and redialed. What if something happened to him before I ever spoke to him again? Finally, he answered. "Dad, I love you. Don't hate me."

"I do not hate you."

"Will you call me?"

"No."

After that, his anger was an ocean away, nowhere near me, almost unreal. I kept calling every few weeks, though, on Sunday afternoons when I knew Cetta and Aunt Sofia were there. In the background my father was always yelling, "Do not talk with her! Hang up!" but he let them stay on long enough to ask, "You OK? Healthy? Are you eating enough?" My father had instructed my uncles in Montemaggiore to have nothing to do with me. But they talked to Carlo every week, asked about me, then my aunts wrote to Cetta and Aunt Sofia and told them I was fine.

I wrote long letters to everyone in Homefield and Montemaggiore. I sent copies of pictures I had taken. No one answered my letters, not for a long time, but I was determined to let them know that I hadn't left them, and to let my father know that in this whole wide world he wasn't alone.

I had found a part-time job with Willy, a British film-maker who was making low-budget educational films. I answered phones for him and did photo research and washed out coffee cups. While I pecked out his business letters, I finally learned how to type. I was paid next to nothing, off the books, but it was my first job and I was near cameras, and when I came up out of the subway at Stazione Termini after a day of work, taking the steps two at a time to get past the boys on the stairway posed like James Dean, the evening was so yellow, so artificially lit, that I felt I was walking up onto a movie set. And this was my life. The rest of the way home I rode the bus, the No. 64, which was always filled with tourists—Americans, Germans, Brits saying things to each other like "What did you see of interest today?" I wasn't one of them. I was at home. To the Italian matrons riding the bus, I looked familiar enough that they'd tell me, protectively, "Signorina, watch your purse." If boys were bothering me, the gruff old women would pull me down into an empty seat next to them, just as they would their own granddaughters.

At Largo Argentina I got off the bus, entered the small streets of our neighborhood. Already, there were neighbors who knew me and waved. Dripping laundry hung over the streets. That last bit of road, walking home to Luca, I slowed down, just to taste it, the delicious anticipation until I got to him again. I'd never headed home to such sure happiness before. Usually I found him lying on the bed reading, and I lay down next to him, kissed him from his mouth to his neck, down his chest. That all-seeing, slit-eyed look of his that had paralyzed me in the early days—now it was home and family and everything I loved.

"Luca, right here," I told him as my head rested on his thighs and I kissed him there too, "here and Rome are my two favorite places in the whole world."

"Then aren't you lucky," he said to me, smiling, "to find yourself exactly where you want to be."

EPILOGUE

The Italian Signora

"CARA SIGNORA" is how the shopkeepers greet me as I go through the neighborhood doing my daily errands. *"E il caro signore, com'è?"* How is your dear husband?

"My husband is fine," I tell them, "thank you," but maybe I'm thinking to myself, He's impossible, if we've quarreled recently; or thinking, Luca, you're amazing, if the night before we made love like teenagers, like fools on the beach; or maybe I smile to myself if I suspect, for the third or fourth or fifth time, that we're expecting a child.

I'm dressed in a good wool coat, camel's hair maybe, if it's fall; or if it's winter, an exquisite earth-brown shearling, light as a layer of moss keeping me warm. A string bag hangs from my elbow and in it I put the warm loaf of bread I just bought; and *panini* for the children's midmorning snack; and a carton of milk; and, rolled in wax paper, a ball of fresh butter; and, floating in milky water in a plastic bag, a big fat *mozzarella di bufalo*.

Between shops, I light a long cigarette and leave a brick-red ring of lipstick on the tip. (Sometimes there is a spot of lipstick on my crooked front tooth.) I exhale and squint my eyes as the smoke rises, and I look as if I know difficult things about life, because now I do. I am an Italian signora. The cobblestones rub the leather soles of my shoes or my high suede boots. My ears are heavy with big round malachite earrings, or dripping turquoise. A Florentine scarf, oversized and paisley print in rich dark tones, is wrapped around my shoulders and a solid gold pin holds it in place.

Even through my coat, my full figure is evident. At night, though, in the bedroom, when I sit before the mirror in my white silk slip, still wearing all my jewelry, combing out my hair, Luca comes and stands behind me, his hands gentle on my shoulders, and he tells me, "You look no different than that morning when you appeared in your aunt's kitchen wearing your robe." And I guess that in his eyes, I don't. Luca is more handsome now than when he was a boy. Very gray at the temples, a little sad around the eyes, but stunning.

It's been years, but still whenever Carlo sees us—every summer the entire family comes together at the beach—he smiles and says, *"Immagina! Di amici siamo diventati parenti."* From friends we became family. The wonder of it never fades.

Luca and I live in Rome. Our house is on one of the fine old streets, through a large wooden doorway, a dark, stone-cold garage and into a messy overgrown courtyard where, when I come home, I find our children safely playing.

"Mamma!" they shout when they see me. "Mamma!" They run to me, and I kiss them, and some are curly-haired and sharp-eyed like Luca, and some are chubby-cheeked like me, and I lift the littlest one and breathe in the sweet baby smell of his neck.

"*Signooo-ra,*" our housekeeper, Natalena, calls from the terrace above, wiping her red hands on a big white apron. "*Il signore* just called. He's on his way home. I think it's time to put on the pasta, Signora Giulia. What do you say?"

"*Si, si,* but remember, not too salty, for my father."

He is often part of our household. He is retired now, living in Montemaggiore very close to his brothers, but he comes to Rome to spend every winter with us. On Sundays, when Luca is free, the three of us take the children to the gardens of the Villa Borghese or to the fountains of Piazza Navona, where they run wild and free. The older ones learn to maneuver their bicycles over the uneven cobblestone, and the younger ones, when they are tired, go to my father, raise their arms. "Nonno," they whine, and he lifts them onto his lap. I always have my camera. I love to photograph my family against the backdrop of Rome.

During the winter I lived with Luca, this dream was one of my deepest wishes. What I hoped to find was that America was nothing, just a detour leading me back home. But that is not what I discovered. I did not become an Italian signora.

In June, after ten months, I left Luca and Rome and Italy. Things between Luca and me, slowly, had begun to fall apart. Our biggest problem, I think, was that we didn't know how to take care of each other. We were only just learning how to take care of ourselves.

We tried very hard, but the little things got us. I remember one November night before an exam, Luca came home late from studying and found me at the sink using soap to wash out the *caffettiera.* He grabbed the small metal coffeepot from my hands. "Didn't anyone ever tell you that you *never* wash this with soap? Do you know what that does to the flavor of the coffee?"

I knew that Luca had gone to Mauro's that evening. We couldn't stretch the money Luca's parents sent him far enough that month. Luca had had to ask Mauro for money, which meant being forced to listen to Mauro yelling, "This thing with the Americana, it better stop. Your grades are going to pay for this mistake." I never had to listen to it myself, but Luca told me, Renata told me. "All right, Luca, all right, I'm sorry. I'll never wash it with soap again."

"Too late," he yelled. "You've already ruined it." He opened the window and sent the coffeepot rolling and clanging down the empty alley.

Hours passed, but finally he said, "I'm sorry."

"And I'm sorry you had to go to Mauro."

He pulled me onto his lap, unbuttoned my shirt. His finger traced where my tan was fading. "You're losing your summer breasts," he said sadly. We had reached a new season, a colder time.

After November first, the Day of the Dead, the rains started. We couldn't even manage to keep each other warm during the night. Our landlord had recently found his wife sleeping with one of the tenants. Rather than punish his wife, the angry landlord cut back on the building's heat. The small, wide-windowed apartment Luca and I lived in, the home we had loved so much, turned on us, got mean. When the heat was off, our shiny tile floors practically formed a layer of frost. Evenings like that, I curled into a ball in the center of the bed with blankets wrapped around me, waiting for him. It was impossible for Luca to study in the cold. Every time he left to go to a friend's warm house, I told him, "I don't even know why you wanted me to stay in Rome. You're never here. We're never together."

"Giulia, what can I do? I have to study. Why don't you get off the bed and do something for a change?"

He slammed the door as he left, and I pulled out our one huge pot, filled it with water and banged it down on the hot plate. I lined up half a dozen carrots on the edge of the sink and chopped off their heads, let their cascades of green hair fall to the floor, then I kicked them under the bed. I dug out all the wilting greens from the refrigerator, held them under a rush of icy water, squeezed them in my fist, tossed them into the pot. I took a small sharp knife to the stalks of celery, pulled the strings through and sent them to the floor with a disgusted flick of my wrist. I found an old onion, chopped it in four, palmed it, tossed it, and just above the pot the onion separated, plopped into the water and sent up four hot, mean splashes.

There was a half-thawed chicken stuffed into our tiny freezer. I put the chicken in the sink and tore the skin off its back. I sliced off the drumsticks. With my bare hands, I ripped the wings off the breasts and tossed them into the boiling water. I threw in the gizzard and the liver and the chicken's heart. Finally, all that was left was the chicken's neck, its thick, coarse, goose-pimpled skin hanging. I hooked my finger inside the skin and yanked it down, inside out, pulled it right off. The skinny neck hung limp in my cold red hand, its small sharp bones protruding. I squeezed that neck until it pinched my skin, then I tossed it in, slammed down the lid, turned up the gas so high that flames licked the sides of the pot and the dripping water sizzled. Only then did I realize how much like Aunt Sofia I had become.

I was still working for Willy, the filmmaker, a few days a week. His films were boring. He always came to work a bit drunk. But without work papers, I couldn't find anything better. Besides, Willy was the only person I could talk to about taking pictures. He always asked to see my photographs. "My girl, you ought to be studying, taking a course with a good photographer." Who had the money for that? But I was grateful to Willy, and when we worked together he always made me laugh.

He was a big, round, flannel-shirted man with a full golden beard. He had crystal-blue eyes, and the whiskey made them sparkle. His face was almost always flushed and warm and red. Week by week, I developed a crush. One Friday afternoon as I was leaving, he said, "Where are you off to so fast? Care for a drink before you go?" Maybe that day he sensed I was lingering. His private office was small and had only one chair. He cleared off a spot on his desk so I could sit and lean my back against the wall. I had never tasted Scotch before. But there was the heavy wood-and-metal scent of it as Willy stood and hovered over me and our mouths met and we kissed.

"Oh Giulia," he sighed, when our faces were still close, "I want to make love to you."

My neck stiffened against the cold wall. No one had ever said this to me in English.

"Willy, you know I live with Luca."

"Darling girl, you seem less than pleased about that love affair."

I knew enough not to argue with him about that, but I was naive enough to say, "But Willy, why? You and I aren't in love."

"Why? Because you're the only woman I know anymore in this bloody country who calls me by my proper name."

"What do other women call you?"

" 'Villì, Villì!' " he imitated, and I had to laugh. " 'Villì, please save me from my horrible husband!' I'd give my right nut for a good English-speaking girl who can belt down a few ales and not worry about dashing home to her mamma and her papà or her husband and kids. With these Italians, I'm a side dish, the antipasto, you know? Their family's always the main meal."

"Oh Willy," I said, sad for him, sad for me, "maybe it's time for you to get out of here, go back home."

Afterward, on the subway, and for days later, I didn't feel guilty for having kissed Willy; we both knew it wouldn't happen again. But that's when I started to notice the American sophomore-year-abroad students. Suddenly, they were everywhere: reading translations of the *Inferno,* sitting under Bernini's columns at St. Peter's, sketching. I hadn't taken a picture in months, and there they sat, at cafes, with their camera bags on the tiny tables in front of them. It was not Willy or some other man I wanted. I wanted to be cured of my amnesia: I'd forgotten how I wanted to live my life.

At Christmas time I called Homefield and told Cetta I wouldn't hang up until my father talked to me. By the time he got on the phone I was crying.

"Have you had enough yet?" he demanded.

"Dad, it's Christmas," I said, and he softened.

"It is probably not too late for you to begin the second semester at St. Helena's," he told me. "I am still willing to pay the tuition."

I almost said yes, just to keep hearing his voice offering me a way back to him, but I remembered enough to say no.

In January, things were hardest—the apartment its coldest, Luca working the longest hours, and I'd sit in our room with him just a few feet away from me, I'd close my eyes and see myself choking him. I hated him for what he had done to me, and wanted to slap him for what he never did for me anymore, bite him for what he might do in the future, what he probably had done in the past. I wanted to kick him for what he was thinking and kick him again, harder, because it seemed he never was thinking about me at all. I'd stare at one page of the newspaper and feel myself crazy, see Luca's face and me holding a hot iron not five inches away from it.

But even then there were moments when I opened my eyes and looked across the room at Luca in his thick green sweater, pacing back and forth, reciting to himself, and the familiar worn-out seat of his brown corduroy pants made me want to go to him. He would glance up from his book, leave his wire-frame glasses hanging from one ear (when I went to Rome with Luca I didn't even know he needed glasses to read), and he'd walk over, hug me, ask me "Would you mind, for a minute, if I recited these idioms to you? Here, look at the book, see if I get them right."

For almost an hour he'd recite. If he forgot even one idiom, he'd get exasperated and grab two fistfuls of hair at the sides of his head. "Calm down, Luca. You'll get it. Let's go over it again." Sometimes it was so easy for us to be kind to each other.

We'd have a few days of calm, a thaw, days close to that September heat, but then there'd be something small, something like taking a walk through the streets at night, and Luca's hand holding on to me—my waist, my shoulders, my neck—would suddenly feel too tight, and my heart chilled. Was this what love would always feel like?

Then one evening close to spring, I was on a bus as it rounded the big fountain at Porta Pia. Through the window, I saw a boy sitting on the edge of the fountain. He looked like Luca. It *was* Luca. But then it wasn't. I was never really sure. I watched a girl walk up to him—whoever he was—and he pulled her arms and he swung out his legs to catch her. He kissed her forehead. I had only a moment to watch, but I saw she was well dressed, a girl from a nice Italian family. I could tell she hadn't spent the winter freezing in an apartment that didn't have enough heat. She was wearing a plaid pleated skirt and flat leather boots, a short jacket. She was small. She stood between his legs, but hesitated to move in closer. He was trying to talk to her. She was looking at him with her head tilted, as if she didn't trust him completely. In the last second I caught her face: that girl was in danger.

I was dizzy as the bus drove on, and a man next to me grabbed me by the elbow. "Are you all right?" Someone stood up to give me a seat. I couldn't focus until we stopped at a red light and I looked out the window and saw a shopkeeper in crisp-pleated pants, standing at the door of his shop. He took a last drag of a cigarette, then with his finger and thumb, without looking to see if anyone was passing, he flicked the lit butt out into the street, and I thought to myself, These men are ruthless.

When I told Luca about the couple at the fountain, he swore it wasn't him. I wanted to believe him, and I almost did believe him, but a few days later I saw the girl again. She was in our neighborhood, talking to a couple of students, friends of Luca's. It was very likely she knew Luca too.

Luca's clothes were packed when he got home that night. "Go to Carlo's," I told him. "You're not staying here."

"It wasn't me, Giulia."

"Get out of here," I yelled, in English.

Carlo came to talk to me. "It wasn't Luca you saw with that girl."

"Now you're lying to me too."

"What is this paranoia you have? Is it American? Is it female? What is it?"

It was like looking at a photograph and its negative at the same time. I couldn't tell the difference between the truth and a lie. "Just get out, Carlo. Leave me alone."

In the apartment, alone, insomniac, the middle of the night, the only thing I knew for sure was that I didn't want Luca to leave me. But I was the one who had sent him away.

With a coat over my nightgown, I ran downstairs to the pay phone under our streetlight. I called Carlo's, woke them all up. Luca didn't get mad. "I need to see you," I told him.

He arrived in ten minutes. Without taking off his coat, he pulled me to him. Thank God, what relief. There was the familiar scent of bed and pillows and sleepiness on his face. Yes, I thought, now we can sleep. But a second later, I had to pull back. I looked at him the same way the girl at the fountain had, with my head tilted, and there it was again, the feeling of danger. "Luca, you have to go now. I'm sorry, I can't . . ."

"Giulia, you really want me to go?"

"No, don't go, Luca."

"I'll do whatever you want."

"You better go."

Was he evil, or was I crazy? There was no peace. Back and forth. Luca, come; Luca, go. Phone calls made with sweaty *gettoni* at midnight, one o'clock, two o'clock in the morning. "Giulia, we can't go on this way. What do you want to do?"

Then one afternoon, early March, the air mild enough for an open window, my day off from Willy's—and I stood at the sink and put a small sharp knife first to one wrist then the other. Just held it there a second, to show myself. See, you won't do it. But I still felt all the nervous energy rushing to those two soft pulsing points. I longed for the action, the cut, the stab, the rip, the break. *Cut deep*, my father had said when I killed the chicken. *You must cut deep or it will never die.*

I tossed the small knife into the sink. Picked up another, a larger, duller knife. Took off my watch, held the knife to my other wrist. Just held it there, the dull point. "See," I said out loud, "you don't want to do this. You don't." I tossed that knife too, grabbed my coat, ran down the steps.

I knew I had to keep moving. Out on the street I put on my sunglasses and forced myself to walk slowly. My heart was pounding, but the streets stretched out empty in front of me. I didn't feel the road under my feet but I was hugged by the tall walls on either side. Narrow, twisting, winding, curving tunnels. They were close and warm, like Cetta next to me on the couch, covering my forehead with her big, cool hand.

I walked looking up, and I began to see things: balconies and the undersides of flower boxes and the flowing tips of hanging vines. And windows, tall and narrow. And above them, smaller, rounded windows with their rounded shutters opened up, forming a triptych. All along the street, shutters closed and shutters opened, and shutters with the bottom panels pushed out. And below the windows, the doors. And cut into the doors, keyholes shaped like the ace of clubs. And above or beside the doors, the house numbers, carved fat and clear, the way the names of the streets were carved into the walls, and each name told you what the business of that street used to be: the street of the carpenters, the street of the trunkmakers, the hatmakers, woolcombers, the street of the pilgrims, of the locksmiths, little street of the chickens, street of the little chairs. And behind everything, still hugging me like a mother as I walked, there was the sunlit

275

sienna surface of the walls. And I realized that these streets were the rooms where my dreams took place, that each night in my dreams for months I had found myself in these streets, but in my dreams the streets were rooms. They were home.

Hours passed. The street I was on ended at a small flight of stairs. I climbed up, went under an arch and came out on Lungotevere, a fast street that did just what it said—rode alongside the Tevere, the Tiber River. It was busy here with small, fast cars and buses and taxis. A break in the traffic, and I ran across, to the sidewalk, which was lined with trees, the tops of the trees joining. I looked up, and the branches were a canopy over the traffic, the leaves overlapping, and the late afternoon light was giving a hundred different shades to what, at first glance, was solid green.

I stood there a long time, looking up at the mosaic of leaves, forgetting Renata's moving-target theory (when I first arrived in Rome, she had told me, "Always move as if you know exactly where you are going. Never stand still, then no one can grab you or take your purse"). I wasn't worried. There was nothing but what my eyes were taking in, and nothing but a feeling of peace, and within the peacefulness, a profound sense of safety. I was safe here out in the world. The only danger was inside, where I lived.

I leaned over the wall that bordered the river, spread my arms and felt the weight of my body press against the stones. Italy had given me this, too—my body, with its bulk and its cravings, its surprises, betrayals, the pleasures it could bring. I watched the river flow toward me, and lying on its surface were the trees, cupolas, towers and houses of Trastevere, the neighborhood on the far side. The undulation of the current made the reflections shimmy, the way I felt my life running through my bones.

And that's how I came to know again what I had known with such surety before I left my father's house. I knew what I needed to do.

By the time Luca moved back into our apartment, I had sent a ten-page letter to Barnard College, along with a batch of photographs, and asked them to send me financial-aid forms. I got so anxious waiting to hear from the admissions office, I took money out of Luca's wallet to make a phone call to New York. I spoke with a woman. She said, "No decision yet, but things look hopeful."

"Please," I said, and repeated, "Thank you for your help," until the transatlantic static ate up my voice.

Willy gave me the names and addresses of a few film companies and photographers' studios in New York, and I wrote to them asking about part-time work. Luca, Carlo, Renata—none of them knew about any of this.

As Luca and I got farther and farther away from each other in the daytime world, we fell more and more deeply into a nighttime world of no words, just touching. All night long we touched, in the dark, not looking. Deep into the night we made love, and often in the morning. Once I woke and found him standing beside the bed. His pants were unzipped, he was touching himself and looking at me.

"What?" I whispered to him.

"Nothing," he whispered back, but his eyes looked glazed. "Will you do something? Will you kneel down here on the floor by the bed?"

"Why?"

"I want to see you like that."

"Luca."

"Please."

It was all murmurs, my faint murmurs of protest, even as I slipped out of bed, his murmurs of encouragement and apology, frighteningly seductive, almost gasping, urgent, as he lifted my nightgown and tossed it across the room. I pulled a pillow in front of me and leaned against the side of the bed.

"Why this, Luca?" I said, but already I was excited. We both felt it: the bed wasn't big enough to contain us.

I couldn't see but I could almost feel the moonlight white across my back. Luca stood to the side of me, just looking, not touching, not saying a word. I didn't know what he was doing and this excited me even more. Then I heard clothes drop, his belt buckle clank the floor.

Three hot fingers moved lightly across my back, brushed the side of my breast. With one quick sweep, he lifted my hair up off my neck, then he was naked all along the back of me, kneeling behind me, his legs pressing tight inside my thighs. Trying to control himself, he pretended he was calming me. "It's OK, it's OK." His voice was so buttery and slow, but with shards of ice at the edges. "Relax," he said in Italian, then it was all dialect. "Just lean forward, into the pillow, that's right, like that, just lean." My knees were numb from the cold tile floor. Our small rug was crumpled under the bed. I tried to rest my feet on Luca's ankles to keep warm, but Luca kicked them away as he spread my legs wider.

I pulled him up inside me and he couldn't get deep enough. We sped each other on, rocking faster. We didn't lie to each other; there were no kisses, nothing like tenderness, and then even his voice stopped. Just breathing, gasping. We had crossed into some new place, close to violence, far from love. We were agreed. He wanted to turn me inside out, I wanted him to touch some spot buried deep, into the darkness and beyond it, into the light. I caught my face in the mirror across the room, saw the impatience in my eyes, my mouth, when, once, he slipped out of me. I heard the anger in his growl, and then saw the determined look in our eyes as both of us, desperately, led him back inside.

We were pushing so hard, the bed got away from us, and we were tired and I stretched out flat, my chest, my thighs, my stomach chilled against the tile floor. Then my back on the floor, then his back, over and over.

Afterward, we lay in bed silent and awake for a long time. By then we had stopped asking each other, What are you thinking? Our silences were cold and private and within them, we were each alone. I was wondering how many times Luca and I had made love during the past year. Innumerable. Soon I would be a woman who didn't make love with Luca. Who would I be? Would I change quickly? Or would I relinquish slowly like an immigrant, with small releases of the fist?

"Luca?"

"*Si?*"

"*Niente.*"

When I showed Luca my college acceptance letter, I tried to explain that I was not leaving *him*.

"So this is what's been going on. I thought you had a lover. Giulia, what can I do to make you stay?"

"Luca, it's me. I want to go to school, just like you. There are things I want."

"What? You can do anything you want here with me."

"Oh Luca, please, help me. I just know I have to do this. But I want you to come to New York, Luca. Even just to visit me. Please, won't you come? Don't you want to see America?"

"America is far away. Do you know what lies before me during these next six or seven years? Do you know? I need you here. Listen, I know you're angry with me. I know this winter was like a nightmare for you. So, if you want, for a while, we won't live together. You take this apartment, I'll find another place. But don't leave Rome."

"I have to go."

Luca and Carlo tried to find out how I could enroll in an Italian university. Renata said she had a second cousin who was a professor who could help me. "Giulia," Renata said, "you and Luca, you've been through so much together. You should be together. How can you leave?"

Even Mauro told me, "Go if you want, but you don't have to."

"I've got to go," I told them.

I had almost enough money for a plane ticket. Without telling my father she was sending it, Cetta wired me the rest. All my father knew was that I had decided to leave Luca. In a letter, Aunt Sofia told me:

> It's such a big relief to your father that you're coming home, but be prepared. He's going to hit the roof at least once or twice, you know that. He's pretty mad. I'm not going to lie to you, it's been a bad year for all of us and nobody likes the idea that you're going to this school in New York City. Why there, Giulia? Can you explain to me? But the only thing we want is for you to be happy, so if that's what you want, God bless you. For your own sake, though, you better not show up at the Cleveland airport with that Luca.
>
> The kids are anxious to see you. We're waiting for you before we have the first cook-out. The sausages came out real nice this year.

I made a reservation for a flight scheduled to leave a few days after Luca's and Carlo's exams, so the three of us could spend some time together. Once we knew I was leaving, Luca and I tried to be kinder to each other, more generous. There was only a week left until the exams and, though Luca was studying hard, he said nothing would stay in his head. I suggested that he and Carlo take the train to Montemaggiore, where they could study in peace while their mothers cooked for them. Luca didn't want to go, but I insisted.

"Mamma mia," Renata told me, "how brave you are."

And I was, until the third morning Luca was gone, when I woke up and realized the apartment was full of nothing but leaving, leaving, leaving. I couldn't bear it by myself. With no coffee, with no breakfast, I ran to the telephone office to place a long-distance call. Crying, I told Luca. "I can't sleep without you."

"Come to Montemaggiore," he told me. "Stay at your uncle's."

"Luca, you don't understand," I sobbed. If I went down there I'd never be able to leave. It was midmorning, an expensive time to call. I wasn't talking, just crying in the soundproof telephone booth.

"Giulia?" His voice so far away, but it felt as if he were talking right into my hair. I had no idea why I was leaving him, only that I felt an ebbing, a pulling back as forceful and uncontrollable as the push that had sent me to him. "Are you there?"

"I'm here."

And then his voice softened. "Giulia, who knows? Maybe this isn't the end for us. I don't believe it is. We were in over our heads. Maybe in a few years . . ."

"Oh Luca."

"Giulia, please, remember you're leaving because you want to. That's what you told me. You have to do what's best for you."

"But I love you, Luca."

"I know, Giulia. I love you, too."

. . . .

After Luca hung up, I called the airlines. I changed my reservation, got a flight for the next day. I spent the afternoon going through drawers, throwing out the heavy flea-market sweaters that had got me through the winter. I packed the few nice things I had left—the crocheted bedspread for my hope chest, the shawl my aunts had given me, a pair of jeans, a denim skirt, two bikinis, some shirts, and my yellow traveling suit. I took all the notes Luca and I had taped on the kitchen mirror. Months before, way in the beginning, we had made a long chain of chewing-gum wrappers. It was Brooklyn gum, and Luca had said, "We will make this chain as long as the Brooklyn Bridge." The wrappers were all faded now, but I packed them too, in a small box with the cameo ring Luca had given me for Christmas.

By 4:45, when the birds started gathering, huge flocks that wove together and filled the sky like a cloud of smoke, I was done. I looked around the apartment—the bare ugly walls stripped of my photographs, the sagging beds. I swept the floor clean, washed the dirty dishes in the sink. I ran out and bought cheese, prosciutto, grapes and a bottle of water to leave in the refrigerator for Luca. Then quickly, without stopping to think, I picked up my suitcases, walked out the door, locked it and slid the key underneath, far out of reach.

I was afraid to go to Renata's. I knew she'd convince me not to leave. The hotel where my family had stayed when my father arrived in Rome was nearby, and that's where I went. The man at the desk remembered me. *"Signorina,* welcome back. This time you are traveling without Papà?"

"Yes, this time I'm by myself."

Without Papà, without Luca or Carlo, without anyone. Alone. I took the smallest, darkest, cheapest room available. I put down my bags and went outside.

An evening in early June, warm as the leftover summer days of fall. The sky was turning soft with color. I walked and walked. It turned dark, but I kept wandering. What do you do, when the thing you're unable to leave behind is something you can never go back to?

My last night in Rome, I realized that the event my family feared had already happened. Our delusion was that we could make choices with America—accept this, but not that; let go here, but not there. Too late. Nicola and Sofia had left Italy for good. America was as real as my mother's death. Why couldn't we learn that? How many times do you have to say goodbye?

I walked until I came to a small piazza in Trastevere that was lit yellow by the candles of two outdoor restaurants. My father would have said I had no business eating dinner out there alone. Aunt Sofia would have said, "At that hour, a young girl, by herself! Where's your head?" But I walked over to the restaurant that looked less expensive, sat at a small table, asked for a menu. I ordered pasta, and then a half carafe of wine, and the waiter said, *"Si, signorina"* and was completely indifferent.

Sad as I was, I knew this dinner was a sort of victory for a girl from a Calabrian family. For years I'd been holding my breath, waiting, and now I knew I'd been right all along—the world was very wide. I had reached a place where I could walk and never feel a hand clasping my arm, never hear a voice saying no. There was consolation in this, but after dinner I passed the stands set up to sell scarves and wallets and gifts. *"Signorina,"* the vendors called to me, "for you, a special price." I didn't want souvenirs. I still wanted someone I could throw my arms around and say *"Mio!"* Mine. Couldn't Luca come speeding up just one more time on his maroon motorcycle, stop me, make it impossible for me to go?

I went to the river and leaned over the wall and watched the lights move over the water. On the bridge nearby sat a night fisherman, patiently waiting for a catch. I might have walked until dawn, but it began to rain. I headed back to the hotel. All night it rained hard, with thunder breaking and echoing and breaking again. I opened my hotel window and tried to look out, but the storm was wiping away all the sounds and scents, the familiar comforts of the Italian night. I pulled in the shutters and leaned my head against the wooden slats.

How dumb you've been, I thought to myself. How stupid. Since the year before, when I took off from Homefield, I'd thought that the force of my anger was all I needed. Determination and direction, and I was off. I had never imagined how difficult it was to simply stand still and say goodbye. That last night in Rome, I learned about the lonely midway station, the inevitable stop between where I'd been and where I was going next. I tried to look forward to college, to New York, tried to imagine myself in a year, but I couldn't see it clearly enough. I wasn't that Giulia yet.

My hotel room was tiny, with four pale walls, an oblong writing table, a firm single bed with a clean beige cotton bedspread. Alone at three, four, five in the morning, I sat on the bed and played solitaire with the *carte napoletane,* laying them down over and over and over again, in an endless variety of combinations.

It was still dark when my wake-up call came from the desk. As I got dressed, I stared at the chubby Italian phone on the nightstand, thinking, I could call him, just one last time. But I was too tired to cry again. I would write a long letter when I got on the plane. I took the elevator down to the lobby. As I paid the bill, the night clerk asked, *"Taxi, signorina?"*

"No, grazie."

I had one more stop to make. It had never stopped raining during the night. I had no umbrella, so I strapped my purse over my shoulder and held my suitcases close. I ran through the still-dark streets, under the shop awnings, until I got to the Campo dei Fiori. The market was almost completely set up. The vendors, wrapped in plastic rain gear, were setting out their fruit and flowers and vegetables. The gates of Renata's bar were pulled open. She was behind the bar pouring water into the espresso machine. Her only customer at the counter was a hung-over vendor smoking a cigarette, rubbing his hand over his face.

I walked in and the bell over the door rang. *"Buon giorno,"* Renata called out without looking.

"Renata, it's me."

She turned. "Giulia!"

"I came to say goodbye," I said, but she didn't hear me.

"How nice you look. I never saw you in that suit before. It's beautiful."

"My grandmother made it for me. It's my traveling suit."

"What are you doing, practicing? You don't leave for another week, no?"

I walked down the bar and stood across from her. "I'm leaving today. Luca doesn't know. But you'll tell him for me, won't you, that I just couldn't—oh Renata—"

I was pressing down hard on the cold marble counter, trying not to cry. Renata rested her big warm hands over mine. Without knowing it, I'd been depending on her to come up with a plan, another scheme, but she was silent. After a long time, she said, "Well, I'm not surprised. It's been too hard, hasn't it?" We looked at each other, our eyes full of tears. Then she took her hands away and came back with a cup of coffee. She handed me a fresh hot pastry. I knew I couldn't eat it, but it felt good to hold.

It was only six in the morning, and Renata's makeup was perfect. "Come on, eat," she said. "You can't fly with nothing in your stomach."

The bell over the door had rung a few minutes earlier, while we were talking, and now a customer was calling from the front of the bar, "Renata! What's going on? Am I supposed to make my own coffee today?"

"Patience! Patience!" she yelled down to him. To me, she whispered, "Imagine his poor wife, what a pleasure her life must be with him."

The bar was filling up. Renata served a few more cups of espresso, then came back to me and handed me her raincoat. "Here, you'll need this so you don't ruin your suit."

"I can't take your raincoat."

"Take it and *basta*. You'll bring it back to me when you return to Rome."

"Oh, Renata, I don't know when I'll come back."

"For my wedding, of course."

"You're getting married?"

"Someday," she said and shrugged, and we both laughed. "That Mauro, how he drags his feet. But you know, I'm almost afraid of the day he will say to me, 'Let's do it, let's get married.'"

"Why?"

"Who knows where Mauro might drag me off to? Calabria, Sicilia. Between me and you—given a choice, I would never leave this miserable bar."

"I'd love it if you came to America some day. Come visit me. Think about it, Renata."

"I'm a coward, Giulia. I'm not like you. You move. You travel. Not me. You know, every day I watch those vendors out there selling fruit. Six days a week, every week of the year, with the rain, the snow, the sun, they put those fruit stands up in the morning, and every afternoon they pull them down again. It's like a circus, but with no imagination, you know? And I say to myself, Renata, you're just like them. What a boring life you lead. Get out of this bar, get out of this city."

"But this is your home."

"Maybe that's why. You know, I've always had the feeling that even though the things I do in my life are so small, doing them here in this place, with so much"—her arm swooped over her head, the wide silk sleeve of her blouse flying, her red nails flashing by my face—"so much history, so much everything, who knows? Somehow it gives my tiny life more importance. If Mauro heard me he'd say I was crazy."

"You're not crazy, Renata. I'm the crazy one. I don't know why I'm leaving. Why isn't it just enough for me to live here and be with Luca? Why?"

"You're leaving because you have things to do, Americana."

"I'm going to come back, Renata. As soon as I can."

"If you want to, you will."

She took away my empty coffee cup. "So, now, we have to call a cab for you, no?"

Over the phone, the dispatcher was trying to say that, because of the rain, there were no cabs available, but Renata recognized his voice. "Luigi, who do you think you're talking to? This is Renata. Get a cab over here in five minutes, for the airport." *Subito, presto,* she told him. Be quick.

She waited at the door with me until the cab pulled up. She covered my shoulders with the raincoat.

"I'll send the coat back to you soon, Renata."

"Don't you dare. I only want it if you bring it in person." We kissed on both cheeks. We hugged for a long moment, and she held her hand on the back of my head, like a mother.

"Buon viaggio, Giulia," she called, and I stepped out into the rain.

The cab driver was stern. He threw my suitcases into the trunk and told me, "You shouldn't be traveling on a day like this." His forehead in the rearview mirror looked angry. He drove fast.

After a while, he demanded, "So, where are you flying off to so early in the morning?"

"America."

"America! For the first time?"

"No, I live there. I'm American."

"Americana?" He glanced into the rearview mirror and showed me his eyes. They were dark, with heavy, folded eyelids, but when he looked at me, his eyes turned kind. "You speak Italian well, *signorina,* but now that you mention it I do notice a little accent. You look Italian, though, you must be of Italian people."

"Yes, from Calabria."

"Ah, Calabrese! Like my wife!" He tapped his knuckles on his head. "You know what they say about the Calabrese, don't you? Hard heads, very stubborn people. It's true, isn't it?"

I shrugged and smiled, and he smiled back at me. "Ah," he said, "I can tell just looking at you that you're one of the stubborn ones. Yes, it's true."

We were driving on the Via Appia Nuova, a wide straight road split by a row of blooming trees, three lanes leading into Rome, three lanes leading out. The traffic was getting heavier; cars splashed us as they sped by. The rain was coming down hard now, in thick blinding sheets. I stared out the window, but Rome was passing: foggy, wrapped in mist, refusing to show me her face.

"It's raining hard," I told the cab driver, just to hear my voice, just to fill the void. "It's raining so hard."

His eyes met mine in the mirror again. "The city is crying, *signorina,* because you are leaving."

Anna Monardo received an MFA from Columbia University's writing program, and is a graduate of Saint Mary's College in Notre Dame, Indiana. Her work has been published in the *Indiana Review, Redbook, McCall's, Seventeen,* and many other publications. She lives in New York.